"Get your hands off ~~me~~," ~~Tonya yelled~~, ~~shaking~~ loose and moving a step back. She looked straight into eyes that were full of regret but she ignored it. All she felt was her own hurt, her own regret—and her anger, as she looked from Jaimer to Cecilia.

"Why," she asked simply. "Why would you do this to me?"

Cecilia spoke first, stepping forward and trying to defuse the situation. The fact that Tonya was standing outside her house, in the front yard, hadn't escaped her. "Tonya, you don't know the whole story."

"I know enough." Tonya walked away from Jaimer and moved toward Cecilia, animatedly using her hands to convey her anger. "You knew all along that Howard was still alive, and you didn't tell me. How long have you been trying to keep him from me?"

"I haven't been keeping him from you, Tonya. Howard has . . ."

Jaimer stepped forward to finish. "Howard has been in the federal witness-protection program for the past three years. Cecilia wasn't keeping him from you." Shrinking from the flash of hatred he thought he saw in Tonya's eyes, Jaimer plowed on. "Tonya, you have to know that no one planned for you to get hurt. Howard Douglass was involved in some extremely dangerous and illegal activities. When the two of you first started dating, Howard was one of the biggest drug dealers in the tri-state area. He was facing drug and weapons charges, so he decided to become a federal witness in order to avoid imprisonment."

"So he was right, wasn't he? You did know him back then. You worked for the government."

The hurt in her eyes seemed to magnify as she began to slowly comprehend the full scope of Jaimer's betrayal.

BEST FOOT FORWARD

MICHELE SUDLER

Genesis Press, Inc.

INDIGO LOVE STORIES

An imprint of Genesis Press, Inc.
Publishing Company

Genesis Press, Inc.
P.O. Box 101
Columbus, MS 39703

ISBN: 13 DIGIT : 978-1-58571-337-0
ISBN: 10 DIGIT : 1-58571-337-6
Manufactured in the United States of America

First Edition

Visit us at www.genesis-press.com
or call at 1-888-Indigo-1-4-0

DEDICATION

To My Best Friends
Cecilia Brokenbough
and
Cynthia Denise Ford
Who help me to keep my Best Foot Forward

ACKNOWLEDGMENTS

To my children, my love for you grows stronger every day. I see you growing into beautiful people, and I thank God for giving me the strength to raise you. It is truly a pleasure.

To my friend, Curtis Bowers, for good conversation and lending your ear in the hard times.

To my family at Restoration Fellowship Church, thank you for keeping me steadfast and focused on my goals and giving me unconditional support.

To my pastor, Darrell V. Freeman, author of *Your Choice Is Your Trouble,* an excellent guide for those seeking maturity in their relationships. Thank you for listening to my doubts and giving me encouragement.

To my friends and family, I love you all.

To Doris Funnye Innis, as always, thank you for all your hard work.

To the Genesis Press family and anyone who has ever read any of my books: Thank you.

And to anyone I might have missed, I'm thinking of you.

PROLOGUE

Tonya wore a huge smile as she accepted the two-carat diamond tennis bracelet from her boyfriend, Howard Douglass. Her brother, Vince, had introduced them two weeks earlier at a Sixers basketball game he had gotten front row tickets to for her twenty-fourth birthday, and they had quickly become friends through phone conversations and emails. They had finally met face to face at a party thrown by a local Delaware bike club. Friends of hers were members of the group, and, after some coaxing, she agreed to go, taking her sister, Cindy, and cousin, Shawnique, along.

At first, she didn't know it was Howard. He caught her eye as soon as she walked in the door, as he was looking good in a pair of loose-fitting jeans and a striped button-down shirt hanging outside his pants. He was tall and lean, the color of coffee beans. She assumed he was attached, but she couldn't tell to whom, because he was seen with a number of women during the evening. But she kept her eye on him, and several times caught him watching her.

Toward the end of the night, he finally approached her and asked for her name. This is when they discovered they had already been communicating with each other for the past week. Though definitely interested, she cautiously waited two days before allowing him to convince her to go out to dinner.

They dined at Zanzibar Blue; Tonya had the blackened catfish with mixed vegetables, Howard the London broil and baked potato. That night, he presented her with a pair of diamond earrings, explaining that a beautiful woman deserved beautiful things. Shocked by this first-date gesture, but not being completely stupid, she accepted the gift and made a mental note to look for signs of any shady dealings. Where she came from and in this day and age, brothas didn't walk around just giving up expensive gifts.

Over the next five months, he showered her with gifts—dozens of flowers, bottles of perfume, and now the tennis bracelet. It was lovely; almost as dazzling as the diamond-encrusted platinum Rolex watch she received for her birthday. Howard had spared no expense—nothing was too expensive, too extravagant, for her. They dined at the finest restaurants, attended the hottest shows, and he had taken her on two shopping sprees.

When asked what he did for a living, he never gave her a straight answer or a specific job title, saying only that he was involved in the banking industry, and she never pressured him for an answer. He lavished attention, respect, love, and gifts on her. Tonya accepted it all at face value. It didn't hurt that he was the most gratifying lover she had ever had.

A collage of tangled body parts, the soft caress of his hands across her nipple, his lips touching her most secret parts, the soft moans of pleasure as they . . .

Suddenly, Tonya's pleasant dreams of Howard turned into a horror show. She began rolling from one side of her bed to the other, causing the bedclothes to wrap around her tightly.

A coarse hand covering her mouth, stifled yells, a hard yank, the string of her tank top ripped, one breast exposed, a soft pillow case over her head . . .

Tonya sprang upright soaked with perspiration; her thin cotton nightgown clung to her body. She began to shake as fearsome images crowded her mind. Quickly, she threw back her covers and turned on her bedroom light so she could better observe her surroundings. Through the panic, she told herself to count to one hundred until she could feel the beat of her heart slow to normal. She left her room and, in her usual orderly fashion, proceeded to check the locks on all her windows and doors. She had her system down pat. Then she stood in her kitchen behind the closed window shutters and made herself a warm cup of tea to calm her jittery nerves.

Four-thirty. She was proud of herself for almost making it through the night. *One day, I'm going to be back to normal.*

She wanted to call someone, talk to anyone, if only to get a compliment on a job well done. If the dream hadn't turned into a horrifying reminder, she would probably still be sound asleep. Cindy would cuss her out; Vince was probably out "visiting," as he called it. She dialed her older sister, almost positive that she would be up. Cecilia faithfully jogged three miles a day, every day.

"Good morning, Summers residence." Cecilia answered the phone with cheerful authority, desperately hoping that it wasn't her partner calling her in to work early. They handled very high profile cases, so her hours were always long, hard, and unpredictable.

"Girl, calm down. It's only me," Tonya replied, laughing.

"Oh. What do you want?" Her police mode vanished, replaced by a casual air of friendship and love.

"Is that any way to talk to your little sister?"

"Girl, it's almost five in the morning. I was on my way out the door for a jog. How long have you been up?"

"That's what I called you about. I *just* got up. I almost made it through the night."

"Really? Tonya . . . that's great. I'm so happy for you."

"Thank you, Cecilia. That's all I wanted. I love you."

"I love you, too. I'll see you later."

Tonya hung up feeling good and confident. Her bad dream forgotten, she felt happy and fully alive. *Today is going to be a good day.*

Cecilia was her rock. When times were hard, she pushed you through. When they were easy, she made you thankful. As a police detective by day, wife and mother by night, Cecilia was one tough cookie. She didn't take or give any mess. After the death of their mother, she and Cecilia had formed a bond stronger than superglue. Happily married and the mother of two beautiful twin girls and one hardheaded boy, Cecilia was living in a peaceful bliss that Tonya wished she had.

CHAPTER 1

Tension crept up her spine, followed by a gripping tightness in her chest that migrated down to the pit of her stomach. Outwardly she was calm, cool, and unruffled, showing little trace of the inner turmoil that had controlled her life for the past three years. She had become good at hiding telltale signs of a nervous breakdown in progress. Perhaps too good.

Too good at accepting the course that her life had taken. Too good at letting herself be absent from the world. Hiding had become second nature, and she could barely remember life before the onset of the paralyzing fear that was now her constant companion.

Tonya Perkins got up from her desk in the corner of her home office for the fifth time in twenty-five minutes and closed the door. She couldn't stand it open. She had once again disappointed herself. No matter how hard she pushed at the boundaries that held her prisoner, she couldn't seem to break through them.

Her house, an older bi-level duplex, was her haven and her prison, depending on how she felt at any given time. From the front door, a wide hallway led toward stairs flanked by a dining room on the right and the kitchen on the left. Halfway down the hallway on the left was the door to the office; across from the door was the opening into a large living room, which connected to the dining room by glass doors. She kept them open. From the kitchen there was access to a restroom, which was located under the staircase. The kitchen led outside to her backyard, and the dining area had sliding doors leading to her porch, which had a roof and was closed in by screening. The second floor consisted of three bedrooms and a bathroom.

This was the day she dreaded each year—the day when her brother and a group of men from his moving company came in her home to remove her living-room and dining-room furniture to make room for their annual family gathering. The men knew about her situation and never bothered her. They tried to complete the task quickly and methodically. But, as in past years, the moment she caught sight of one of them walking past, she immediately froze, an unimaginable icy fear clutching her heart.

The crunching sound of the men walking across her hardwood floors had her nerves standing on end, and she had an irrational urge to run for her life.

Be strong, girl. Be strong, Tonya told herself repeatedly for the next three minutes until she mustered up the courage to walk back to the office door and open it. Then she repeated this routine when her nerves began to fray. It was an unending cycle of insecurity that she wished with her whole heart would end.

Staring idly at her computer's blank monitor, she abandoned any thought of completing any work today, not with her brother and his crew scurrying around her house. She mentally prepared herself for a late night with her computer and notepad. A freelance writer, Tonya had found a respectable niche for herself writing short stories: romance, horror, and sci-fi. She was good at what she did and had contracts for future pieces with four different magazines.

Her writing career had started only a few years before the incident that had changed her life, opting to work for herself rather than for the pompous oaf who had hired her fresh out of college with an accounting degree. It seems corporate America wasn't comfortable with her strong will. Her routine consisted of working during the day on her short stories and at night on her novel. But today was going to be a no-novel day. With five romance novels sold, Tonya was now writing her first mainstream thriller, a challenge she welcomed.

Cautiously, she crept out of her office, intent on telling her brother that they would have to leave. She had awakened that morning to the sound of her ringing door-bell. She knew then it was going to be a long day, and it was now eleven in the morning.

"Yo, you all right, girl?"

Tonya panicked at the sound of the male voice, but she relaxed when she realized it was her brother. Sounding somewhat breathy, she replied, "Yeah, I was just, uh, wondering how long you guys would be."

"I didn't mean to scare you. Sorry. You all right?"

"Yeah," she replied, trying to sound brave. *No,* her heart whispered, the tension on her face clearly projecting how she truly felt.

"Don't worry, we're almost finished in here. Cindy called me, by the way, and said that she would be here in an hour, so be ready for her and the girls."

"Oooh, I don't know why I put myself through this. Why don't you just have the party somewhere else?" Pleading had never been her strong suit, but as of late, she found herself resorting to it more and more. And that, along with being secluded in her house, was something else she was getting tired of.

"Because then you wouldn't be there," he replied, hardly surprised by the suggestion, which she made every year. Tonya knew better than to think they would relocate the gathering. "There's an easy enough solution to this problem, Tonya. All you have to do is walk out the door."

"That's easy for you to say, Vince." Easy for anyone who wasn't in her position to say. Anyone who had never felt the agony of helplessness and defeat, or the absence of will. She could go on all day trying to explain, but he still wouldn't understand. She looked with helpless eyes at the front door to her home. "I can't," she said, not for the first time. Her desire and trepidation could be seen in the dullness of her pain-filled eyes, and in her defeated posture.

"It's all right, girl." He gave her a hug. "Take your time. You know we're all here for you."

Tonya hugged him back. She was thankful for the support she received from him and the rest of her family over the past few years. But nobody knew how badly she wanted to battle her fears and get her life back to where it had been.

"Vince, I have been trying to fight it," she said sternly, unwilling to accept what she felt was pity.

"I know you have," he agreed. "Hell, I noticed that when you allowed us to keep the front door open to move your stuff, which, by the way, I will be bringing back on Monday. And don't worry about it this time. I'm taking very good care of it."

"I'm not worried. I ordered four large subs from the deli down the street for you and the boys. When you finish, have one of them walk down and get it. The money is on the counter. I'm going to be in the office trying to get some work done. I got a deadline that I don't think I'm going to make."

"Are you going to leave the door open?" he asked, looking hopeful.

"I think it's for the best. I've already pushed myself to the limit," she answered, walking toward her office.

"Well, it's only me out here. By the way, remember the guy I told you about who is going to be renting the house next door? I'm meeting with him today."

"Your friend from school?"

"Yeah, he's a good guy. You'll like him. I'm glad he'll be around here; maybe he can help me with some of the upkeep." He put up his hand to cut off what he suspected she was about to say. "Before you say anything, like I said, he's a good guy. I wouldn't have him around you if I didn't trust him. I invited him to the party tomorrow." He waited for the retort he knew was coming.

"Vince, you know I can't have strangers running around my house. It's bad enough I have to get through these two days. God, it's tiring." She made no effort to hide, or even soften, the annoyance in her voice.

"Sis, you'll be all right. After you meet him, he won't be a stranger. He'll be living right next door. You should get to know him."

She let her shoulders drop in silent resignation, now not really caring one way or the other. "Whatever."

She looked at Vince with his dark-chocolate skin, clear complexion and black eyes that shone like onyx, and wondered why he had never found someone to love. He was six feet even, only three inches taller than she, had a slim build, a full six-pack and shapely arm and leg muscles due to hours of push-ups and weight lifting. Looking at him, she could picture their father. Vince was the mirror image of his namesake. It was too bad he hadn't stayed in their lives; too bad he had opted to become a stranger instead.

Dozens of women had tried unsuccessfully to capture that steel heart of Vince's. As far as she could tell, he was a love 'em and leave 'em kind of guy. He had brought only a few around her, none of whom lasted long. His excuse was that they became too clingy, which was a turnoff to him. He wanted a strong, independent woman—like their mother. That was funny, considering Tonya remembered them arguing almost every day from when Vince turned fifteen to the day she died five years ago. They definitely loved each other, but they were too much alike, both being extremely strong-willed and independent.

"Did anyone get in contact with Aunt Bea to see what time her plane was coming in?" She moved to sit on the bottom stair step as one of Vince's workers walked past. She knew he was safe, but something deep inside was not so sure.

"Cecilia is going to pick her up," he answered her. "Her plane will be here six in the morning. They'll be here first thing tomorrow to help decorate."

Tonya looked toward her dining room as two men walked out, each carrying one of her six dining-room chairs. She was totally oblivious to the suspicious look that passed over her face. The room was bare except for the chairs' matching china cabinet. *It will take them a while to dismantle it,* she mused. Her china and glassware had already been packed, and the living room was empty except for two huge paintings on the walls.

Using pictures she had saved over the years, she had commissioned a talented young painter to create one of the large oil paintings. It was a collage of her great-grandmother, grandmother, and mother during different periods of their lives. All were dressed in navy blue. The other painting was of her and her siblings, and showed the four of them as children. As the keeper of all family heirlooms, she had the honor of safeguarding these, and many other pictures and valuables for her family.

Tomorrow night the portrait of three generations of motherhood would hold center stage as it did every year when her family gathered to honor the memories of her great-grandmother, Louise; grandmother, Elizabeth; and mother, Anne. And what a family she had, Tonya thought, as she tried to mentally prepare for the commotion that would begin at six o'clock the following evening.

Her great-aunt Bea, now the family matriarch, was a petite woman whose mouth in no way matched her physical appearance. She was one easy-to-love-but-hard-to-deal-with woman. And no matter how mad she made you, the minute she was gone, you missed her.

The person she wanted to see the most was her Uncle Butch, her mother's brother. He had always been her favorite. He was her "buddy," as they always referred to one another. Even when she was younger, and he was on that *stuff*, coming to their house and making her laugh and stealing her birthday money out of her piggybank, she had loved him. Now, her uncle was a big-time minister down in Maryland with a thousand-member TV ministry. He still had his sense of humor, and still owed her birthday money.

Yeah, that's family.

"I'm going to go to my office and rest while you guys finish up. Maybe I'll be able to get in a few minutes of shut-eye before Cindy arrives."

"Good luck," Vince replied, knowing that Tonya wouldn't sleep a wink while people were still in her house. He watched his sister walk away, wishing, as he had for the past three years, he could do something to help her. Maybe he couldn't, but he was sure his friend Jaimer could.

His boy seemed to be the same as he had been in college—always trying to do the right thing and looking out for others first. Vince also tried to do what he thought was the right thing, but not at the cost of placing himself in a bad predicament. You take care of home first. Except for his sisters, he wasn't moving heaven and earth for anybody.

Jaimer had always been different. In school, he hadn't been exactly slow; he'd had his share of college booty. But he hadn't been the dog Vince and their other frat brothers had been. Because of his own occasional carelessness for the opposite sex, Vince found himself standing between two screaming girls once or twice while attending the University of Maryland Eastern Shore. Although he never thought women went to school specifically to service him, it wasn't until he messed around and got whipped himself that he began to mature. But Jaimer was a gentleman at heart. He was respectful and always sensitive to his girl's feelings.

Tonya needed a good man in her life; he was going to give her one. Besides, Jaimer's life was probably so boring and dull that he would welcome the pick-me-up.

After lying quietly on the sofa in her office for an hour, Tonya opened the door and was greeted by her younger sister Cindy and their cousins Jordan and Shawnique. Each was carrying metal folding chairs.

"Hey, girl," Cindy yelled. "What's up?"

"Nothing is up. Where's Vince? You need to let the guys bring those in." Annoyed, she looked toward the dining room to see if her brother was there, but he was gone.

"That's okay. We got it all—"

"But you're pregnant, Cindy. You shouldn't be carrying that. Here, give them to me," she said sternly, holding out her hand. Concern for her little niece or nephew was evident in her tone.

"It's only three chairs, Tonya. I'm all right," she said firmly, rejecting Tonya's offer.

Jordan came up behind Cindy. "If you're all right, please keep it moving. We got more in the truck. Tonya, you're welcome to go get a few," she added, smiling sarcastically.

"Smartass. Cindy, you could have left her home," Tonya said, giving Jordan the evil eye.

"I love you, too, cuz," Jordan said, giving Tonya a quick peck on the cheek.

"Me, too. I love you, girl," Shawnique echoed, putting her chairs down.

"We got a lot of stuff to unload, Tonya," Jordan said. "My grandma said she expects more people this year." Jordan's grandmother was their great-aunt Lu on their grandfather's side, and had been their grandmother's best friend.

"Yeah, and Aunt Bea said that all of her kids were coming this year with their families. Plus her brothers are coming with their families, too," Cindy said, not even trying to add the numbers up in her head. The family had grown a lot in the last ten years, and she had stopped trying to remember all the faces and names.

"Damn, that's a lot of people. Are we going to have enough room?" Tonya asked, her voice rising hopefully. They just might have to move the party to accommodate the possible overflow.

"It's going to have to be enough room—unless you're ready to go out," Cindy replied, dashing any expectations Tonya might have had. She watched her sister take a step back. Her sister's actions infuriated Cindy, but she kept her anger to herself. In the past three years, her sister had changed from the person she most admired into one she most pitied.

Tonya once had been outgoing, flamboyant, and fun to be around. She was popular throughout high school and college, was well liked at the clubs they used to frequent, and had her share of love-struck wannabe suitors. They used to jump into their cars and travel at a moment's notice. But after the incident, Tonya had become increasingly afraid of everything, and she had eventually just shut herself off from the world. Cindy wanted her sister back.

And she damn sure didn't want to have to pick between Jordan and Shawnique's silly asses to be in the delivery room with her. Shawnique would laugh at her, and Jordan would cry more than she did. Uh-uh . . . if Tonya didn't get it together soon, she would have to go it alone. Cecilia had already said she wasn't going.

Cindy had made such a terrible scene when she visited Cecilia, who delivered twins with her first pregnancy, that she was banned from the birth of the second child. It was a small argument with a nurse on staff who was flirting with her man and a charge for bodily harm, big deal. How was she supposed to know the chick worked there?

"Well, is there going to be enough food?" Tonya asked, bringing her sister back from her mental wandering.

"You know there is, girl. Stop worrying. I paid the caterer last week. They'll be here to set things up tomorrow at four." Seeing uneasiness on Tonya's face, she added, "Dayton and I are coming to help decorate in the morning. I'll bring my clothes and get dressed here so I can stay with you when people start to arrive. Cecilia will pick up Aunt Bea at the airport and drop her stuff off at the house, and then they'll come here. Aunt Bea's kids are driving down from Chicago, but she said she was flying. She couldn't stand being cooped up with that many kids for the long drive."

"I don't blame her. I don't know how she did it last year," Tonya laughed.

"Remember when Josh's son Jeremiah was her only grandbaby?"

"Yeah, he's not a baby anymore. Now Jeremiah is twenty-two."

"Really?"

"Yeah. Tiana has two teenagers, Annie has five kids . . ."

"She still married to Marvin?" Tonya asked, remembering her older cousins.

"Yup, and Mike got three."

"Right, and Josh had two more."

"Damn, that is a lot. No wonder Aunt Bea's hair is white as snow," Jordan piped up.

"Aunt Bea ain't thinking about them kids. You know she cusses their behinds out just like she used to do us."

"You're probably right," Cindy said, laughing loud and hard. "Remember when she used to bite us on our cheeks? I hated that shit."

"You never told her to stop," Tonya said, also laughing loudly.

"Neither did you or Vince or Cecilia," Cindy replied.

"Hell, no. I'd rather just deal with the pain and get it over with." Tonya laughed even harder. Her sister watched her, loving the glimmer of her pre-incident sister.

"Me, too . . . Anyway, things are going smoothly. So don't worry."

"I just feel so useless." The sudden slump of her shoulders showed her frustration. She moved back into the office, her sister close behind.

"Tonya, didn't we go through this last year? When you're ready, we'll be waiting for you. Nobody is pushing you to heal overnight. Just like your therapist said, you have to take your time. We want you to take your time. Don't rush and everything will fall back into place."

"Cindy, you don't know how bad I've been wanting to go out that door and be me again. In my heart, I feel like I'm ready to live again, but my head won't let me do it."

"It will happen." Cindy said, wrapping her big sister in an embrace of love and patience. "Just take your time."

"Hey, what's going on in here? Nobody invited us." Jordan and Shawnique bounced into the room and formed a group hug, rocking back and forth in unison, until silly Jordan began to chant:

"Oowshi, waila waila; Oowshi, bang bang; Oowshi waila waila; Oowshi bang bang."

Laughing, they broke out of the hug and began talking about old times as they finished setting up the serving tables for the party.

CHAPTER 2

Tonya paced the length of her spacious bedroom, pausing long enough to give herself the once-over in her full-length mirror. She was glad to see that she had successfully hidden the dark worry lines under her eyes. However, the nagging uneasiness plaguing her refused to still as she clenched and unclenched her hands and rotated her neck to ease her tension. It only helped a little. But she pressed forward, slipping on her pumps, thus changing her hippy five feet, nine inches to a more slimming six feet even. She was pleased with the final results. The paisley Barcelona-style skirt set fit her perfectly, accentuating her hips and rounding her behind nicely. The red of the outfit matched her lips and made her mocha skin glow. When she heard the doorbell ring, her face paled and her nervousness returned.

＝

"Hey, girl . . . how you doing?" Cindy said, opening the front door wide and hugging Cecilia.

"Baby girl, look at you all fat and pregnant," Cecilia said, patting Cindy's stomach. She was disappointed when she didn't feel a kick. For all her complaining, you'd expect that Cindy had gained a hundred pounds during her pregnancy. In truth, she had gained only twenty pounds thus far, carrying her load right in the pit of her belly. Her legs weren't fat, her breasts hadn't swollen to the size of watermelons, and her ass hadn't spread across her back. Envious, Cecilia added, "Girl, you look good, but I'm not surprised. You always look good."

"Thank you, sis." Cindy turned around slowly, showing off her seven months of pregnancy in a black velour catsuit covered by a sheer, sterling silver beaded V-neck poncho. Shorter than Tonya at five feet seven inches, the girl was dressed perfectly for the fall weather, matching the ensemble with a pair of black tapestry T-strap pumps.

"Where's Tonya? I was just telling Aunt Bea in the car about her almost sleeping through the night," Cecilia said, turning to see Tonya creeping downstairs. "There she is." Arms outstretched, she met Tonya at the bottom of the stairs and embraced her. "Congratulations, girl. This is going to be a great night." Tonya fell into her arms, easily accepting the comfort and familiarity of her embrace. Cecilia couldn't stop being a mother hen. Although there was only a five-year age difference between them, it must have come from helping their mother. Tonya loved her for it.

At five feet, eleven inches, Cecilia was the tallest of the girls and the thickest, having more hips and behind. But they were basically all cut from the same mold. However, while Tonya had thin eyebrows and eyelashes like their mother, the other two had thick brows and long lashes like Vince. And his were the thickest, longest, and most luscious of all.

"Yeah, I think it's going to be great, too. You're looking good. Where's everybody?" Tonya asked, checking out Cecilia, who was wearing a brown, tan, and black asymmetric tunic pantsuit that showed off her fit figure. "Where's Aunt Bea?"

"She's coming," Cecilia responded.

As they walked toward Cindy, who was still at the door, their Aunt Bea walked in carrying a large grocery bag.

"Hello, ladies," their rambunctious aunt called out to them, putting her bag down. Cindy and Tonya rushed into her arms and hugged her tightly.

Bubbling with joy, Tonya held on extra long. It was Aunt Bea who had flown down right after the incident and had stayed with her for two weeks. It was Aunt Bea who had sat up with her all night and allowed her to cry out her fears and who had stood by the bathroom door without complaint while she relieved herself or showered. It was Aunt Bea who had sat in the living room with her the first time her therapist came to visit. And it was Aunt Bea who came back once a year to stay with her for a month each winter.

Their Aunt Bea was a piece of work. Five feet, three inches of fun and the mouth of a drunken sailor. She was their grandmother's baby sister. Tonya could remember when her aunt still lived in Philadelphia. As youngsters, no matter how much Aunt Bea picked at them, made them mad, made them cry, they wanted to visit her. Her mother used to say that it was like that when she was growing up, too. Nobody could get enough of Aunt Bea's good-natured laughter or her tendency to be overly dramatic.

"Dirty, you're looking beautiful. Pregnancy suits you, baby."

"Thank you, Aunt Bea," Cindy said, answering to the nickname her grandmother Elizabeth gave her when she was a toddler because no matter how many times she was bathed, two seconds later, her face was covered with food, dirt, or whatever she could get her hands on again. After her grandmother's death, Aunt Bea and her mother were the only ones she allowed to call her by that name.

"Tonya, I hear you're doing better." Aunt Bea turned to her, beaming with pride.

"Yes . . . I'm so tired of being locked up in here."

"Well, good, cause it's time for you to get your ass up out of this damn house." Aunt Bea hugged her again. "Now, let's get ready for these folks. You know how this family is. Everybody wants a plate. Half of them didn't even send all their money."

"Actually, they were your people first, Aunt Bea," Cindy joked.

"Hell, I don't even claim half of them. That was your grandmom who always had folk up in the house, this cousin, that cousin."

"Mommom Lizzy did know everybody," Tonya agreed.

"Yeah, well, I didn't know, don't know, and don't give a damn about ever knowing them," Aunt Bea replied. They knew she meant every word. "Hell, and the ones I do know, I don't trust." She snapped her eyes for extra dramatic effect.

"Stop," Cecilia said, giggling. "Aunt Bea, behave. Tonight is all about family."

"Family, yeah, all right. And see how many extra relatives y'all gonna have tonight." She laughed and then changed the subject. "I'm sorry we couldn't make it this morning to help decorate, but Cecilia got called to the station, and I stayed to help with the kids."

"That's all right, Aunt Bea," Cindy said. "We had plenty of help. Everything is all ready. The caterers just left; two of them are staying behind to oversee the food table. People should be arriving any minute."

Two hours later, the party was in full swing. Everyone was having a wonderful time eating, socializing, and catching up on the family gossip. But the house was overcrowded. Aunt Bea was right; a lot of extra relatives were floating around. Tonya dealt with it best she could because she was in her home. Although she didn't know everyone in the house, she kept reminding herself that she was among family. It was a good thing her office door was locked; otherwise, she would probably be in there right now. Instead, she was forced to face her fears.

Standing near the bottom of the steps talking to one of her cousins, Tonya looked over the crowd. People were everywhere from her foyer to her large living room, and from her equally large dining room to her closed-in patio, which ran the length of the house and was well lit.

Their father passed away three years before their mother, and although he bought the connected homes after their divorce, some twenty years earlier, he left both homes to her. Their mother refused to move into either house, and never explained her reasoning. Their divorce had been kind of strained, but Tonya had assumed relations were better after both remarried.

Both houses had been rented out until their mother's death. After that, it didn't make sense to pay rent for a house when they had two that were mortgage-free, so Tonya and Cindy moved into one and Vince the other. Cecilia was already married and in her own home. Later, Cindy moved in with Dayton, whom she had met at the same party that Tonya first saw Howard. Dayton was a member of a Philly-based bike club. Then Vince moved into the apartment above his office, which he had obtained when he bought the building for his company.

Over the past two years, they had rented out the house next door. Unfortunately, the last tenants were divorcing. The wife was moving back with her first husband. The husband was getting back with his old boyfriend. Life is crazy.

On one of her sweeps of the crowd, Tonya glimpsed Vince talking to a tall man. His back was to her, so she couldn't see who he was. A few inches taller than her brother, he had broad shoulders and a bald head and was wearing a well-fitting beige linen suit. Real nice, from what she could see of him, anyway. Almost as if sensing her gaze, he turned slightly, looking over his shoulder at her. Even through the bobbing heads of the dancers between them, they made eye contact. Before looking away, she saw intense interest in his eyes.

Tonya felt an unfamiliar stab of longing, followed by an unexpected surge of warmth. Surprised by her reaction, she tried to compose herself. She watched apprehensively as her brother led the tall stranger toward her; she couldn't take her eyes off him. Vince must have thought something was wrong, because he appeared to be anticipating the worst.

"Sis, are you all right?" he asked, holding her by the elbow to steady her.

"Ooh . . . yeah," she said, feigning interest in an invisible spot on her top. "I thought I spilled something on my blouse. What's up?" *Real smooth, girl.*

"Well, um . . . this is my boy, Jay, the one I was telling you about. He's going to be renting the house next door." Vince stepped aside so that tall, dark, and handsome could move into full view. "This is Jaimer Lambert. Jaimer, my sister, Tonya Perkins."

Jaimer extended a hand, but Tonya hesitated before taking it. His gaze was direct, intense, his brown eyes slowly moving from her face to her chest.

"Hi, Tonya. It's nice to meet you. I've heard a lot about you." The voice was smooth and deep, with just a touch of raspiness.

"Nice to meet you, too. I can't say I have heard a lot about you." She smiled weakly at her lame rejoinder. *I gotta start getting out of this house.*

"Tonya, I told you about Jaimer," Vince reminded her. "We went to school together."

But then, they had never visited Vince's campus. He used to say that he didn't want his sisters exposed to the kind of men that were at the college. But then again, he probably hadn't relished the idea of being caught in the middle of some relationship gone south.

"And, that's all I know," she said, unaware that her hand was still in Jaimer's until he placed his over hers.

"If Vince doesn't mind, I'd love to tell you more about myself, Tonya," he smiled.

Ooh . . . that smile. It was wide with perfectly even white teeth framed by full, smooth lips. "He doesn't mind," Tonya said, pushing her brother aside and leading Jaimer to her side patio.

They found empty seats near the back corner of the room. Tonya sat with her back to the corner, occasionally looking over the crowd of familiar faces, unsure of what she was doing. The only thing she knew for sure was that she was going to enjoy this man's company and that she was surprising herself.

It had been a long time since she had entertained the idea of male companionship, but crossing back into that territory seemed smoother than she had thought it would be. If nothing else, Jaimer Lambert was reminding her of what she was missing while "locked up." His smile had her wishing for long walks through the park. His laugh had her thinking of bike rides along a nature trail. And his body had her imaging passionate candlelit nights.

Nothing was actually stopping her from having candlelit nights. But how was she going to meet anyone with her self-imposed imprisonment? And who would want to be in a relationship with someone who was terrified of opening her front door?

Something about this man had her thinking of things she hadn't done in years. She had thought about doing them, but they were close to impossible to do without a partner.

"So, Jaimer, tell me about yourself," Tonya said, forcing herself to be just a little forward, testing both herself and him.

"Well, there's not really much to tell," he began, his voice echoing his warm smile. "I'm just a regular guy. I went to school with your brother. We met our sophomore year while we were pledging the same fraternity. Um . . . after graduation, I went into law enforcement. I was in that arena until two years ago, when I was wounded."

"Not seriously, I hope," Tonya said, a tinge of concern in her voice.

"No, not serious. It was only a shot in the arm, but it was serious enough to make me realize I needed to get out of the game before it got too late."

"So now you're retired?"

"Yep. Now I own a small security consulting firm. The apartment I was renting got to be too small. I saw your brother a couple of months ago at a frat reunion, and we got to talking, and the place next door came up. And that's basically all she wrote." He smiled again, this time a little wider, showing more pearly white teeth. *Sexy.*

Tonya wasn't satisfied with his too-brief synopsis. She found herself wanting to know more. "Well, what about family? You don't have any around here?" She glanced down at his hands, openly looking for a wedding ring.

Jaimer watched her, intrigued by the question behind the question. His mouth twitched with humor. He flexed his fingers, showing her that he knew what she wanted to know. "Nope, no family around here. I only have a sister. She lives in Virginia with her husband and two kids. That's it. No wife, no ex-wife, no kids, no dogs or cats. It's just me and this business that I'm getting off the ground."

"And why is that? You seem to be a very nice, definitely attractive man. Why haven't you settled down?"

"Honestly, I've only met one person in my life I have felt strongly enough about even think about settling down."

"And she didn't feel the same way?" Tonya asked curiously.

"Actually, she never knew that I existed." He looked away, catching a few curious glances aimed at them.

"Well, why didn't you approach her and at least let her know how you felt?" After some hesitation, she placed a comforting hand on his knee for comfort, thinking he didn't want her to see his pain. Then, pulled it back as a small electrical charge hit her fingers.

He turned back to her and smiled again. "You're a romantic."

"Well, I guess I am." She laughed.

"I couldn't approach her. It wasn't the right time. But sometimes I wish I had said something to her back then. Anyway—" he cut himself off, sensing a need to change the subject. "Can you tell me something?"

"I'll try my best." Tonya felt herself relaxing around him. She was so absorbed in her conversation and the presence of Jaimer, she was paying no attention to anyone else. Any other time, she would have been restlessly scanning the crowd.

"Why do I get the feeling that we're being watched?"

Then she remembered that they weren't alone on a secluded island somewhere. She heard music playing in the background and chattering voices all around her. Tonya blinked and glanced around the room. She smiled as she closed in on her sisters and her aunt standing at the patio entrance watching them. Crossing her arms in front of her, she stared back at them.

"That's because we are." Narrowing her eyes, she tilted her head to the side just long enough to show them how annoyed she was. "See, my family thinks it's pretty amazing to see me sitting here talking to a man."

"They've never seen you talk to a man before?" Jaimer asked. He knew what she meant, but wanted to hear her say it. Her short laugh at his question was unexpected, and it both unnerved and intrigued him.

"Uh, let me explain something to you." Tonya let out a short, world-weary sigh before continuing. "I'm what you would call a recluse. I don't go outside. I'm afraid to. I don't like strangers around me."

"Yeah, I know." Jaimer looked around the patio. She couldn't possibly know everybody in the house. But then again, Vince did say it was all family. "Your brother mentioned that to me when he suggested that I come here tonight. He said that I had to meet you first and get your approval before actually moving in. He also said that if you didn't feel comfortable with me living next door, then it was a no-go."

She laughed. "Vince is crazy. I wouldn't have turned you down." She stopped talking for a minute as questions careened through her head. *Could this all be a setup by Vince? Was he intentionally trying to hook her up with this man? And could they all be in on it?* "I'm not worried about what goes on outside. I just don't go out there. I can't."

"But whatever happened has you locked in here, right?" His question had a subtle but detectable note of impatience. "I mean, that's why you're not going out, right? Because of something that happened when you were outside."

"Yes, but . . . okay, let's change the subject. I don't want to get into that right now," Tonya replied, trying to disguise her annoyance. This was not a good topic for her to be talking about with a complete stranger. That's what she paid her therapist for. Jaimer didn't know what she was going through or had gone through these past three years. This wasn't the time to try to make him understand.

"I'm sorry. I just thought that maybe you wanted to talk about it. Let me just say this." He spoke with quiet but distinct firmness. "In our lives, we tend to give people and things more power over us than they have or even want. Don't let anyone or anything have that much power over you."

Tonya took a sip from the wine glass she had forgotten she was holding. He made a lot of sense. She was lending power to the outside world—a world that didn't know she existed, wasn't paying her any attention, and was oblivious to her problems. She had built her fear up so high it had become an inseparable part of her daily life. She had just accepted the fact that she was afraid instead of earnestly trying to deal with that fear. It was time to start dealing with her fears.

≈

"Um . . . Dirty," Aunt Bea said, repeatedly hitting Cindy's elbow. She stood between Cindy and Cecilia. Nodding toward the corner of the patio, she spoke just above a whisper: "Who is that handsome man talking to your sister?"

"I don't know, but he looks good as hell. Don't he, Cecilia?"

"I think he's the guy who is moving in next door. They seem to be pretty interested in each other, don't they? He is sharp," Cecilia agreed, squinting her eyes. "He looks like . . . nah, never mind," she said, chasing her unfinished thought away.

"Who?" Cindy asked curiously.

"Nobody. A couple of years ago, I was at a convention in D.C. on new surveillance equipment. He looks a little like the keynote speaker. But that guy was a former DEA agent, had done work with the CIA and the FBI, and had even invented some new surveillance devices."

"Well, we know that ain't him. Why would somebody like that be here? Besides, that guy doesn't look harmless at all. And look at how taken Tonya is with him." Cindy and Aunt Bea moved further into the patio area to get a better look and hear a bit of the conversation. They were not very subtle.

Cecilia hung back, shaking her head at the two of them. They were too much alike. She would listen to Tonya yell at them later for being in her business. Before going in search of her husband, Cecilia took another long look at the mystery man.

A couple of hours later, the party showed no sign of slowing. Leftover food had been put away, and an assortment of desserts was brought out and arranged on the large table left by the caterers. There were pies and cakes brought in by various family members, a large tray of pretzel salad, and Aunt Bea's famous rice pudding.

Tonya glanced at the wall clock in the kitchen. *Ten o'clock.* She had a long night ahead of her. Her family was one of those families that didn't know when to go home. But this year, unlike the two previous years, she didn't mind them lingering. In fact, she was surprised to find herself dreading the evening's end.

When the music turned from the slow, old-school R & B to a new-school upbeat tempo and rap, chairs were folded and taken to the basement. Immediately, the living-room floor was filled with couples dancing to Beyonce's "Baby Boy."

Tonya stood on the sidelines watching her brother dance with Marcia, the woman he'd invited to the party. Also standing on the sidelines was the woman he hadn't invited. She stood with her arms crossed, leaning back on her hip and tapping her foot against the hardwood floor. Her oval-shaped jaw line visibly tensed as she watched him enjoying himself. Tonya had a mind to tell her to take it easy on her polish, but just then, Cindy wobbled off the dance floor.

"What happened to that gorgeous man you were talking to earlier?" She looked at Tonya with mischief in her eyes.

"I wouldn't know. He's not my child for me to keep an eye on, Cindy." She looked at her sister, annoyed. "Besides, I was just making friendly conversation." Giving up, she smilingly said, "He's over there by the table drinking a cup of cran-grape juice."

"I knew it. You like him. I knew it. I knew it. I knew it," Cindy crowed, excitedly pinching Tonya's upper arm.

"Ow! Stop it. I don't like him. I don't even know him." She hit Cindy's hand away.

"You're getting to know him. He's been around you all night. He's looking at you now."

"Then he must see you standing over here acting like a fool. Go find Dayton."

"Don't look now, but he's on his way over here."

Cindy stayed put and watched Jaimer slowly make his way over to them, staying as close to the edge of the dance floor as he could. But at times, he had to move through the dancers in order to make any progress.

Moving in beat with the music and dancing along with different couples, he finally made it to his destination.

"Well, one thing I can say for you—you got rhythm. That's a good thing," Cindy laughed, extending her hand. "Hi, I'm Cindy, Tonya's younger sister."

"Hi, Cindy. I'm Jaimer, the friend of Vince's who will hopefully be renting the house next door." Releasing Cindy's hand, Jaimer looked pointedly at Tonya. "Um, your aunt told me that I should come over here and ask you to dance."

Tonya didn't answer.

"Tonya, I think he's talking to you," Cindy said, nudging her sister.

"Me? Oh, no. It's been so long since I've danced, I wouldn't know what to do."

"That's nonsense," Jaimer replied, pushing her out onto the dance floor ahead of him and leaving Cindy to smile after them.

As soon as they found a spot on the floor, the music changed. Tonya hesitated, but Jaimer's hand on her back urged her forward. "A slow song will be easier for you," he whispered close to her ear.

Easy for you to say!

A few couples left the dance floor. Tonya became highly conscious of the fact that she was standing board-stiff, afraid to let Jaimer any further into her personal space. She could see Cindy, Dayton, and Aunt Bea watching from the sidelines. Even Vince, who had switched partners, stopped dancing to watch them. She became even more self-conscious.

"Tonya, look at me," Jaimer said. He stood directly in front of her with his arms spread wide. He wasn't oblivious to the group of spectators. "All you have to do is watch me and concentrate on us." He could tell from her tense expression and wandering eyes that she was uncomfortable. "I'm not going to hurt you." He stepped closer to her, talking the whole time. "I'm going to put my hand on your waist. Relax, it's just me." His hand rested on her hip. "Here's my hand. I want you to put your hand in mine, and your other hand on my shoulder. Just concentrate on me and feel the music."

Tonya did as she was told and stepped into his strong arms, which felt as if they could take hold of her worries, her fears, and her burdens and carry them for her. It felt good for once to be able to let her guard down—if only for a minute—and let somebody else worry. She was astounded at how this strange man was willing and able to help her forget about her problems. She almost felt like her old self again.

She allowed him to pull her further into his embrace as the beat of "When I'm with You" by Tony Terry vibrated through the speakers. Halfway through the song, Tonya began to relax against Jaimer's body, feeling the strength of his muscular chest. She felt little shivers when he lightly caressed her back.

"I'm starting to remember what this feels like," she admitted, letting herself be lulled into the bolder rhythm of Prince's "Adore." In total contentment, she sighed against him and let her body move in unison with his through the high and low notes of the provocative song.

Leaning back to see her face, Jaimer asked, "What do you mean, you're starting to remember?"

"It's been a very long time since I've danced like this in a man's arms, been around a man, period."

"Because of your illness—if that's what you would call it?"

"Actually, it's called agoraphobia. I call it a condition, one that I am slowly but surely fighting. And yes, because of it."

"Well, now that you trust me, I would be happy to have you in my arms anytime."

Tonya became flustered and, unsure how to respond, simply said, "Thank you for the dance."

"As I said, anytime." Following her off the dance floor, Jaimer chided himself for doing exactly what he'd promised himself he wouldn't do: move too fast.

"Girl, you looked almost like your old self out there on that dance floor tonight," Cindy said after the party.

"Yeah, right. I did have fun, though," Tonya admitted.

"It showed. Aunt Bea must have watched you all night. She was so happy to see you having a good time."

"I know. I think I've been missing something in my life cooped up in this big old house."

"Duh. You think? Hell, as good as he looked, I think I might be missing something, too. Dayton had better step up his game," Cindy responded, delighting in the change she saw in her sister.

"Yeah, right, I know Dayton is giving you everything you need," Tonya said, watching her aunt walk over with a tray loaded with coffee, cream, and sugar. "Ah, just what I need to help me get to sleep tonight."

"I thought you two could use some coffee. Cecilia has the pie."

"I just locked the front door. Vince said he will come by tomorrow to help clear stuff, and he'll bring your furniture back on Monday," Cecilia said, taking a seat on the sofa in her office beside Aunt Bea. The four of them were having a sister-power session before separating.

"So, Missy," Aunt Bea began, turning to Tonya. "By all appearances, it seems that you had a wonderful time tonight. Did you enjoy it as much as it looked like you did?"

"I did."

"And?"

"And, what?"

"Don't play with me. Do you like the damn man, or not?" Aunt Bea always went straight to the point.

"He's all right. Yeah, I like him, but I don't think that I should be trying to get to know anybody until I can get myself together."

"Girl, please, it's been long enough," Cindy interrupted. "You can only play with one of those toys for so long before you're ready for the real thing. And it has been three years. I think the girl is long overdue."

"Cindy!" Cecilia managed to say before they burst into laughter. "You know what? You're a mess."

"I'm just telling it like it is. Y'all might want to sit around and act like you don't know, but I'm the youngest in here, and if I know, I know damn well you all do. She needs a man fast before she messes around and electrocutes her damn self." Cindy took a fake sip of her drink, desperately trying to keep up a serious facade.

They all threw their heads back and roared with laughter. Unable to suppress her giggles, Tonya joined in.

"Ah, damn," Aunt Bea screamed, still laughing, "girl, if you had any sense, you'd be crazy."

CHAPTER 3

At three forty-five in the morning, Jaimer breezed into his tiny two-bedroom apartment humming Prince's "Adore," which had instantly become one of his favorite tunes. He closed the door and leaned back against it. He shook his head from side to side, trying to clear his mind. *Not so fast, boy . . . get a grip. You're not in there yet.*

Looking around the cluttered apartment reaffirmed his decision to rent the large house next to Tonya's. But best of all, it afforded an ideal opening to step back into her life. Well, not exactly *back* into it, but closer than he had been. Approaching her at the party was the beginning of their friendship for her, but Jaimer had been in her life much longer than that.

Pushing aside the boxes he had spent all day packing, he made a path from the door to his sofa. Once there, Jaimer pushed aside packets of the bubble wrap that he had used to protect his delicate electronic equipment and fell exhausted onto the soft cushions.

The black leather three-piece living room furniture was the second-largest purchase he had ever made. It came in as a complete set with end tables, lamps, and a coffee table. He had bought it the same day he retired from the agency as a sign that he was committed to stabilizing his life.

When he was younger and more sure-footed, the new kid on the block, a shooting ace and new shining star from the bureau's training classes, he had been too eager to prove himself to even think about women, let alone a family. Then as a lead agent, he had to work extra hard to stay ahead of the next class of possible wonder kids. Occasionally, he dated—out of necessity, not love. Back then, a warm body was all he needed to get by. That wasn't enough any more.

After fifteen years of service, Jaimer realized that he was missing something very important in his life, something that would make him whole and complete. He saw it when he visited his sister and at functions held at the homes of some of his co-workers. He was missing something in his life and was tired of no longer being satisfied with just a career. And he definitely didn't want to wait until he was too old to enjoy the fulfillment that a family, his own family, would bring him.

As he lay back on the sofa cushions and allowed his tense body to relax. Jaimer thought about the tangled web he was weaving and prayed that a good ending would be the final outcome.

He first saw Tonya Perkins three years ago when she unknowingly walked into the path of his camera's telescopic lenses at the annual Unity Day festivities at Benjamin Franklin Parkway. She was talking to his surveillance subject. They seemed to be having a good time—walking hand in hand; checking out the wares of various vendors and making small purchases; eating an array of foods.

He and two other agents had taken turns tailing the unsuspecting couple, suspecting Howard would use the crowded festivities as an opportunity to make contact with the man they expected him to eventually testify against.

Upon learning her family name was Perkins and that she lived in the area, he had his men dig for more information about her, and sure enough, his suspicions were confirmed. She was the sister of his old college friend. And she was in the middle of one of his department's biggest investigations. He could do nothing to warn her, couldn't even contact his old friend after all these years. The department couldn't know that he had any ties whatsoever to the case. To get the man responsible for the murder of his partner, he needed Howard Douglass. His decision wasn't a hard one to make.

So he had kept quiet and stayed on the case, hoping for the best—at least for his friend's sake. After several more weeks of surveillance, it became apparent that Tonya wasn't involved in or aware of Howard's drug activities. She seemed to be exactly what she was, his girlfriend. Through surveillance photos and the tape recordings from the bugs secretly placed in Howard's apartment, Jaimer could tell that the man cared for her very deeply. And she appeared to have strong feelings for him. Jaimer found himself envying Howard for having her love.

"Ugh . . . enough of that," Jaimer said out loud. "This is a new day." He stretched and went into the bedroom, which was also filled with boxes. Pushing aside a few discarded articles of clothing, he found a clean pair of sweats and a T-shirt and headed for the shower.

In the shower, through the thick fog of steam from the hot water, with his head down and his eyes closed, thoughts of his magical night with Tonya drifted back to him.

He had spotted her standing in a corner of the room as soon as he walked into the house. Her huge jet-black eyes, filled with worry, roved over the crowd, pausing here and there to take in particulars of this or that person. He could see from her rigid stance that she was on guard, it seemed, waiting for something to happen. She was tense and unsure. Jaimer wanted to comfort her.

Vince was standing a short distance from the doorway in the company of an exotic and sensual-looking caramel-colored woman. When he saw him, he immediately left her to greet him. "Hey, brother, what's up? Glad you could make it."

The bone-thin woman with a model's build sashayed away after glancing at Jaimer. She looked oddly familiar to him, but he paid it no mind. "Thanks, frat. After giving it some thought, I decided that you were right. It would be better for me to be introduced to your sister around a group of people. I don't want to scare her or anything."

"Man, it's cool. You can move in on Tuesday. But I still want you to meet."

"This is definitely a large crowd. Is it always like this?"

"Every year we have this big blowout. It's more people than last year, but it's all family." Vince paused when a tall, and voluptuous dark-chocolate woman came by and kissed him on the side of his mouth. "Well, almost all family," he corrected, grinned.

"I see some things never change," Jaimer said, smiling tolerantly.

"I can't help it, man. Every time I try to fly straight, they keep drawing me back in. Did you bring anybody with you?"

"Nah, man. Are you kidding? Not with you here. It's been a long time, but I remember how you used to do."

He didn't know why, but just then, Jaimer turned and looked across the room. And there she was, standing on the other side near the staircase. Her curious eyes seemed to draw him in, and with considerable regret, he knew that he was going to have to play his friend to get what he wanted. He just hoped that in the end, things would work themselves out.

"Yo, man . . ." he said excitedly, hitting Vince on his thick shoulder. "Who is *that* standing over there next to the steps?"

Vince looked up, thinking he was missing something. "Where?"

"Over there. I don't want to point. The pretty mocha sister in the red outfit by the steps."

Vince strained to find this mystery beauty his friend had spotted in a group that supposedly consisted of only his family. Not that the women in his family weren't all beautiful, but by the way his friend was acting, this lady wasn't someone he knew yet.

"The one with the small frame glasses and long braids, a small birthmark near her left eye."

Realization hit Vince immediately after Jaimer's brief, but precise description. Laughing, he said, "Man, that's Tonya, my sister."

"Your sister?" Jaimer already knew the particulars of the Perkins clan, but had to continue playing the role of innocent newcomer.

"She's the one who lives here. The one I was telling you about. You're here to meet her."

"Good, I think I'll like that," he replied, pushing aside the twinge of guilt he felt. "Well, no time like the present."

"Whoa, slow it down, man," Vince cautioned, grabbing Jaimer's arm when he began walking away. "Let me explain something to you. You getting all excited about the intros and what not, but that's my little sister. As I told you, she has been through a lot, gone through a really hard time. She's still going through a thing or two, but she's working on it. I don't want her sidetracked, so don't go trying to holla at her or doing anything to spook her."

"I'll make you a promise," Jaimer said, holding out his hand. "I won't go any further with your sister than you did with mine. Is it a deal?"

"Hell, no, it ain't no deal," Vince replied, pushing Jaimer's hand away. Jaimer knew the whole truth about how things had gone down between his sister and Vince. That girl had Vince wrapped around her finger so good and tight it was still embarrassing for him to remember.

It had only lasted for a semester in his junior year, but for that brief time, Vince had put his pimp hat on the shelf, stopped calling his other lady friends, and lived for the weekends that the former Ebony Lambert came to visit them at school. She was a couple of years younger, but wise way beyond her years. And if she hadn't broken it off, he would probably still be lapping after her like some lovesick pup.

"Okay, since we're both consenting adults, how about I just tell you that I have no intention of hurting your sister. I was just interested, that's all."

"Just remember, frat, I got my eye on you." Then Vince quickly changed his joking tone into a more serious one. "I'm not too worried, though. Tonya might be housebound, but she's far from blind. She can spot a player a mile away. Remember, she was brought up with the best."

Laughing, they headed toward the object of Jaimer's desire.

Eager to finally meet her after all of these years, Jaimer all but forgot Vince was still standing there once Tonya spoke. He was immediately entranced by her.

His eyes took in everything from head to feet. The soft braids caressing her shoulders made him want to wrap his fingers around her hair, pull on them to make her head fall back and conquer the smooth, slightly parted lips beckoning him with their shiny gloss.

Although she stood proudly erect, the rise and fall of her chest was a bit erratic. He watched as her breast rose with each intake of new air. He could see his hands easily fitting around her small waist and sliding just as easily over her wide hips and down her smooth thighs and shapely legs. Tonya swayed back and forth uncomfortably, making him aware that she had noticed his unabashed inventory of her.

Vince broke the silence with introductions and then was whisked away by the dark beauty who had kissed him earlier. Vince introduced her as Marcia Jones.

With Vince gone, he was free to get to know Tonya Perkins, free to uncover the person behind the beautiful face, the lovely body. He found himself falling in love with the real Tonya this time, not the outward shell. If Jaimer had thought he was in love before, by the end of the evening, he knew that the game he played had risen to another level of seriousness.

They talked a little about the past, a little about the present. Her laugh captivated him, her sadness touched him, but she opened up to him freely once she got past her initial hesitation. And they had danced. Holding her in his arms had felt so good once she let her body relax against his. They fit perfectly together; she had to know that. The response of her body to his hands made him believe so.

He could only imagine the degree of passion she possessed before her disorder left her housebound, as her brother put it. Even when he felt his own body tighten and respond to her, she still moved against him willingly.

Jaimer awakened to the cooing sound of a small pigeon roosting in his windowsill. He was annoyed it had picked that exact moment to rouse him, but then he remembered there was much to do in the two days left before his move-in day.

Vowing to make the day productive, he set out to finish packing his office equipment and papers. He intended to use the first floor of his new residence as his office; the second floor would comprise his living quarters. He and Vince had already discussed this, and other details. Vince had nixed the posting of a business sign in the front yard, but had accepted most of Jaimer's alteration ideas. He would be allowed to put a business sign on his front door—but only to keep potential clients from unwittingly disturbing Tonya.

It was finally happening for him, and he was excited about the possibilities ahead for his company. An expert in the areas of surveillance and security equipment, he was a highly respected former agent, and was well known to those in the field. He was still called on to assist in different areas of intelligence gathering. Eventually, his name had become known to, and his services sought by, large corporations and other high-profile clients.

He didn't like the necessary travel, being too much like his old job, but it paid the bills. Philadelphia and the surrounding areas could offer him only so much business. The higher-paying customers weren't your everyday, run-of-the-mill companies. In any case, his small staff of fellow ex-agents and ex-police officers would soon have to be doubled to keep up with the demands of his clientele.

Two more days became a refrain as he stacked boxes in corner after corner. Jaimer's phone rang just as he was about to take a break around two o'clock. Answering on the third ring, he wasn't surprised to hear his sister's voice on the other end of the line. Like clockwork, she called every couple of days just to be in his business, using the excuse that they hardly ever talked anymore.

"Hey, boy, what's up?"

"Hi, Eb . . . what's going on?"

"Nothing much. I just called to see how you were doing. I haven't heard from you lately."

"I talked to you three days ago. I'm still doing well. How is everybody down there?"

"Good. Your niece is being bad again, but besides that, everything is okay."

He laughed. His niece *was* a handful. "What happened this time?"

"She got into a fight with one of the boys in her class. I told her that she shouldn't go around fighting. It's time for her to start acting like a young lady. The boy tried to hug her, and she kicked him in his privates."

"That's my girl. That's . . . my . . . girl," he laughed.

"Well, your girl got herself suspended for a week."

"He shouldn't have put his hands on her," Jaimer said, adamantly defending his niece.

"Jaimer, the girl is in the sixth grade. This little boy just likes her."

"So she should let him touch her?"

"I'm not saying that. But there are other ways to handle things. I wish you hadn't started teaching her

43

karate, kung fu, or whatever you got her practicing every day."

"You're a mess. You better be glad that she knows that stuff. One day, it just might come in handy. You tell her that Uncle Jay said for her to keep right on practicing."

"Whatever . . . did you get packed?"

"I'm finishing up the last of it now. I'll be all moved in by the end of next week. Sis, I can't wait to move."

"What's her name?" His sister didn't miss a beat. The excitement in his voice was a bit too much.

"Huh? Whatdayamean?"

"You heard me. Somebody has got you just a little too eager."

"Oh . . . no, I'm just tired of being in this mousetrap." Jaimer played it off as best he could. His sister didn't know what he was up to, and there was no need in telling her. She would only put in two cents that he didn't want or need.

"Oh, I'm wrong? Okay." She decided to let it go for now. "Well, get settled, because I'll be up there in three weeks for a book signing, and I need someplace to stay. You got me?"

"You know I do, sis," he said apprehensively. If she got wind of his little scheme, it would be the end of everything. *Three weeks. That should be enough time to gain Tonya's trust.*

"Jay . . . Jay?"

"Huh? What did you say?"

"I said that I had to go. Big Daddy just pulled into the driveway. It's time for me to get myself together so I can pay my man some attention."

"Oh, please. Go on with your ol' nasty ass," he laughed, relieved to have her off the phone. That was one little homemaker if he ever knew one. His sister Ebony was the happiest person he knew. Except for the occasional book conference or signing, she stayed home, tending the house and sitting in front of her computer.

After the phone call, Jaimer finished packing his limited collection of dishes, his clothes, and the personals from his dresser, did his laundry, and was showered and in bed by nine-thirty. Tomorrow, he would be doing the same thing all over again. And that was fine with him, because he was determined to be ready for the moving van on Tuesday morning.

CHAPTER 4

Wiping the sweat off her brow, Tonya stoically ignored the heat from the sun as it hit her skin. The sun's unforgiving glare through the window of her front door caused her to squint her eyes, but she wouldn't let it deter her. She was going to make it this time.

Okay, girl, step . . . step . . . look straight ahead. You can do it. Don't stop.

The same nervousness that had her heart beating furiously caused her hand to shake violently. But she continued on. She pulling the heavy wooden door open and allowed the sun enter her domain.

Let it go, girl. It's just a door. It's been opened before. Now, step . . . closer, closer.

She was at the screen door. This was the closest to the outside she had been in three years. Making it this far gave her strength. She wanted her life back. It was so close, she could almost touch it. With nervous fingers, she closed her hand around the knob of the screen door and pushed it open.

One step, girl . . . You're gonna do it . . . You're gonna . . .

Tonya lifted one foot and lowered it over the threshold. She fell forward. She didn't feel the side of her head hit the porch's wooden plank floor. And she did not move when the screen door hit hard against the side of her body.

Jaimer pulled up in front of his new home, ready to unload his boxes and quickly make a second trip before meeting the moving van. He put his truck in park and was walking around to the back of the truck when he noticed that Tonya's screen door was open. Not knowing why it was in that position, he decided to go over and investigate. It only took him a split second to notice her seemingly lifeless body.

He sprinted over the three-foot fence that separated the yards and was quickly by her side. Jaimer knelt beside her and felt for a pulse.

Good, she's still alive.

"Tonya. Tonya, can you hear me?" He lightly shook her. "Tonya, can you hear me?"

She moaned and moved her head toward his voice, but didn't open her eyes.

"Just relax. I'm here." He lifted her into his arms and held her close while talking to her the whole time. "Tonya, I'm here. Can you hear me? Everything is going to be all right."

Just as he was about to enter the house, he heard a braking sound from a car pulling in front of the house. He turned around and saw Vince jumping out of his truck and running toward them.

"Hey, hey!" Vince yelled, slowing down when he realized it was Jaimer. "Hey, man, what the hell happened?" Vince moved with Jaimer into the living room.

Jaimer lowered Tonya onto the sofa before he spoke. He checked her pulse, which had slowed to near normal. "Tonya, are you all right? Do you hear me, baby?"

Vince was taking note of how Jaimer was handling his sister. *Baby?*

"Vince, I need a washcloth, cold."

"No problem. You got it."

When he came back into the room, Jaimer was still talking to a groggy Tonya. His hand was on her forehead, lightly touching the small bruise caused by her fall.

"What happened, man?"

Jaimer finally answered him. "I'm not totally sure. When I pulled up, she was passed out in the doorway. Here, let me have that rag." He put it on her temple.

Tonya responded to the cold cloth, suddenly shaking and feeling chilled. She began to warm when her favorite blanket, the hunter-green throw she kept in the living room, was placed around her shoulders.

"Tonya?"

Jaimer wasn't surprised, but he was relieved, when she finally opened her eyes.

"Hey, lady," he smiled at her. "Feeling better?"

Tonya looked into his sparkling brown eyes. He looks happy. *Could it be because he is near me? The sun makes his eyes more hazel than chestnut. The sun.* She remembered what she had been doing. Closing her eyes, she let her head fall back onto the sofa pillow.

"Oww. I feel like such a fool."

Vince came up behind Jaimer. "What happened, Tonya?"

"I don't even want to talk about it. It was so stupid."

"I think it would be stupid if you didn't talk about it." Jaimer was still sitting next to her on the sofa. He moved a stray strand of hair off her face.

Vince stood back watching the two. This was happening a little faster than he had expected. He wasn't sure if it was still a good idea or not. But it looked to be pretty much out of his hands. For now, he would just sit back and see what happened.

"How long was I out?" She looked at her brother for the answer.

"Don't know. Jaimer got to you first."

Tonya turned to him.

"I don't really know, either. I arrived approximately ten minutes ago, but you were already passed out. I don't know how long you were there."

"I thought I could just walk out the door and take a stroll down the block like it was an everyday thing. That was crazy."

"Maybe it was just too soon, sis."

"I know, but I really thought I could do it," Tonya replied, looking at her brother. "Vince, I slept through the night. And . . . and, I guess I was a little too excited about it. Like I was suddenly cured or something." She tried to sit up on the sofa, but Jaimer kept her in place.

"Whoa. You should stay there for a while. There's a pretty nasty bump on your head."

"What? Damn, I think I hurt something else, too. I got a sharp pain on my side."

Without hesitation, Jaimer bent down and lifted her shirt to take a closer look. He touched it lightly.

Tonya flinched, but didn't recoil in pain.

Vince watched closely, amazed his sister was letting this quote-unquote stranger be so intimate with her.

"You're going to need a bag of ice for that. It only looks like a bad bruise, though." Jaimer turned to Vince. " Is there an ice bucket in the freezer?"

"I'll get it, man." Vince couldn't wait to get home to call Cindy and Cecilia and tell them what was going on.

"I guess I need to thank you for rescuing me."

"No thanks necessary. Why were you trying to get outside?"

Tonya's eyes fell. There was no way she was going to tell him the real reason. "Don't you think it's time? I've been cooped up in here for three years. I'm so tired of not having a life. I need, no, I want to get out there and live a little bit. I'm going crazy in here night and day."

Jaimer looked at her. Slowly, he turned her head back toward him so that he could see into her eyes. "You don't get it, do you? Tonya, your life isn't what's out there. Your life is in here," he said, lightly tapping the spot where her heart was. "Everything you need is here."

"That's easy for you to say." Her perplexing problem lay buried within her.

"I know, but listen. The important things in your life are right here. Your family, your friends. God, your people had a whole party, which should have been held in a hall or someplace, right here just so you could attend. They come to your aid at the drop of a dime.

Girl, the people who love you *are* your life. We're all right here."

Tonya looked at him, stunned. *Yeah, she had heard right.*

Jaimer realized his slipup too late and didn't know how to fix it. Should he even try? Thankfully, Vince walked back into the room with a plastic bag of ice wrapped in a small towel. The timing was perfect.

"Here you go," he said, pausing in mid-step, sensing that he'd intruded on something.

"Well, um, here," Jaimer said, taking the ice from Vince and placing it on Tonya's side. "I'm going to go on over and start unloading my stuff. Vince, I'll holla at you. Tonya, you should stay put and keep that ice on for a few more hours. I'll, um, check on you later if you'd like?" He was slowly backing out of the room.

"That would be nice, Jaimer, and again, thanks for being here."

Tonya folded the newspaper after reading for three hours. She had relaxed enough to doze off for two hours before she began reading. She was tired of relaxing. There was work to be done. Her stories weren't going to write themselves. She had deadlines for a reason.

The local newspaper wasn't interesting, anyway. After dissecting it section by section, only one article, about the death of Jackson Melbourne, had caught her attention. Jackson Melbourne, or Meltdown as he was called, had been involved in several criminal enterprises, including drugs, prostitution, and loan sharking. He was one of the most successful criminals of his day. She had never met him, but as with most legends, his reputation was larger than life. He was very well known in Philadelphia and most East Coast cities. Even while locked up, he was able to keep control of all his street interests. That is, until somebody named Marion Brittingham decided to shank him in the prison shower.

Tonya remembered Howard telling her he had a cousin named Marion and wondered if it could be the same guy. There weren't too many men with that name. She thought he was talking about a girl until he corrected her. But if this was Howard's cousin, why was he in jail? Why did he want Jackson Melbourne dead? Could Jackson have had something to do with Howard's death? Numerous possible explanations came to mind, but none of them seemed viable. She had nothing to go on other than the newspaper article. People got paid good money to investigate murders. The police, for instance, had probably already come to the same conclusions she had, and they, too, had probably dismissed them one by one.

Mr. Melbourne had been in jail for only two and a half years. Tonya recalled the trial and the newspaper coverage. It had taken a court order to keep all reporters out of the courtroom the day the prosecution had produced a surprise witness. In the end, Meltdown was found guilty and sent up the river on racketeering charges— thirty-three years mandatory. Already fifty-five, he would have most likely died in jail anyway.

～～

Tonya rose painfully and walked slowly through the living room. She felt her bruised side tighten with every step. The few steps had been an agonizing journey. The cup of tea she had gotten up to make didn't seem so appealing, and she didn't need to use the bathroom anymore. Although Tonya didn't relish the thought of sitting on the sofa all day, she now believed that it was probably the best place for her. She turned around and headed back to her haven.

Propped up by several plush throw pillows Vince had stuffed behind her before he left, she could see Jaimer standing on the back of his pickup truck, which he had parked right in front of his front door. Apparently he was trying to figure out how best to move a large computer desk into the house. She assumed he had given up when she saw him go into the house and return with a toolbox.

The truck seemed to fit his personality perfectly. It was a Dodge truck with an extended cab built high off the ground like an SUV. The windows were tinted. There were step-up rails and big fat tires. She didn't know the names of all the accessories, but the total package looked good. He apparently took very good care of it.

He's working really hard. See how the sweat-drenched T-shirt is clinging to his body. Damn. On impulse, Tonya leaned forward and tapped on the windowpane to get his attention. It did.

When Jaimer he heard the tapping sound, he looked up and saw Tonya was the source. He dropped his screwdriver and made a mad dash for her house. Rushing through the front door, he slipped on the rug runner, fell flat and began sliding down the hallway, coming to an abrupt halt at the bottom of the stairs.

Not knowing if he had been hurt, Tonya tried her best to hold in her laughter.

Jaimer stayed where he was until he was sure he hadn't hurt anything other than his pride. When he finally looked up, he saw that she was just barely holding in her laughter.

"Go ahead and let it out. I'm okay."

She did, for a long time, before finally apologizing. Wiping her tears, Tonya said, "I'm sorry, Jaimer. I know it's not polite to laugh at people, but you didn't see yourself come sliding down the hallway with your legs all up in the air." Another fit of laughter hit her.

Moments later, Jaimer joined in as he got up off the floor and straightened the runner.

"Damn it, girl, I thought something was wrong with you."

"So you came busting through the door like a knight in shining armor?" she asked, still giggling.

"I had to get to you, didn't I?" He sat next to her and noticed that she was blushing a little.

"I'm fine. I was just wondering if you wanted something to eat. It's the least I could do for this morning."

"I told you. You don't owe me anything for this morning. But I'll take payment for that good laugh you just had at my expense. What do you want to eat? I need a break, anyway."

"I saw you out there working up a good sweat."

"I wanted to get done today. All I have to do is take this desk apart and move it inside. Tomorrow, I'll start working on my papers, setting up my office, things like that."

"Well, what do you want for dinner? I would cook, but my side is still a little sore. What if I order out, my treat, for your taking such good care of me today?"

"That sounds great. Next time, I'll cook. Do you want me to pick up the food, or is there someplace nice around here that will deliver?"

"Jaimer . . ."

"Call me Jay, please."

"Well, Jay, there is one advantage to being a recluse. Most of the local restaurants know of my situation, so they're more than willing to deliver to me."

"So restaurants that don't normally deliver, deliver to you?" he asked.

Tonya nodded, picking up the phone and dialing the number for Red Lobster.

"Please tell me you like seafood," she said, second-guessing her decision to call without first asking his preference.

"Love it. Just order me whatever you're having. I'm going to run over and take this desk apart and get it into the house. I want to jump into the shower, too."

"Yeah, that would be a good idea," she replied, pinching her nose with her thumb and index finger, not once thinking it abnormal for her to be joking so famil-iarly with a near-stranger.

"Oh, you got jokes. I'll be right back." Jaimer strode out the house and went back to dismantling his desk. A few turns of the screwdriver and the desk was apart. Two quick trips into the house and his task was complete.

Tonya wished she could quickly set the dining-room table or retrieve a bottle of wine from the rack in her kitchen, but her side was so painful she doubted she would be moving off the sofa at all. Her best bet was to try to position the pillows the best she could and straighten up her nightclothes—an old Delaware State University T-shirt and worn sweatpants, which she was still wearing from this morning. *Oh, Lord. This is embarrassing.* She straightened her braids, which she had pulled into a ponytail.

Waiting for the food to be delivered and wishing for a bath, she wondered if it would be too forward to ask Jaimer's assistance. *No, no . . . I can't do that.* Instead, she picked up the phone and called her sister.

"Hello?" A masculine voice came over the line.

"Hello yourself, Dayton." Tonya loved his voice, smooth and deep with a strong hint of his Trinidadian accent still intact. "Is my sister there?"

"Hey, yo, what's up, girl? Heard you had a spill earlier. Is everything cool?"

"Yeah, I'm fine. I just need a little help from Cindy."

"Hold on. I'll get my baby for you."

She heard the rustling of bedsheets and giggling.

"Hey, girl, what's up?"

"Am I interrupting something?"

"No, I was just getting my daily massage and rub-down before he runs off to work. You know a sistah has to get creamed with the cocoa butter. I'll be damned if I end up with stretch marks after this pregnancy. You need me for something?"

"Not now, but I haven't bathed or anything since this morning."

"Tonya, it's only five-thirty. I'm sure you don't need a bath already."

"No, but later I will."

"Oh, he got your juices flowing, don't he?" Cindy laughed. "I'm just kidding. You can't wait until the morning. Never mind, I'll be there later. A hot soak will probably help you with your side, anyway. So what are you doing now?"

"Lying down. I tried to get up earlier. It didn't work. Jaimer is on his way over for dinner."

"Ooh, that sounds romantic. What y'all having?"

"I ordered from Red Lobster. I wanted to thank him for helping me this morning. And believe me, if you could see how I look, you'd know there was nothing romantic about this evening."

"Well, it's still nice. I don't know what you were thinking."

"Me, either. Oh, there's a knock at the door. Don't come out tonight. I'll just get Jaimer to walk me up the stairs before he leaves."

"Ask him to help you bathe, too."

"Bye, Cindy."

"Love you." Cindy's good-byes always ended this way.

"Love you," Tonya replied.

"Miss you."

"Miss you, too." It had started when she was about six years old. Their mother worked far from home, and Cindy would always say that she would miss her from the time she called them to tell them she was on her way to the time she eventually arrived.

The young man dressed in a red polo shirt with the Red Lobster logo across his chest looked frightened when Jaimer ran out his front door to get to him before he rang Tonya's doorbell. He didn't want her to have to struggle with getting off the sofa.

"Hey, man. Sorry about that. Here you go. I got it." He handed the guy fifty dollars and told him to keep the change. Announcing himself as he entered, Jaimer was stunned to find her very slowly moving across the floor. Her evident discomfort and fatigue made him feel sorry for her. "Tonya?"

"I know, I know. Sit down."

"Right, sit down. I already got the food. Is it still very painful?"

"Hell, yeah. I need some more ice."

"Maybe you should sit in a hot tub for a while. I don't know why I didn't think of that earlier. That'll help your muscles relax."

Tonya looked at him as he took her by the arm and helped her back to the sofa. "I was just thinking the same thing."

"Well, do you want to go up now or after you eat something?"

"After we eat."

"Okay, after dinner, I'll help you to the bathroom."

She opened her mouth to say something.

"I'll stay out here until you finish and help you to bed."

"Jaimer—"

"Jay."

"Jay, I can't ask you to do that. We just met and—"

"No problem, that's what friends are for, right?"

"Right." Tonya felt a rush of relief. "You must be my guardian angel."

"Maybe I am." He smiled and took the bag of food to the table.

"I wanted to set the table and get a bottle of wine, but I couldn't get up."

"It's all right. Believe me, compared to the way I'm used to eating, this is like paradise." After making sure she was comfortable on the couch, he brought her food to her, set up one of her meal trays, retrieved the bottle of wine she had mentioned and poured them each a glass before settling down next to her. "This is nice just like this."

"You're right. So is everything okay over there so far?"

"Perfect. Once I get the upstairs set up and the offices downstairs organized, my business should run much smoother. I scheduled my employees to come in on Monday."

"So you gave them all a week off?"

"Yep. I like to do most things myself. You know, set up the office and stuff." He paused, looking up from his plate of fried shrimp, lobster tail, and crab legs. "Do you want to talk about this morning now?"

The switch of subjects caught her off guard. She wasn't sure how much she wanted to tell him. Jaimer was too good at making her feel comfortable. If she weren't careful, he would know everything about her before the evening was over.

"You wouldn't understand."

"Now, how do you know that? Try me," he urged, testing her trust.

"Well, last night, I had a really good night's sleep, and I kinda let it to my head."

"A good night of sleep?"

"Jaimer, for the last three years," she explained, awkwardly clearing her throat, "I have not been able to sleep a whole night. When all of this first started, I couldn't sleep at all. Eventually, I began to sleep one or two hours a night, then four or five, six or seven; it's been a steady progression. Last night, I actually slept the whole night through. I went to bed at ten and didn't wake up until nine. When I got up this morning, I was so psyched I mistakenly thought I was cured. I was scared, but I knew that I had to try it. The next thing I knew, I was hearing your voice."

"Tonya, you don't have to tell me if you don't feel comfortable, but what exactly happened?"

"It's all right. I can talk about it now. Three years ago, the guy I was dating was killed in front of me."

"Killed?" Jaimer asked, feeling apprehension stirring. *Killed?*

"Yeah, we were on a date. Were having a lovely time. Then all of a sudden, men came out of nowhere, jumped on us, put a blanket or pillowcase or something over my head. But I could hear Howard, my boyfriend, fighting them off. Then it was silent, and I was let go and standing all alone on a side street."

"Okay, okay. Tonya, breathe. Just breathe."

She was unaware of how fast she had been talking as she relived the night that had changed her whole life. Obeying his command, she inhaled deeply, resting against the pillows before releasing the air.

"I'm sorry. That was the first time I've ever really let it all out like that."

"It's okay. You never talked to a shrink or somebody about this?"

"Yes, but I've only been seeing her for the past year. I didn't want to see anyone when it first happened. I didn't want to talk about it."

"What about your family?"

"Well, actually, they found out everything from Cecilia. She's on the police force. When Vince found me, I was hysterical, babbling about what had happened. Cecilia was on duty at the time. She met us at the hospital. Then we went to the police station. It was a terrible time in my life. At first, they didn't believe me. A full investigation was conducted before it was assumed that Howard had been killed. The case was closed. His body was never found."

Jaimer sat back quietly. He knew the police department had been instructed to inform anyone inquiring about Howard Douglass that he was murdered. But how was he to know that placing Howard into protective custody and the relocation program would lead to her becoming a recluse and going through all this pain and suffering?

Even though he could easily rationalize that he wasn't responsible for Tonya's illness, he still placed a huge burden of guilt on his shoulders for his part in the whole scheme.

After dinner, Jaimer and Tonya sat on the sofa and talked about their families and made a plan of action for gradually getting her out of the house.

"I just want you to be ready for this."

"I'm ready. I hate being in this house. It's time for me to get out of here." She said, determination hardening her tone.

"Okay, we'll start slow. One step at a time. First, we'll start tomorrow morning by opening some of these curtains. This whole house has windows that you have kept shut all these years. Let's start by letting the outside in. Then we'll get you out."

"You sound like a therapist or something."

"No, I'm just looking out for your best interests; I want you to get better." He sincerely meant it. There were places he wanted her to see. She was missing so much by being in this house all day, every day. And it was his fault she was there. "But first, we've got to get you better. So I'm going to go up to the bathroom, start the water running, and then help you up the steps."

"You don't—"

"Yes, I do. Now, come on. I told you I was here for you."

"Okay," she said, submitting to the inevitable.

CHAPTER 5

"One step at a time, hon."

"Don't call me hon," Tonya said icily. "I hate that."

"Okay," Jaimer said, recognizing the signs of pain, misery, and helplessness. Obviously, Tonya wasn't used to being this needy.

"Jaimer, I'm sorry," she said, apologizing for her sharp tone.

"That's okay. I'm just here to help you."

She took two more steps toward the staircase and then stopped and rested against him, exhausted, feeling like she had just ran a marathon. "I may have hurt myself a bit more than I originally thought."

"Do you want a doctor or something?"

"No, I'll wait until tomorrow before I do that. But I don't think I'm going to be able to make it up these stairs." A stabbing pain shot up her side.

"Want me to carry you?"

He said it so nonchalantly that Tonya didn't take him seriously until he bent down.

Even as she said, "Nooo," she was being lifted into the air. "Jaimer, it's not neces—"

"Just be quiet. You know, you talk too much sometimes." He held her securely against his thick, solid frame, but was careful not to hold her too tightly.

"No, you didn't just tell me to be quiet," Tonya said, nonetheless enjoying the feel of him next to her. Then she laughed. "You know what, we're not going to get along. I can just tell."

"Oh, you think not? Just because I told you to be quiet? That's too bad, because I'm a really nice guy once you get to know me."

"I just bet you are," she replied as he started up the stairs.

They reached the steamy bathroom, and he sat her down on the closed toilet seat. "Is there anything you need out of your bedroom?"

"No," she said quickly, horrified at the thought of him rummaging through her personals.

"Oh, please, don't be so dramatic." He stood over her with both hands on his hips. "I've seen underclothes before. This is about getting you settled in for the night, not whether or not I'm trying to make a move on you."

"You're not trying to make a move on me?" she teased.

"No, not today." He smiled down at her. "Come on, woman. What do you need?"

"Just get my robe off the back of my bedroom door. Second door down on the left. It's navy blue with light blue writing on the sleeves."

When he left to get the robe, Tonya lifted her T-shirt to take a peek at the long purple-and-blue discoloration of her skin. Hopefully, a soak in the hot water would make it feel and look better. She didn't hear Jaimer come back into the bathroom. Jumping in surprise when she saw him—and more than a little self-conscious—she quickly pulled her shirt down.

"It's not polite to spy on people," she chastised, giving him an accusatory look.

"That's how I make my living. Sorry, I guess it's force of habit."

"Yeah, well, don't make it a habit around here."

"Whatever," he said, dismissing her comment. "Here's your robe. Where's a towel?"

"In the closet behind you."

He got one and handed it to her.

"Thanks."

"Do you need me to do anything else?"

"No, I think I can handle the rest by myself." *She couldn't ask him to help her into the tub, could she?*

"Well, if you don't need me to help you get into the water," he smiled mischievously, "I'll wait outside the door until you let me know you're safely in the tub. Then I'll go downstairs and start cleaning up until you holler for me. I'll help you into bed and then leave."

"Thanks again for the help. I really mean it." As helpless as her disorder made her, it still bothered her that Jaimer so willingly offered her his assistance. For some reason, help from him made her feel much more an invalid than help from her family did. But she needed him today.

"No problem," he replied.

Jaimer stood next to the bathroom door and listened to her groans and grunts as she struggled to take off her clothes and lower herself into the bath water. Once she said she was in, he finished straightening up downstairs and waited for her call.

⸺

The water was a blessing. She could feel it soothing the tightness around her side as well as the tension in her body. Resting her head against the bath pillow, she closed her eyes and let the feel of Jaimer's body rush back into her mind.

His chest was hard and solid. He obviously worked out to keep in shape. She hadn't felt muscles like that in a long time. He was built like her brother Vince, but had more meat on his bones. Vince was cut with muscles and a six-pack, but with clothes on you would never know it.

Jaimer's built was unavoidable to the eye. He had those things on his neck like football players did—those muscles that make you look like the Hulk. Not real big ones, but they were well defined. When he was carrying her, her arm went around his small waist and rested on his back. It was tight and thick with muscles.

She could only imagine what the rest of him looked like without the baggy jeans. He had to have a tight little rear end. Strong, thick legs, muscles rippling. Goodness, he had to be a close replica of that famous sculpture *David*.

Letting her mind stray a bit further, she hoped that was all that resembled that centuries-old masterpiece. Though she had never seen the sculpture in person, the pictures she had seen did not do the poor man justice.

Nah, she would rather imagine Jaimer being more Mandingo than David. She smiled sheepishly. *Why am I sitting here in a tub of water thinking about things like this, anyway?* It had been three years since she'd been with a man. Hell, she probably wouldn't know the first thing to do to get the man interested in her.

Jaimer sat on the top step, waiting to hear her call his name. He wished he had the nerve to go to the door, knock, and ask if there was anything she needed him to do. Wash her back, her feet, sit there and watch her bathe herself. He was open to any of it, really.

But he couldn't do that. She didn't seem to be turned off by him—had even flirted a little. All he had to do was make a small move to let her know that he was interested. Maybe it would have led to something.

But he refused to take advantage of her situation or mess up his own. She had been locked up for three years, thanks to him. The last thing he wanted to do was hurt her more by moving too fast. He had all the time in the world—three weeks. So to help her and himself, he would make sure she was out of the house by that time. With the right kind of slow-paced motivation, she could do it. He was sure of that. She had enough determination. He just had to focus on her need to get better instead of his need to have her.

Jaimer jumped when he heard a sudden splash of water. In an instant, he was up and at the door. His hand on the knob, he was about to turn it and walk right in, but he stopped himself.

"Are you all right in there?" he yelled, swallowing hard.

"Yeah, I just slipped trying to get out, but I'm fine. I'm almost ready."

Jaimer put his head against the wall next to the bathroom door and closed his eyes. *I'll be dead before this is over.*

"Okay, I'm ready. You can come in," Tonya yelled.

Jaimer opened the door to the smell of honeydew melons. He wanted to see for himself that she was fine. He was about to say something when he saw a drop of water slide down the side of her face and onto her shoulder.

Tonya saw his eyes moving over her and pulled the top of her robe closer to her neck. She bent to pick up her discarded clothing, and the pain in her side made her groan.

"I'll get them," he volunteered.

"No. No. Leave them there." Why would any lady want a strange man to be picking up her dirty clothes? He had to know better than that.

Apparently, he didn't. Scooping up the clothes, Jaimer looked at her questioningly while the crotch of her drawers hung over the edge of the pile.

Tonya was horrified.

"Where's the hamper?" he asked innocently.

"In my room," she said in defeat, knowing she couldn't bring his attention to her undies. *Oh, God. Why*

69

couldn't this have happened on a day when I was wearing my silk hipsters or even a thong instead of my granny Hanes-Her-Ways?

"Well, let's get you into the bed so I can lock up."

"Okay," she agreed, taking his arm and praying her drawers wouldn't fall to the floor. Her aching muscles felt better after soaking in the hot water and Epsom salt.

"You smell good," Jaimer commented.

"Thanks . . ."she replied, sounding shy and feeling ill at ease.

"Look, Tonya, I'm not trying to make this uncomfortable for you."

"I think we're a little past that already." She took the last couple of steps into the room and pointed to the hamper in the corner. She needed for him to get her personals out of his hands ASAP.

"Okay, to bed with you." He moved past her, threw the clothes into the hamper, and then walked with her to the bed and pulled back the bedcovers.

"Nice bed, by the way," he commented, smoothing out the sheets on the four-poster oak bed. For a girl who didn't get out, she had a lot of nice-looking things in her room. They looked newly purchased. He wondered who did her shopping for her. The bed had sheer curtains hanging down from all sides. Only the curtains at the foot of the bed were drawn back and tied.

"Thanks. We have to tie the side curtains back. I can't sleep with them closed like this."

He obliged her, moving swiftly around the bed and drawing back the curtains. "There. Is that better?"

"Yeah, thanks. And when you lock up the house—"

"Tonya," he put up a hand to stop her. "Remember when we said we were going one step at a time? Well, the first step is trust. I know how to lock up a house, okay? Don't worry about it. No," he said, stopping the retort that was on the tip of her tongue. "Trust me."

"Okay. I trust you." In her mind, she said the words over and over again. *Trust him.*

"Now, get in bed." He was standing right behind her, smelling the fragrance of her body oils each time she moved. He wanted to put his hands on her, but hesitated until he saw that she needed help climbing into the high bed.

The robe that Tonya was so desperately trying to keep closed wasn't cooperating. To get into the bed, she was would have to either push her bashfulness aside or fall flat on her face. Not wanting to look like a clumsy fool, she let the ends of the robe go. At the same time, she lifted her leg up to get in. Tonya was shocked to feel his hands around her hips.

Jaimer couldn't put his hand on her waist to lift her because of the bruise, so he did the next best thing. Whether it was best for him or her, he wasn't quite sure.

"I got you," he said, helping her to flip around onto her back. "There you—" The words dropped off as her robe opened wider, leaving Tonya's left breast exposed. Being a gentleman, he tried to act as if it didn't matter, but it was hard not to notice the cinnamon-colored, cantaloupe-shaped mound topped with a plump darkened areola. Her flat stomach was still beaded with little ringlets of water. His eyes automatically traveled further down to the beginning of short, nestling. . . . He turned away, licking his lips.

Tonya righted herself as fast as she could and pulled as much of the sheet up over her as possible. Embarrassed wasn't a good enough word for how she felt at that moment. *Just let me die already. Good grief, what else could possibly happen?*

After taking a couple of quick breaths, Jaimer was under control again, back to his old self. He turned back, reaching over and pulling the sheets and comforter the rest of the way over her. All this was done without eye contact.

"Okay, well, since you're all tucked in, I'm gonna be heading out."

"Okay, um, thanks again, Jaimer." She didn't make eye contact, either.

"Um . . . okay." He leaned forward to kiss her on her forehead. "You sleep good." Jaimer moved away slowly and looked down at her.

She was looking up at him. "I will," she said softly, the words caressing his face.

Damn. Jaimer lowered his head once again.

The kiss was a soft, clumsy brushing of lips that quickly ignited the desire of both participants. They were left breathless and confused by its sharp intensity.

"I'll, um, see you tomorrow, Tonya," Jaimer said, backing away from the bed. He felt a surge of electricity, of excitement, shoot through him because the kiss confirmed what he already knew. She was for him.

With that done, Jaimer fought hard to stay focused on the front door. He went through the lower level of the house, opening the curtains so the house would be full of sunlight in the morning, and checking the door locks. Back in his house, he worked off his desires and frustrations by moving around office furniture and filing papers.

Tonya woke with a smile on her face. The sun was already high in the sky, and its rays were bathing her room in warmth. She had done it again. Slept through the night without the slightest hint of unrest. It was going to be a good day. She could feel it.

Jaimer must have lifted her shades while she was in the bathroom the night before. She hadn't noticed. Never had it been so bright and alive in her bedroom, anytime. She was fine with it. No apprehension, no nervous twitches in the back of her mind.

Jaimer. Last night, he had kissed her. Admittedly, she wanted him to, but she hadn't expected him to. He kissed her on her forehead like some little kid in a Hallmark movie and then pulled away when he looked into her eyes. She was holding her breath, hoping that he would make some kind of move. Then he lowered his head until their lips met.

At first, her mind went blank. She knew what to do, but she was afraid to. But he moved his mouth over hers, softly, like a feather over her skin. In seconds, chill bumps

73

were rising on her arms. She returned his kiss, then slightly opened her mouth when she felt the tip of his tongue glide over her lips. He took the initiative and deepened the kiss, urging her to join him.

Then, he was bent down over her and her arms were around his neck. If it weren't for the fact that they both needed air, the kiss wouldn't have ended. But Jaimer let go of her lips and kissed her face and neck before putting a stop to their impromptu act.

He whispered in her ear, "I think I'd, um, better leave."

Tonya was silent, not trusting herself to agree.

"I'll see you tomorrow," she remembered him saying.

Well, it's tomorrow. Tonya made her way out of bed and into a hot shower, testing the soreness of her bruise. It was feeling better. She figured the more she moved around, the better it would get.

When she stepped out of the bathroom, the phone was ringing. She knew it was one of her siblings. And it was—Vince.

"Hey, girlie. How you feeling this morning?" he asked cheerfully.

"Fine. You sound in too good of a mood. Who were you with last night?"

"Come on. You know I don't kiss and tell. I'm on my way to the office. I was just calling to see how you were doing."

"I'm fine."

"I mean after your fall."

"I'm fine."

"I was trying to get back over to you last night, but I got sort of tied up."

Tonya laughed. "Yeah, right. Just make sure you strap up, brotha."

"Safe sex or no sex. You know me," Vince laughed. "I have to say that you sound like you're in a good mood, too. What gives? Did you get into something last night that I need to know about?"

"Nothing gives. I didn't get into anything."

"This is me, Tonya," he said, already knowing she would only tell him so much. "Anyway, did the girls come over to help you last night?"

"No. Actually, your boy helped me out."

"My boy? Who, Jay?"

"Yeah. I bought dinner and invited him over. He stayed and helped me to bed and locked up for me."

"Word. How long did he stay?"

"Until I told him to leave. Mind your business."

"Oh, it's like that. I'm going to have to holla at him."

"Mind your business, Vince. Like I said, he helped me out a lot last night."

"Yeah, all right. But I got my eye on him. Know that. We cool, but we ain't that cool."

"When I need you, I'll call you. You stopping by later?"

"Probably. I got a meeting today with Meltdown's widow. She wants to hire us to move her back to Atlanta. Then I have another move to assign. I'll stop by, but it might be late."

"No problem. I'm feeling better today. After my coffee, I'm going to jump on this computer. I have a lot to make up for after not working at all yesterday."

"All right, sis. Love ya."

"Love you, too."

She hung up the phone and went to her office, feeling a little bit more chipper with each step. The downstairs was just as well lit as her bedroom, and it gave her a sense of accomplishment to walk through the rooms without pause. She lifted the curtains to the windows in the office as well.

Although she hadn't yet been able to actually stare outside for long periods of time, she was letting the outside in. That was step two. Once she felt comfortable enough with this, she would take the next step.

Cindy showed up within the hour. Tonya was on the last paragraph of a short story she was writing for *True Confessions* magazine when she heard the front door open. Fighting her impulse to jump up and hide, she made herself wait to hear her sister announce herself before she got up and walked to the office door. She was careful to remain calm and appear nonchalant.

Cindy walked through the front door and looked to the right and left for Tonya. When she didn't immediately see or hear her, she got worried.

"Tonya, where are you?"

"Oh, I was in the office, hon." She leaned against the office door nonchalantly. "I was finishing up a story for this deadline. What's up?" Trying to look as if everything was normal, as if she hadn't had a close encounter of the nicest kind the night before, she purposely made her face blank, unreadable.

"I told you I would be here this morning. Is everything okay?" Cindy looked at her suspiciously. She looked around and noticed all the window curtains open.

"I couldn't be better. How are you feeling with the baby and all?"

"I'm just fine. Everything is moving along like normal. Um, Tonya, why are all the curtains up? What's going on around here?"

"Oh, it's part of this plan that Jay and I came up with yesterday." Tonya went into the kitchen to fix herself a cup of tea. "Want some tea?"

"Who is Jay? And what plan are you talking about?" Cindy followed her and sat on one of the stools at the wooden island in the center of the kitchen. She plucked an apple from the fruit basket.

"Jay. Jaimer. We came up with a plan for me to get out of this damn house. Taking it step by step instead of in one big leap like I tried to do yesterday."

"Oh, well, that sounds good. At least somebody around here is thinking straight. What else happened? Why do you have that big-ass smile on your face?"

"Nothing." Tonya took a seat across from her.

"You know something or you did something." Then realization struck. "Tonya, you slept with Jaimer."

"What? Are you crazy, girl? And shut up before he hears you." She hit her sister on the arm. "I . . . did not . . . sleep . . . with . . . Jaimer. Don't be ridiculous."

"Well, you did something with him." Cindy studied her sister closely "What did you do? Look at you, all glowing and everything. Hell, I wish I could look that happy without doing anything with Dayton. Not that my baby doesn't please me, but goodness."

"Look, Cindy, nothing happened. He came over last night for dinner, which I owed him for helping me, then he helped me to bed."

"I bet he did."

"Girl, you're too much. How long are you staying?"

"Not long. I told Shawnique and Jordan to meet me here. We're going baby shopping."

"You haven't turned seven months yet. You got until the end of the month before you can start shopping. Couldn't you can't wait for it to get here?"

"You know I don't believe in superstitions."

"Yeah, right. All the same, just put the stuff on lay-away. You don't need to start filling the house up yet. Let Dayton finish the room first. Have you decided which one is going to be the godmother?"

"No. It's hard. Jordan is my girl. We go way back to Sesame Street days, and Shawnique is your girl. She wants to be the godmother only because she is tired of waiting for you."

"Well, if I were you, I would pick Jordan. Shawnique is just going to have to keep waiting. And by the look of things, her wait might not be as long as she thinks it will be." A small smile hovered around her lips long enough for Cindy to see.

Cindy was surprised Tonya had made such an admission. "Ow, you did do something." She was smiling, happy to see a glimpse of her sister's old self. She reminded herself to congratulate her brother for the excellent idea of introducing the two. "Have you talked to Cecilia?"

"What I mean is that I'll be out of this house real soon. Cecilia called yesterday afternoon to check on me. Is everything all right with her?"

"Yeah. She told me she was the lead detective working on the Meltdown case. It's probably taking up most of her time."

"It probably doesn't help any that she was engaged to the man's son. Has he come back to town yet?"

"He's back. Just as conceited as ever and looking just as good. I never did like him. You can see the snake in those green eyes of his."

"Yeah, Darius Melbourne always was slippery. Remember when Vince went after him that time?"

"Which time? That little punk was so scared of Vince it was pathetic."

"That's because Vince is crazy. It didn't matter who Darius's dad was, Vince was determined to get him for hurting Cecilia like that. It's a good thing Cecilia got to him first."

Cindy laughed. "I wish I had seen her beating him up in the schoolyard. Imagine, as fly as he thought he was, as tough as he thought he was, getting beat up by a girl."

"Well, in all honesty, Cecilia never did fight like a girl. What time is it?"

"Almost eleven, why?" Cindy asked curiously.

"Nothing. I was just wondering."

"Wondering where your man is?"

"Don't start. He's not my man."

"Yeah, right. I don't know what's going on, Tonya, but I'm going to tell you this: I like it. It's time for you to start enjoying life again."

Almost as if his name had been called, Jaimer he walked into the house, calling out to let her know he was there.

"Hello, hello. Tonya, it's me. Are you decent?"

Cindy looked at her, smiling. Tonya blushed.

"We're in the kitchen. Come on back," Tonya answered.

The ladies were treated to a tasty sight as Jaimer strolled into the kitchen wearing a tan double-breasted suit with a peach shirt and matching tie. Tonya almost had to use both hands to keep her mouth closed. He looked good. The peach shirt was in perfect contrast with his dark, glossy skin.

"Hello, ladies. Cindy, it's nice to see you again."

"Nice to see you again, too, Jaimer." The look that passed between him and her sister didn't escape her. "Where are you off to looking all debonair?"

Feeling just a little self-conscious, he replied, "To a meeting with a potential client."

"You always dress like that for work?"

"Only when I have a meeting. Usually, it's jeans and a T-shirt. Most of my work is manual labor, setting up equipment and stuff."

"Oh, right? You're in surveillance, right?"

"Right. I didn't mean to intrude," he said, turning to Tonya. "I just wanted to make sure that you were okay before I left."

"I'm fine." She unconsciously moved her hand to her side. "It feels a lot better, and not nearly as stiff as it was yesterday." She looked at him with undeniable emotion in her eyes.

"Okay. All right, then. I'll just be on my way, and I'll see you later." He was about to leave, but he wanted to kiss her first. So here it was, he thought, a decision to make. Either he had to kiss her in front of Cindy, which he knew she wasn't ready for, or . . . "Um, Tonya, could you walk me to the door?" He grabbed her hand, not giving her a chance to decline.

Cindy sat on the stool and smiled as she watched them walk out together. She figured it wouldn't be long before her sister was back.

At the front door, Jaimer stopped and turned to her. "That was probably a little forward of me, huh?"

"Not really forward, but definitely not subtle," she replied, grinning.

He took both her hands and pulled her a little closer. Since last night, he had wanted to do just this—touch her. "I wanted to have a second with you before I left." He felt like an awkward teenager.

"That's all right. What time do you expect to be back?"

"It should only take about two or three hours. How was your morning? I mean, how did you do with the window shades and curtains open?"

"It didn't faze me one bit. I like the sunlight coming in. I didn't realize how much I've missed it." The fact that he cared enough to ask that question made her feel more joy than the sun possibly could. It gave her bottomless pleasure to know that he truly cared.

"Good, now, how do you think you'll do if we keep the shades up again tonight? I mean, they were all up last night, but you didn't know it. How do you feel about knowing it?"

"Let's just do it and find out," she replied, willing to try anything. His concern gave her confidence. "Is your phone on yet?"

"No. The telephone man is coming tomorrow before noon. Will you be all right?"

That wasn't the response she was hoping for. "Let's just talk about it when you come back, okay?" Letting the subject die was in her best interest. What was she going to do? Ask the man, a total stranger, to stay the night?

Jaimer moved a hand over her temple. "You look beautiful today, very happy and stress-free."

"That's a good thing. That's how I feel today." She lowered her head shyly. "Thank you."

"Hey, I'm not doing it." He wasn't about to take credit for her accomplishments. "You are. Look, I gotta go."

"Okay."

"Are you going to look at me or my chest?" His mouth twitched with amusement until she turned her head up, her eyes reflecting the same desire he was feeling.

Jaimer swooped down and captured her mouth, pulling her against his hard body. Her arms circled him. She spread her hands across his back as the kiss progressed.

Tonya was up against the wall with one of his arms around her. He had placed the other on the wall and was using it for support while he leaned into her. His lapping tongue slipped through her lips to caress the inside of her mouth.

She closed her eyes, enjoying the feel of his full body flush against hers. She moaned softly when she felt him tighten against her stomach.

They were so absorbed in the interplay of their tongues, neither heard the screen door open and Jordan and Shawnique come into the house. The clearing of a throat brought an end to the kiss. But to Jaimer's credit, Tonya thought, he didn't jump away from her as if he had been caught doing something wrong. Instead, he stayed where he was, putting his head down on her shoulder briefly to get himself together.

Being ignorant and nosy as usual, Jordan and Shawnique didn't move at all. They stood right where they were. And it was quite a sight to take in: The window shades were up, the front door wide open, and their recluse of a cousin was standing in the hallway in the arms of a complete stranger.

Hellooo, what the hell is going on around here?

When Jaimer realized the ladies had no intention of moving, he rose to his full height and looked down at Tonya. Kissing her on her cheek, he said, "I'll see you later." Then he walked toward the door. "Ladies," he said, stepping between the two and wearing an irresistibly devastating grin.

After he left, they let out a collective sigh.

"Daaamn. Tonya, you know you got to tell me how you did that without even leaving out the house," Shawnique said.

"Girl, he is fine. Does he have a brother or something?" Jordan asked, following her cousin to the kitchen.

"Jordan, didn't you say that you just met someone? Someone, by the way, that no one in the family has met yet."

"No, I have a friend that no one has met yet, but I want one of those." She pointed back at the front door. "Can you help a sister out?"

"He doesn't have any brothers. Sorry," she replied, shaking her head.

Cindy was trying to sit back down when they rounded the corner to the kitchen. Tonya stopped dead in her tracks. "You're caught, Cindy."

"I—"

"Don't even try it. I know you were spying on us."

"Y'all left me back here by myself. I got lonely," she said pouting pathetically.

"Whatever. Didn't y'all take off work today to take this girl shopping or something to do?"

"Oh, it's like that," Jordan interjected. "Got a new man, now you gonna kick us out."

"Pleeease," Tonya replied. "I've been kicking y'all out for years. This shit didn't just start."

CHAPTER 6

Tonya sat in front of her seventeen-inch computer monitor and struggled to finish her story, but the memories of the heavenly kiss from Jaimer kept intruding. But he was the next-door neighbor. Should she be letting their relationship become so intimate so fast? True, she felt the chemistry between them, and they seemed to click well together. Tonya was definitely interested, definitely wanted to get to know him better. She just wasn't sure if this was the right time. She had to concentrate on getting over her fears before new ones invaded her subconscious.

Her long self-exile and the events leading up to it had made Tonya skittish about relationships. But in the past, she was anything but. A no-nonsense sort of girl, she never had time for the games men play, so she was always honest but very firm with her male friends. She spent time with them when she wanted to, and when she didn't want to be bothered, they weren't to bother her. Before Howard came along, she was a very independent woman. But this was different, even more different than it had been with Howard. She wanted Jaimer around her all the time. Despite knowing him for less than a week, she was just about certain she wanted him around for a long time, if not forever.

Around five, a light tap on the door roused Tonya from a comfortable slumber on the cushiony settee. She moaned and rolled over to her side. The second knock was a little harder; this time she sat up and checked the time. Five-ten; she had slept longer than intended. She knew it had to be Jaimer. Tonya jumped up, straightening her clothing on her way to the front door.

Jaimer stood at the door holding a grocery bag. He was being impulsive, but he figured it was his turn to treat. Besides, he wanted to spend time with her. He was in a very good mood after gaining a new client. What better way to end his evening than dinner with her?

Was he moving too fast? Probably. Would it be worth it? He hoped so. Although this was all new to her, in his head, he had started a relationship with her three years ago. This wasn't too fast for him, but he had to be careful not to frighten her away.

Once he heard movement in the house, he waited patiently for her to open the front door.

"Hey, Jaimer," Tonya said, pinning her eyes to the floor as she opened the door. "Come on in."

"Thanks." He stopped in front of her to block the doorway and gave her a brief kiss on her cheek.

His simple gesture surprised her, but it probably shouldn't have. They had seemingly taken their friendship to the next level. A silent concession must have been conveyed. "What's in the bag?"

"Oh, it's dinner. Since you treated last night, I thought tonight would be on me."

"You didn't have to do that. I could have whipped up something."

"It's not much. Just a couple of subs, chips, and soda. I also thought that we could watch a movie."

"Movie? What did you get?"

"*Barbershop II.* You haven't seen it already, have you?" He was suddenly worried that he hadn't thought about that while he was at the shop. Maybe she had seen it.

"As a matter of fact, I haven't." Smiling at his release of breath, she added, "I've been meaning to get Cecilia to pick it up for me."

"Well, now you got it," he said, clearly relieved. "So, you good?"

Nodding, she watched him move through her house. His stance, his walk, and his smile exuded confidence as he retrieved two tray stands, cups, and ice. He was very much at ease in her home. But it didn't bother her in the least. She was happy to see him, realizing that she had missed him just a little while he was gone.

They dined on Italian subs, Ruffles barbecue potato chips, and Tahitian Treat soda, Tonya's favorite thrown-together meal. But how did he know that? She figured he must have gotten his information from Vince. Her brother was probably in cahoots with Jaimer. He was always telling her that she needed to get out so that she could find a good man. She must have been taking too long for him.

By the time they started watching the movie, Jaimer had removed his shoes and was resting comfortably on the sofa. The movie had them laughing and arguing over the different relative merits of the characters.

She tried to concentrate on the movie, but having Jaimer so close only made her awareness of him grow stronger. Throughout the movie they flirted constantly until they eventually stopped paying attention all together.

For the last ten minutes of the movie, Jaimer had concentrated on Tonya. He moved from her hand to her neck after positioning her to lean on his chest while watching the movie. Perhaps he was moving too fast, but he was enjoying it. Obviously she was, too, because she didn't stop him

His lips against her wrist made her realize her hand was pressed to his face. She started to pull it away, but he grabbed it and kept it in place.

A tremor moved through her when his tongue grazed the same area, followed by little nips from his teeth. Tonya's her heartbeat quickened as he turned her hand over and kissed her palm. *Oh, God. It's been such a long time since I've felt anything like this.*

Jaimer inhaled the sweet essence of honeydew from her skin while he kissed the back of her neck and side of her face. Eventually, her tightly wound body relaxed. When he moved further down her neck, she shifted her head to give him better access. This emboldened him. They wanted the same thing—to be together.

Testing his ground, Jaimer turned her so he could see her. She was still a bit uncomfortable; the shyness in her eyes showed it. He was so sure she was ready, but something in her eyes told him that he should back off.

She wanted this—to be in his arms, to be showered with affection. When he hesitated, Tonya made the next move. Leaning forward, she placed a soft kiss on his lips and then moved back and looked into his eyes. She smiled at him and moved forward again. Instead of two mature adults, they were behaving like goofy teenagers on the verge of their first sexual encounter.

This kiss was light and feathery at the start. He put his arms around her and drew her closer. Tonya began to feel quivers in the pit of her stomach.

He used his tongue to outline the fullness of her lips. The honeydew aroma held him captivated with a hunger that was long buried. The delicate softness of her silky brown skin drove him insane just wanting to be closer to her.

Her lack of shyness surprised Jaimer considering that she hadn't been near a man in three years. He thought he would keep this intimate play at a slow pace, but was quickly taken over when the exchange became unexpectedly heated. He was thankful to be the recipient of such affection.

Their tongues played a dangerous game of Twister; their hands roamed over each other's bodies, trying to commit texture and contour to memory.

Jaimer slid his hand under Tonya's shirt and covered her breast. A throb began gradually between her thighs. As his hands squeezed her soft globes harder, her hips twitched with an old familiarity.

Jaimer lifted her T-shirt over her head. He unhooked her bra and let her firm breasts fall into his hands.

"You're beautiful, Tonya," he said, lavishing kisses on her face and neck.

A gasp left her throat as she felt his tongue repeatedly swirl around the brown nub of her areola. "Oh, please don't stop, Jaimer."

The soft moan that Jaimer heard nearly drove him insane. He wanted to hear more of that, feel the vibrations of the moan as it escaped from her throat. Concentrating more on bringing her pleasure than himself, Jaimer was unaware that she was pulling his T-shirt off until it was bunched under his arms.

Tonya finally saw what she knew was there all along—rippling muscles. She had to feel them, taste them for herself. She was not apprehensive that the early evening sun's glow was flowing through her front bay window or that she was newly discovering a man's body. Tonya moved over Jaimer's chest as if it was a forbidden city. She wanted to explore all his nooks and crannies. *What makes him shake and moan? Would he, for me?*

Her first question was answered as soon as she maneuvered a wet finger trail down the center of his body over his taut six-pack, ending just above his left hip. He was shaking all right—with laughter.

"What's so funny?" she asked, slightly annoyed. Here she was trying to make a lasting impression, and he was laughing at her.

"I'm sorry, baby, but I'm ticklish."

"Why didn't you stop me?"

"Because at first it felt good. I was trying to hold it in. Come here." Jaimer rolled her onto the sofa and lay on top of her. Amid the kissing and groping, Tonya's pants became unfastened. Jaimer tried to take his time and enjoy the moment. He covered her neck, chest, and stomach with kisses, loving every minute of her muffled sighs. Did he dare go a step further, even with her lying under him pliant and wickedly willing?

Still moaning, Tonya shifted beneath him, making his already palpable state of arousal even more unbearable.

She was still attractive, still desirable after all this time locked up without the least bit of companionship. His face had a look that she had forgotten a long time ago: This man wanted her. That knowledge alone was powerful.

Twisting her sideways, his hand pried through the tight band of her jeans, wrestling with the elastic band of her panties until he felt the beginning of soft curly hairs at the tip of his fingers.

Yes, Tonya thought. *Yes,* her mind screamed.

Breathing hard, he kissed her as he moved his hand through the small mound of teasing shag. Then he froze.

The footsteps became louder by the second. From the shadows crossing the far wall, he could tell there were children, two girls, one boy, and an adult, female, coming toward the front door. Quickly, Jaimer jumped off Tonya, who was still in something of a daze.

"Tonya," he whispered, dipping behind the front of the couch so as to be unseen by the intruders. "Tonya," he said again, louder this time. He was reaching for his T-shirt when she finally opened her eyes, still in a state of awe. With a nod, he indicated that they were no longer alone.

"Oh, shit," Tonya hissed, burrowing down into the sofa and reaching for her bra. Through the window, she could see Cecilia moving toward her front door.

DING-DONG.

"Oww, she sure does have perfect timing, doesn't she?" Trying to fix her clothing and forestall Cecilia using her key, she yelled, "Just a minute!"

"Well, maybe it's best that she did stop us."

Tonya stopped clasping her bra and looked at him. "How can you say that?"

"I mean, I think that maybe we were rushing things just a little?"

"You think?" she asked sarcastically, looking irate.

"Tonya, I'm just saying, we only met about four days ago. I just don't want something to happen that we might regret."

"Yeah, I could tell you were real worried." Her bra and T-shirt back in place, she walked toward the door just as the bell rang a second time.

"Tonya, why are you mad at me? I couldn't stop myself. I didn't want to, but—"

He stopped talking just as Tonya opened the door and Cecilia's kids ran in to give their auntie a hug. Getting himself together, Jaimer busied himself getting the movie out of the DVD player. When he stood up, he was alone with Cecilia in the room.

"Tonya took the kids to the back for ice cream. I'm sorry if I interrupted something." She looked at his stance. *Typical cocky son of a bitch. He thinks he has my sister wrapped around his little finger already. I don't trust him.*

"No. Don't worry about it. We were just, um, watching a movie." *She is interrogating me. Me. This is one tough chick. She's going to be the hardest to get on my side. But I'm up to the challenge. Okay, let's play.*

"Didn't look like the TV was on to me."

"Were you looking through the window?" Jaimer sat back down on the sofa. He put his shoes on.

"What do you think? When I walked by, I saw a foot on the window sill."

"You know, your sister is a grown woman. She might have a problem with you being in her business. Besides, she wasn't fighting me off, was she? In fact, I think she was enjoying herself more than she has in a long time."

"True, she is grown, but she is still my sister." Cecilia stood with her arms crossed.

"Do you ever stop being a cop?" He smiled up at her when her facial expression darkened.

"No. But speaking of cops, would you happen to know someone by the name of Archie Dallas?"

"No," Jaimer responded after feigning serious thought. "I can't honestly say I've ever heard of him."

"You know, you remind me an awful lot of him. He was a speaker at a seminar I attended last year in Baltimore. Mr. Dallas is considered an expert in the surveillance field. That is your specialty also, isn't it? I can't believe you've never heard of him."

"That's just what I do for a living." Jaimer moved closer to the doorway, realizing his mistake and knowing that he was busted. She didn't believe a word of what he was saying, as was evident by the smirk on her face. But he couldn't let her in on his secret. Years ago, he was given his alias, as were a number of other men and women who had elected to live in the undercover world of the federal government. He didn't think that alias would follow him into his personal life after leaving the agency.

"Don't you think it strange that you wouldn't know of a man who is one of the foremost experts in the field in which you make a living? That's like a writer not knowing who Maya Angelou is, isn't it?"

"I guess," he shrugged, trying to show her that the matter was unimportant to him. "Look, I'm going to go and let you spend some time with your sister. Tell her for me that I'll stop in tomorrow morning."

"No problem." Cecilia watched him leave the room. Her instincts told her she was right, and she had learned to always trust her instincts. When she heard Tonya approaching, she turned to face her.

"Don't give me that look," Tonya said flatly. "Did he leave?"

"Yeah, he said he'd be by tomorrow morning," Cecilia reported truthfully.

Tonya nodded her approval.

"Where are the kids?"

"In the kitchen. They wanted brownies with their ice cream, so I popped some into the microwave. They're cooling."

"You spoil them."

"That's what they're here for."

"Tonya, have you thought about this? I mean, really thought about what you're doing?" Cecilia asked fretfully.

"What am I doing?"

"Carrying on with him like this. You've known him less than a week."

"And? Cecilia, look, I don't butt into your personal life. I wish you would stay out of mine. I might be locked in here, but I'm not a mental case. I have a mind of my own."

"But . . ."

"No buts. I like him. That's the end of it."

"Well, I don't trust him."

Tonya laughed. "Who do you trust?"

Cecilia laughed, too, but let out a long sigh after taking a seat on the sofa.

Tonya sat next to her, knowing her mood had to do with something bigger than finding her and Jaimer together. "So, when did you see Darius?"

"This morning," she confessed after a moment's thought. "He came into the station demanding to speak with the detective in charge of investigating his father's murder."

"Was he surprised to see that it was you?"

"I'd say. He came in prepared to snap and ended up apologizing to me about the past and asking me out to dinner."

"Do what?"

"Yeah, he said that he always thought about me, that he still loves me, and that he just couldn't deal with what

95

happened. When his father gave him an out, he took it. He moved to Atlanta, ran a couple of the clubs down there. He got married about six years ago and divorced two years ago. Said he never had any more kids."

"Are you all right?" Tonya placed a sympathetic hand on her sister's knee.

"Yeah, you know. For a minute there, while he was holding me in his arms, it seemed as if we had been transported back in time. Everything was good, we were in love again. But then he kissed me, and I knew it wasn't."

"He kissed you?" Tonya automatically began whispering as if the kids could hear her.

"And yes, it was just as good as it used to be."

"Are you going to dinner with him?"

"Nope. At first, I said yes, but then I thought about things. Tonya, if I were to go to dinner with Darius, it would be like saying that I want back what once was; that I'm not happy with my life. And I am. I love Curtis. I love my children. And regardless of what happened in the past, I don't want to change anything. I've dealt with my past, and I've come to terms with what happened."

"Are you sure?"

"I'm positive. Let me tell you something, big sis to little sis. When you find the right man, you know it. You don't let anything or anyone turn you from that. I mean, Curtis and I have had our share of problems, but when I need him, he's always there. When I'm down, he lifts me up. And he has my back. That's a real partner. Darius might be all sophisticated, suave, and handsome as hell, but he's no Curtis. With the potbelly forming and the receding hairline, I know I got a strong man in my corner. When God blesses you, you got to see it, right?"

"Right. I'm glad you've made the right decision. Of course, I had no doubt, but I was wondering how you were going to deal with Darius being back in town."

"It's a done deal. I already called him and canceled the dinner. I told him that I would work my hardest to have Marion Brittingham prosecuted to the fullest extent of the law."

"I thought it was an open-and-shut case."

"No, the defense is contending that it was self-defense. They say that Meltdown had been harassing Mr. Brittingham for months before the confrontation."

"Why?"

Instead of going deeper into the conversation, Cecilia changed the subject. How was she going to bring Howard Douglass's name up when her sister finally seemed to be happy and doing much better? "I can't go into all of that. Police business." That excuse always worked. "So do you want me to help you close up the house before we leave?"

"No, girl. Haven't you heard? I'm leaving the shades open at night, too, now. Within the week, I plan to be outside playing with my nieces and nephew. It was Jaimer's idea. We plan to start slowly and work our way outside."

"Hmm. I guess he's good for something."

"Hey, what's that supposed to mean? If it weren't for him, I'd probably still be lying around like some helpless little kid."

"Don't give him too much credit, Tonya. Didn't you call me the night before the party all happy about sleeping almost through the night? You started this road to recovery, not Jaimer."

"What do you have against him, Cecilia?"

"Nothing. I just don't trust him. It seems like he's making himself at home around here."

"That's because I told him to."

"It's only been four days, Tonya."

"All right, let's stop before this gets ugly. I appreciate your concern, but really, it's not warranted."

"We'll see." Cecilia stood in the hallway. "Come on, kids. Put your dishes in the sink. We gotta go."

After Cecilia and her family left, Tonya locked the front door and went upstairs to the bathroom. Under the hot, steamy water, she tried to let her mind go free, but Jaimer entered her brain again. Thoughts of his hands and mouth caressing her body brought a rush of mixed feelings and desires.

CHAPTER 7

After two days, Tonya's confidence was soaring. With her windows and the heavy front door wide open, she moved through the house putting things back in their proper places. The salt and pepper shakers were on the counter instead of on the spice carousel by the stove. She found pens in the living room that should have been in her office. The phone book was on the living room table, not in the kitchen on the phone stand. Friday was her cleaning day. She had already mopped her kitchen floor, washed dishes, and wiped down her counters. So, the kitchen was done.

Spurred by her newfound independence, Tonya had even opened the back door wide enough to throw out her area rugs. Pride blossomed in her soul as she ignored the sweat on her palms and the twitching nerves bunching in her back. The trick would be to get the rugs back inside. But she was willing to try with Jaimer's help.

Over the past two days he had helped her deal with her fears, and she was hoping that soon she would be ready to take that final step into the outdoors. He came over every day after finishing whatever work he was doing to prepare for the opening of his office on Monday. They usually ate together, talked, and then watched a movie. But the strong sexual attraction they shared was kept in check. Tonya felt that it was mostly his doing. Maybe he didn't feel ready for that kind of relationship. That would be a first. She was a recluse, but she knew men. He was under no obligation to her. She never asked him to be. If Jaimer thought that she was trying to maneuver him into a serious relationship, all he had to do was tell her that he wasn't ready for it. Men could be so taxing.

Banging his finger while stubbornly hammering the wrong-size nail for a picture he was trying to hang only added to Jaimer's frustration. With all his unpacking and filing finished, he was trying to blow off steam by changing the office furniture around. Again. Jaimer wanted to find things to keep him occupied rather than become a nuisance to Tonya.

For two days, he had been holding back from being intimate with her. In all honesty, he wanted nothing more than to make love with her. Jaimer was falling more in love with her each day, but how could he tell her that? How could he say that he had been in love with her for the past three years when she had only known him for seven days? She would hate him. He knew it.

For that reason alone, at evening's end, he always shied from taking their goodnight kiss a step further. Guilt made him want to stop this game of deceit and secrecy, but love made him continue to try to win her heart.

Looking at the clock, he saw that it was still before noon. He had promised himself that he wouldn't knock on her door for at least two more hours, and it was not even noon. His house phone rang just as he was looking for something else to do.

"Yeah."

"Yeah? Is that any way to answer the phone, Dallas?"

"Excuse me, sir," Jaimer answered, immediately changing his tone after recognizing the voice of his former supervising officer. "I wasn't expecting—"

"Dallas, I know I'm the last person you expected to hear from today."

"Yes, sir. Especially since the phone was just turned on a day ago."

"You know it's not hard for me to find anyone I truly want to find, which brings me to the first topic of our conversation. You never registered your new address and number with the agency. You know that's a violation of the terms of your retirement."

"I was going to get around to doing that today, sir," Jaimer lied, knowing his mentor would not believe any excuse he gave.

"Rules, my good man. Rules."

"Sir, the reason you called?"

"Uh, yes. Yesterday, I received a call from someone at the witness protection program. Seems that one of our placements has suddenly vanished. They think that he might be headed back to the Philadelphia area. Agents are in the area, but I thought that I would let you know just in case you crossed paths during the course of the day. He was one of yours."

Jaimer's heart skipped a beat. "Don't tell me. Let me guess. Howard Douglass."

"Correct. I don't know how you knew, but you're correct. It seems that Mr. Douglass skipped his appointed location approximately four days ago."

"What's the big deal? Send some men out to pick him up."

"Can't do that. We don't know where he is, yet. Also, according to the local precinct, his name has been mentioned in an ongoing criminal investigation. Victim is a Jackson Melbourne, prison inmate killed by a Marion Brittingham, Howard's cousin. As you know, it was Howard's testimony that enabled the prosecution to make the charges against Melbourne stick."

"Yeah, I read about Melbourne's death in the paper. So you think Howard had something to do with the murder?"

"I wouldn't be surprised. Melbourne's death makes it possible for Howard Douglass to step right back into his former lifestyle."

"True," Jaimer replied, his mind suddenly filled with thoughts of what Howard's old lifestyle entailed.

"So just be on the lookout, old man. You know him and his past whereabouts better than anyone. You might want to report to the precinct and introduce yourself. Maybe they could use the help of a man with your expertise."

"No, thank you. I'm retired from that, remember."

"You might be able to take the man out of the agency, but you can't take the agency out of the man. The detective to contact is a Cecilia Summers."

"I'm not surprised," Jaimer mumbled, exasperated. *I can't seem to get a break.*

"What was that?"

"Nothing. I'll think about it, but I gotta tell you that this isn't exactly what I had in mind when I retired."

"It never is. How's the surveillance business going?"

"Getting off its feet quickly. Just acquired another big client, so we're well on our way."

"Good to hear it. You know, if you had kept your alias instead of reverting to your given name, your business would be swamped. Everybody knows the name Archie Dallas as it relates to our world."

"I couldn't do that. That was one life, this is another."

"You're a good man, Lambert. I wish you the best of luck."

"Thank you, sir." Jaimer hung up, surprised by the use of his given name. In the fifteen years he had known Jacob Johnson, if that was his real name, the man had never referred to him by anything but his agency name.

Sitting in front of the computer in the reception area of his office, Jaimer thought about what Howard's presence in Philadelphia might mean to him. He wondered if Howard would try to contact Tonya. And if he did, what would be her reaction. She believed Howard had been kidnapped and killed three years ago. It was the reason she was still unable to leave her house. And it was all because he had been doing his job. How many other lives had he affected the same way over the years?

What am I going to do? The web he had helped weave was closing in around him.

~~~

A shiny new white Dodge Durango was pulling into Tonya's driveway when Jaimer stepped onto his front porch. Jaimer was on his way over there, too. Wanting to know who this stranger was, he dawdled in his front yard, giving the stranger enough time to get out of the truck.

His first thought was that it was Howard returning, but he relaxed when he saw Vince getting out of the driver's side.

Damn that phone call. Now he would have to be on constant guard in case Howard tried to reenter Tonya's life. It was inevitable, of that he was sure.

"Hey, man. What's up?" Vince exclaimed cheerfully when he saw Jaimer walking toward him.

"It's all good, frat. What you up to?"

"Not a thing. Just stopped in to see how little sis is doing. I hear you're taking pretty good care of her." Vince stepped a little closer to Jaimer, giving him a knowing look, which Jaimer didn't miss.

"Yeah. Well, she's a good person, you know." Not sure what was *really* being said, Jaimer decided to keep it light. He was sure Vince knew about the kiss by now, which could make this conversation turn serious real fast. Cindy didn't seem like the type to keep things to herself. Cecilia, on the other hand, didn't seem the type to tell a lot of what she knew and saw. She herself was trying to catch him doing something wrong. Either way, he was in the hot seat, and that was a place he didn't like being.

"Yeah, I know." Deciding to change the subject for now, Vince switched moods on him. "Look, man. I'm going to a new club tonight, a gentleman's club, with my cousin Rhashad and some other frat. How about it?"

"Nah, man. I've got some things to do tonight." Jaimer lowered his head slightly so that Vince couldn't see directly into his eyes. *Why am I even trying to hide the fact that I like her?* He knew the answer was guilt. If Vince ever found out that it was he who had caused Tonya all that pain for the past three years, he would never forgive him. Frat brother or not, blood was thicker than water.

Vince was oblivious to the torment going on inside Jaimer. "All right, man. Maybe next time. You coming in?"

"Oh, yeah. I was on my way over to check on things." He fell into step with Vince.

"Things?"

"Yeah. The girls didn't tell you about our little experiment?" Of course they had. Jaimer knew it.

"Experiment?" Vince continued to play dumb.

"Yeah, to get her outside. Believe me, it doesn't take that long when it's something you really want. You know, Tonya has been trying to break herself from this house for a while now. Luckily, she worked on her willpower. She was just moving a little too fast; hence, the incident Monday. But we've taken a few steps back and some giant leaps forward."

"You almost sound like an expert on the subject, Jaimer." Vince opened the screen door, surprised that the heavy wooden door was wide open. Inside, he immediately noticed that the window shades and curtains were open. So were the windows. A nice soft breeze flowed through the house, making it feel comfortable and relaxing. Vince had heard about the changes, but his surprise still caused him to turn around and raise an eyebrow at Jaimer.

"I've had to learn to open a few doors myself over the years. All it takes is love and patience."

"And you're giving her that?" Vince tried to make the question sound inconsequential.

"No, she's giving it to herself. The love and support that all of you have shown her was only a start. To get better, Tonya had to begin to give herself that same love."

"Could you please stop talking about me like I'm some lab experiment?" Tonya came out of her office just as they walked into the living room.

"Hey, sis," Vince said, walking over and giving her a brotherly kiss on the cheek.

"Hey, man. What brings you around here?"

"I left work early. Wanted to show you my new ride."

"Why did you need a new ride?"

"I just saw it and had to have it. It's not brand new, but it only has 15,000 miles on it. 2007 Dodge Durango. Something for me to do my puttering around in."

"Yeah, I know what kind of puttering you're doing. I swear, Vince, one day somebody is going to come along and knock you so far off your feet that you're not going to know what hit your ass."

"But until then—"

"Yeah, whatever. Jay, I didn't expect you over this early."

"Jay?" Vince looked from one to the other, wondering exactly how far this friendship of theirs had gone. He knew about the kiss. Cindy had called him as soon as she got into her car that day, but maybe it had gone a little further than that by now.

Even though he had been the one who had hatched the idea of hooking them up, Vince didn't like the idea of his boy taking advantage of Tonya. The girl had been a recluse for so long that she was sure to fall prey to any slick line thrown her way. But he didn't think Jaimer was the type to do that—unless he had changed since college. People did change; sometimes for good, sometimes for worse. They were definitely going to have to talk.

Jaimer finally joined in the conversation after watching the easy rapport between the siblings. He missed having his sister near him. While working for the government, his visits with Ebony were few and far between. He was never able to drop by for no reason. All his visits home where planned and usually involved a great deal of traveling.

Unsure if it was a good idea to show Tonya any affection in front of her overprotective brother, he stood at a safe distance. "I just came over to see if you were all right with the progress you're making."

Tonya smiled at his uneasiness. Well aware of what was going on, she didn't try to force him any further than he was willing to go. After all, she could understand what he was going through. Vince was his frat brother. Maybe not his oldest or best friend, but close enough for him not to want to cause any unnecessary problems between them.

She, on the other hand, didn't really care who knew what was going on between them. If she knew her family, Vince already knew, anyway. So did Aunt Bea, all the way in Chicago. She was surprised that she hadn't received a phone call by now.

"I'm doing just fine, as you can see. While I was cleaning this morning, I even opened the back screen door and threw out my rugs. I was going to wait until you stopped by to get them. I wanted to do it myself, but just in case I got a little dizzy or faint, I wanted somebody to be around."

"You did what?" Vince smiled a little, but worry still showed on his brow.

Smiling up at her big brother, she repeated herself. "I opened the screen door and threw my rugs out."

"Tonya, that's great." Jaimer gave her a big hug. "Are you sure you want to bring them in? You're ready for that, right?"

"I'm more than ready. I'm sick of being in this house." Her excitement was contagious, and Jaimer and Vince laughed along with her. "Let's do it now. I want to be out of here by next week."

They followed Tonya to the back door. She looked out the window, trying to muster up her nerve and confidence.

"Vince, I never really noticed what a good job Mr. Abernathy does with the yard. Until a couple of days ago,

I didn't know my backyard was this beautiful." Mr. Abernathy, an old friend of the family who once owned a greenhouse, earned his money by working on yards throughout the neighborhood. Tonya wasn't sure if they were paying him enough for the curved stone walkway leading from her back door to a white swinging lounger lined with rows of tulips. Violets surrounded the lounger, and a number of rose bushes were near each corner of her freshly painted white picket fence.

"Yeah, he does do a good job," Vince agreed, patiently waiting along with Jaimer as her hand reached out to touch the door handle.

Tonya turned the knob, telling herself to breathe and concentrate. *Stay focused.* Pushing the door open, she kept her eyes on the rugs, which were only a couple of feet from the door. *One step at a time.* She put her left foot out the door, and pushed it a little wider. *You can do it, girl.* Her right foot followed. *Breathe.* Holding the door wider, she moved her body in line with her legs. *Breathe.*

Jaimer's breath caught in his throat as he watched her bravely accomplish her task.

Struggling with himself to remain in place, Vince stayed strong enough not to attempt a rescue mission.

Tears slowly slid down her cheeks when she heard the sound of the screen door click shut behind her. Her pulse was racing, and she felt beads of sweat form at her temple. The nerves on the back of her neck stood up, and goose bumps rose on her arms as the wind softly caressed her skin. The thought of turning around and running into her house never once crossed her mind as she looked around her backyard, feeling totally free for the first time in a very long time. This was what she had been wanting since the day she decided it was time to move on with her life. *I'm really outside. Oh God, thank you.*

The tears running down Vince's face weren't easy to hide. Overwhelmed by what he had just witnessed, he couldn't hold them back. His sister, his little sister, the sister he had gotten so used to protecting, to taking care of, was a strong, brave woman. She was just like their mother, only he had never seen it until this day. With Cecilia's overbearing posturing and Cindy's self-absorbed tenacity, it was easy to see they could take care of themselves. But Tonya had always been the one he thought he would have to safeguard forever.

He had been wrong.

Jaimer placed a comforting hand on Vince's back. He knew how it felt to not be needed in the same way anymore. When his sister got married, he had felt it just as strongly. There was nothing closer than that bond—sibling to sibling. After a minute, Jaimer pulled Vince back into the kitchen. They sat at the island, where they could watch Tonya as she reacquainted herself with the outdoors. Jaimer moved around the kitchen, preparing to make coffee. Vince noticed how familiar he seemed with her house.

"This is unbelievable," Vince whispered, watching Tonya, who was still standing in the same spot, her arms wrapped around herself. "I know that she was trying to make it there, but I have to say that I believe you had a lot to do with this, frat."

Jaimer turned around to face him. He knew where this conversation was headed, and no matter how much he wanted to avoid it, he knew it was a topic that was going to have to be addressed sooner or later. And rightly so. She was his sister, and Jaimer, a complete stranger to her, had come into her life and practically taken up shop in only a few days. They all had to wonder at his intentions. He and Vince had been really good friends, and even though it had been years since they'd really seen each other, Jaimer thought that all of his trust should be forthcoming. But he knew how Vince felt about her. He wanted to let his boy know that he had nothing but good intentions toward her. So, yeah, they did need to talk. Jaimer preferred to just get it out of the way.

"I'd like to think I had a little to do with it, but believe me when I tell you, Tonya did this all on her own."

"You really do like her, don't you, man?" Vince sat back, staring at him intensely because he truly needed to know that his sister was in good hands.

"Man, I love her. I have since . . ." Jaimer stopped himself. *A little too much to soon.*

"You what?" Vince pressed on.

"I have since the day you introduced us," Jaimer finally said. Stretching the truth wasn't necessarily a bad thing. "Call it crazy, call it love at first sight. I don't know, but I do know that I care for your sister very much."

Not knowing what to believe, Vince decided to play it safe. "Just because it has never happened to me doesn't make it impossible. I guess if that's how you feel, it's real.

I heard about the kiss, so I was wondering where you were planning to go with this."

"I know what you're thinking, Vince. But we're not in school anymore."

"Jaimer, in school you were far more of a gentleman than any of us, but you still had your share of liaisons."

"I know, but this is different. Frat, I have no intention of hurting your sister. You don't know, but I've been through a lot. It's time for me to make a few changes in my life as well, and I plan on starting with your sister. I really like her, and I want to get to know her better."

"Just be careful. I know that she likes you, but she's been out of the game for a while."

"That's just it, Vince. This is not a game." He stood by the island watching Tonya bend down to smell a tulip along the walkway.

Vince saw the look in his eye, which answered any further questions he might have had.

Tonya sat on the stone pathway, loving the feel of the soft air running through her hair and causing her braids to move to and fro across her shoulders. Simple things amazed her. The wind in her hair, the grass between her toes, the sound of the birds in the tall oak tree, which had been in the yard for years. She had forgotten about it. Each little observation brought waves of memories back to the forefront of her mind. The days she and her siblings wasted playing tag, hide-and-seek, and jumping rope came back to her.

For almost an hour, Tonya sat in her backyard enjoying sights and sounds she had forgotten existed. An airplane flew overhead, a ladybug landed on her shoulder. And she was taking it all in, unaware that she was being watched, being loved.

CHAPTER 8

Howard Douglass walked through the crowded bus terminal thoroughly pissed off. *Where the hell is my ride?* It was bad enough that he had to bus across the fuckin' country like a damn pack rat, squished among a bunch of sniffling kids and coughing adults. Smelling everything from dirty diapers to funky armpits wasn't how he had planned to spend the first few days of his new freedom. *God, how I hate cramped spaces.*

It was hard work lollygagging around the small hick town, its only claim to fame being its desert resort and spa. He had worked there as a masseuse, catering to the rich and famous who frequented the place. At times, he wanted to yell out that he was also rich and famous—in Philadelphia. But he held his tongue for the greater good, and that was hard work, too.

Even having secret affairs with a multitude of the hotel's ritzy clientele had been hard work. He had to fake interest in the majority of them. As the new beefcake, his attention had been much in demand. He was creative enough to keep them coming back for more, bringing with them plenty of gifts. Yes, it was hard work, but a brother had to live properly.

Even harder than the physical act of keeping himself erect and willing for each obese, nasty, or just ugly woman who came looking for him was being ordered around like a cabana boy. He was used to being the one giving the orders. Being ordered around and keeping your mouth shut was hard work. He took his anger out by pounding the backs out of the old broads, but that only had them coming for more.

Occasionally, he would luck up and be treated to a delectable young beauty, a niece or granddaughter and maybe a friend would join in, but for the most part the young and rich partied someplace else.

He should have been on an airplane in first class, relaxing comfortably, watching a movie or two and enjoying the fruits of his labor. Lying low was the safest way for him to travel, or so his cousin Dominique had said. He, however, didn't favor the idea of coming back to his old stomping grounds in anything less than style. Howard was all about glamour and glitz, but again, for the greater good, he'd made a concession to her plans.

For three years, that damn witness protection program had him locked away in a strange town, surrounded by people he didn't know or trust. They were probably all federal agents. He had been pulled out of his familiar surroundings, everyday life, and from the woman he was beginning to develop strong feelings for.

Years of resentment against the powers-that-be forced him to make the phone call that initiated a long chain of events until he was able to make the move he was now making. The move back home and into his former life.

Yeah, he had plans of his own. With Meltdown out of the way, Howard planned to take over the business with help from Dominique, whose college degrees in finance and business from Clark University in Atlanta would help him take his business to the next level—integrating into corporate America. For three years, he had been losing money while on vacation in that small town south of Phoenix, Arizona. Howard knew he had a lot of making up to do and very little time to do it in.

Dominique had kept his interests in good standing while he was locked away. He trusted her more than any of their other relatives because, along with book smarts, she was street smart and devilishly conniving. While the trial was going on, she had vehemently pledged her loyalty to Meltdown to the point of telling him that she would find out where they were hiding Howard and have him murdered. She and Meltdown were already lovers. That, too, was part of the plan.

Not knowing the two were in cahoots, Meltdown decided to put Dominique in charge of his whole operation while he was locked away. His mistake was trusting Dominique's beauty. It had cost him his life.

Dominique's beauty was surpassed only by her love of money. Glowing, caramel skin and gleaming hazel eyes did well to hide the deceitful vixen underneath. With a body like Beyonce Knowles, a face like Janet Jackson, and a brain like Oprah Winfrey, she was a formidable ally. And a very dangerous lady.

After trying for over a year, one of their cousins had managed to end up in the same prison as Meltdown. Everything had gone as planned with Meltdown's death and his cousin's cry of self-defense. Because no one else was around at the time of the incident, it was hard to establish a case, especially since his cousin had also been severely wounded. A security guard from the prison had even stepped forward claiming that Marion rushed out of the showers bleeding, but telling them to check on Meltdown first. That was not the action of your usual murderer.

But none of that mattered now. How it all came about wasn't important. He was back home where he belonged, and he intended to get back everything he missed. First order of business: Tonya Perkins.

Scowling, Howard curtly acknowledged the driver of the Lincoln Town Car that had just pulled up at the curbside.

"You're late," he said, ripping out the words impatiently.

"Sorry, sir. Traffic was terrible," Jimmy, a new driver, said, apologizing profusely.

"Next time, leave much earlier. You never know what might happen on the way anywhere. It is best not to keep the one who pays you waiting. And just so you know, I don't like to be late, ever."

"Yes, sir," the kid mumbled, rushing to open the door for his boss. Just being in the presence of Howard "Brick" Douglass made his palms wet. "Miss Dominique is waiting for you at the office."

"Before heading there, I would like to go by this address," Howard replied, passing a white piece of paper to the driver.

After talking to Jaimer, Vince decided it was time to go home and prepare for the evening. Tonya had finally brought her rugs in and was returning them to in their proper places, smiling brightly all the while. And with very good reason; she had accomplished something great today.

"Baby sis, I'm about to leave. I love you, and I'm proud of you." He hugged her quickly, not wanting to get too emotional, and gave her a quick peck on the cheek. "Yo, man," he said, turning to Jaimer, "it's not too late to change your mind."

"Nah, I'm good." Jaimer glanced at Tonya.

"Change his mind about what?" Tonya asked.

"Oh, I wanted Jaimer to go out with me tonight to a new gentlemen's club. A lot of frat will be there," Vince responded and then waited for her reaction.

Tonya didn't know how to react, simply shrugging and turning to Jaimer. "Hmm, are you going?"

With nothing to hide, Jaimer answered honestly. "No, I was planning on spending some time with you."

The smile she tried to hide was nonetheless seen by both men.

"All right." Giving up, Vince walked to the front door. "I'm outta here." He knew when he wasn't needed or wanted. Oh, well, he still had places to go, things to do. He was supposed to have been at Marcia's house two hours ago, but he just couldn't tear himself away from his sister's joy. She would have to understand. Or she wouldn't. He really didn't care one way or the other.

Climbing into his new car, Vince secretly wished that Tonya's prediction would come true. Nobody would believe it, but he did want to find someone that he could love forever. Distracted, he put the truck in reverse and almost slammed into the front end of a black Lincoln Town Car that was moving slowly past the house. If his good reflexes hadn't kicked in when he heard the other car's horn, he would have wrecked his new automobile.

"Let's go out to eat," Tonya suggested. Her stomach became woozy at the idea of being that far away from the sanctuary of her home.

"Are you sure you're ready for that?" Jaimer asked, amazed by her courage.

"No, I'm not, but it sounded good," she laughed. He actually believed she could do it. "Okay, what's for dinner then?"

"Whatever you want. I'll go get it. I think we deserve a fabulous meal with wine or champagne included. We need to celebrate tonight." Jaimer came up behind her and draped his arms around her waist.

"Celebrate?" She turned and faced him, not fully comfortable with his gesture, although she liked how it felt.

"Yeah, your breakthrough," he answered, quickly dropping his arms.

"But I'm not done yet."

"No, but you're more than halfway there." His arms at his side, Jaimer lowered his head and kissed her lightly on her cheek. His promise to go slow still uppermost in his mind, he reached up and caressed her chin as he pulled her closer. But when he felt Tonya's hand grasp his back, Jaimer knew that promise had flown out the window. Changing the innocent kiss, he allowed his tongue to lavish her mouth with quick traces before lacing with hers.

"I'd better go and get our food." He tried to move away from her, but her grasp was unyielding.

"Are you in that much of a hurry?" Tonya nibbled at his chin, working her way toward his earlobe.

"I'd better go before I don't go," Jaimer said, moving away and giggling.

"You really are ticklish, aren't you?" She asked, laughingly. "Okay, let's decide what we're having."

"How about the Olive Garden this time? I saw a commercial earlier advertising their stuffed chicken marsala. It looked as good as I-don't-know-what."

"Okay, Olive Garden sounds good to me. Tomorrow I'm cooking you a real meal. You've been so good to me, and I want to do something special to show you how much I appreciate it."

"Can you cook?"

"Of course, I can cook. I've been cooking since I was ten years old."

"Is there anything special you want?"

"No. The stuffed chicken marsala sounds good. I'm going to take a shower while you're gone."

Leaning back against the sofa, Jaimer sighed contented and slowly undid the top button of his Levi jeans. "I'm so full," he said happily. "That was good."

"Yeah, it was," Tonya agreed, lounging next to him.

"I better clean up that mess before I get stiff here. I won't be able to move a muscle soon," Jaimer commented.

"Are you sure about that?" she asked, reaching over and landing a solid kiss on his chin.

Jaimer looked down at her quizzically. Where had that come from? She probably didn't know she was playing with fire. "Tonya, are you flirting with me?"

"What if I am?" she asked teasingly. It was only nine o'clock. Jaimer was beginning to feel crowded as the air in the room seemed to grow warm. "You did say you were going to spend this evening with me, didn't you? Are you trying to back out of that now? You're thinking that maybe you should have gone with Vince to the strip club instead? Maybe I got it all wrong; maybe you don't really want to be with me after all."

"No, you don't have it wrong at all. You know that I want to be with you. I'm just not sure if this is the right time."

"Well, if now is not the time, when will be? Jaimer, I want you now, right now. But if you don't want me, then please just let me know." Tonya couldn't believe that she was almost pleading with him.

Jaimer looked at her. "I just want you to be sure."

Tonya stood up and pulled on Jaimer's hand. When he was standing beside her, she moved in close to him and whispered, "I'm sure."

Needing no further assurances, he kissed her deeply.

Dishes forgotten, they stumbled their way up the steps, holding each other and shedding their clothes along the way. By the time they reached her bedroom, Jaimer's shirt was off, as was Tonya's printed sundress. She was now wearing only a red matching bra and panty set.

They looked at each other. Grasping her around the flare of her hips, Jaimer pulled her close. He kissed her shoulders as he pulled each bra strap down, then he covered his hands over her breasts. He squeezed her and held her in his palms.

Tonya's hands moved from his chest to the band of his jeans, quickly loosening the last few buttons of his jeans, eager to see what was hidden beneath. Her tongue twisted with his as they kissed.

Once his pants fell, Jaimer stepped out of them and kicked them to the side. Tonya gasped, sending shivers up his spine. She liked what she saw. So did he. Following the trail of his hands, Jaimer's mouth covered her breast. Slowly, he used his lips and tongue until her nipples stood hard and stiff. He hooked the band of her panties with his fingers and pulled them down.

Tonya pulled his boxers down, and took several steps back; she wanted to get a good look at him. She couldn't take her eyes off him as he took purposeful steps toward her. His body was hard, thick, solid. Like a moving Greek statue, his abs flexed with step, his thighs tightened; the overall effect was hypnotic.

Jaimer lowered her onto the soft bed. Falling beside her, he planted kisses all over her stomach and then moved up to her breasts. Moving up to her face, he mumbled, "Baby, are you sure about this?"

The length of him pressing against her outer thigh made it difficult for her to think. Instead of answering, she kissed him greedily, silently urging him to continue. Their legs were intertwined, his chest half crushing her breast, his heart beating in rhythm with hers. "Please, Jaimer."

Using his fingers, Jaimer pried her legs open and then traced small circles along her inner thigh. He kissed her neck, her shoulder, her left breast, and the side of her belly, working his way to the essence of her femininity.

Tonya lay back, relaxed and clutching her stomach muscles as Jaimer's exploratory moves grew deeper, more intense. Her moans became louder and louder as she fell captive to his magnetic charms.

"Wait a minute," Jaimer whispered, moving off the bed.

"Wha—what? Where are you going?" Tonya asked, stunned by what seemed like abandonment.

"The condom is in my jeans." He hastily retrieved the foil package and returned to her. As she opened her arms and her thighs to receive him, Jaimer knew something extraordinary was about to happen. After all the years of waiting, he was where he wanted to be—next to her, surrounded by her, a part of her. She had his heart, now he was about to hand over his soul.

Tonya felt him heavy against her opening. The pressure of him didn't hurt; it aroused her, causing the liquid of her excitement to flood her canal and make his entry easy.

With his eyes closed and his teeth clenched, Jaimer slowly slid into her tightness. He felt the muscles surrounding him as they began to relax. The soft quivers that racked his maleness drove him to distraction. To maintain control of himself, he froze until he felt his emotions settling.

"Oh, Jaimer," Tonya moaned when he drew back and took his first plunge deep into her abyss. The old familiar sensations came back full force, her gyrating hips taking notice of his rhythm.

Gripping the sheets on both sides of her head, Jaimer forced himself to concentrate. He didn't want to think of how luxurious her body felt under him, or the feel of her hot breath against his right ear, and certainly not the moistness he was slipping into over and over again as he picked up the pace of his lovemaking. He tried to focus on the calm ocean and the sports game he had watched the night before, knowing if he didn't do this, her first experience since the incident wouldn't be as good for her as he wanted it to be.

It was an old trick his dad had described to him years ago. To this day, it never failed to elicit anything but praise. Not all men could do it; some weren't strong enough to concentrate on inconsequential things when the feel of a tight, wet, and willing tunnel of satisfaction lay beneath them. But Jaimer would do it for her. *Tomorrow, I want her looking forward to my afternoon visits and be more than willing to express her feelings for me in front of her family. And I want her to look at me and remember our time together.*

Tonya was soon at the end of the rope holding her sanity together. As wave upon wave of desire crashed through her, with her hands tangled up in her hair, her whole body clutched tightly, she released years of doubt, confusion, and pent-up tension.

Jaimer held onto her through her climax, but continued to concentrate so that he wouldn't cause his own release prematurely. Instead, he decreased his speed and increased his pressure, applying long, deep, lazy strokes until he had her on the brink of another overwhelming orgasm.

This time, when her muscles convulsed and tightened around him as he continued to bury himself deep within her, he only thought of her legs wrapped around his hips and Tonya meeting his every thrust, her hands grabbing and kneading his back and her nails digging into his bottom, urging him closer to her. Jaimer dipped, banged, and ground into her until they had both succeeded in opening the door with love and crossing over the threshold.

Lying in the afterglow of their lovemaking, Tonya was happily satisfied that things had turned out exactly as she had hoped they would. She watched him make his way back into the bedroom after going to the bathroom. It was her turn to wipe off the evidence of their time together. As she passed him, Jaimer reached out and lightly tapped her on the behind.

〰

Tonya exhaled slowly. Under the stream of heated water, she smiled and did a quick jig in a circle, too excited to just let the event go uncelebrated. She pumped her fist in the air, whispering, *"Yes! Yes!"* She was overwhelmed by what she had just experienced. The feel of him moving over her, him inside her stretching and reaching into her very essence, washed over her in one quick rush.

"Whoa, girl. Okay, calm down, just calm down," she giggled, trying to retain a bit of dignity. It was just sex, right? There was no reason to be acting as if she had found the pot of gold at the end of a rainbow, right?

Like hell, Tonya thought. It had been three years, but she remembered what good sex felt like, and Jaimer had definitely given her something to think about over the next few days.

And although she was starting to make progress with her illness, Tonya could honestly admit that it was her feelings for Jaimer that made her want to speed up the process. It was her trust in him that made her try things that she would have easily put off before. And it was her lust for him that had her wanting his touch.

Even now, drying herself off with a thick, purple towel, she tingled as the cotton cloth passed over her breasts, her thighs, and each part of her body that Jaimer had shown attention. She still felt his lips on her breasts, her thighs. His hands had left pressure marks along her hips and on her stomach.

Before she once again became overheated by memories, Tonya finished drying off and then wrapped the towel around her. Unfortunately, she wasn't as shameless and comfortable with her nudity around him as he seemed to be with her.

She glanced in the bathroom mirror, wondering if she looked any different, because she felt totally different from the woman she had looked at that morning.

Everything was the same, except the corners of her mouth lifted a bit higher when she smiled. Her eyes sparkled a little brighter, and the set of her shoulders was just a little straighter.

Another thought came to mind, and the smile faded and panic set in. Was he satisfied with her?

How was she supposed to find out if he was thoroughly satisfied? Looking back, Tonya realized she hadn't been her old wild and crazy self. Sure, there were things that she could have done, but this was their first time together and her first time in years. He couldn't have expected her to do too much. She wasn't that used to him yet. But she didn't just lie there like a stiff board, either. She responded to him and his movements. She had no choice. God knows she made enough noise for it to sound like he was killing her, which he practically was.

Tonya smiled again.

"What took you so long?" Jaimer asked as soon as she stepped into the room.

"I didn't realize that I was taking that long. I guess it was feeling good under the water." She took the glass of champagne he handed her.

"I got something that will make you feel better." He moved closer to her, still undressed except for his boxers and still bulging everywhere. *Everywhere.*

"I just bet you do."

"This is the last of the champagne." Jaimer didn't know why he said that, but he knew that he would have to ask the next question. He could tell she was just as unprepared for the rest of the evening as he was. Before he could continue, she interrupted him.

"Are you staying?" The question was asked shyly, and clearly did not match the determination he saw in her eyes.

Jaimer looked down at her trembling hands grasping the glass. He took it from her and took both of her hands in his and walked with her to the bed.

Tonya readily followed, thinking he was going to pull her into another play session.

"Baby, I would love to stay with you tonight, but I don't think you're ready for someone to invade your privacy. I mean—"

"My privacy? Jaimer, you've been invading my privacy since the first time we met. In my house, my head, you're everywhere."

"I know. You've been doing the same thing to me. But—"

"If you leave me, it'll seem like this was just a booty call."

"Tonya, you know better than that. I mean I don't have any problem with staying. I just don't want to hurt anything we've started." Seeing the hurt in her eyes, he conceded. "I'm staying, but if you get too uncomfortable with me sharing your bed, just let me know. I don't want you trying to deal with something just for my benefit. If you can't take it right now, that's fine."

"I'll be all right." But just to be on the safe side, she retrieved her wine glass and quickly downed the smooth liquid. She had to do *something* about her fraying nerves.

CHAPTER 9

Impressed and surprised by the classy decor of *Waterfalls: A Gentlemen's Club*, Vince moved through the spacious, well-lit lobby followed by two of his frat brothers, Sean and Nairobi, and his cousin Rhashad Burton. Men were dressed to the nines in their Versace and Armani suits and multi-colored alligator shoes. But not to be ignored, the ballers were flossing the latest in RocaWear tracksuits, Sean John dress shirts, and Timberlands. The atmosphere was comfortable and filled with excitement over the attractions gracing large posters, which lined the lobby hallway. Each poster was encased in a lighted metal frame, adding extra effects to the beauty in the center.

In navy blue slacks and a pale sky blue Avirex dress shirt, Rhashad drew the same attention to the group as he always did. The light-skinned basketball star stood six feet, eleven inches tall and was a starting forward in the NBA. He was Shawnique's older brother, and he and Vince had grown up together thicker than thieves. By his second year in the league, Rhashad was an all-star after being traded by Philadelphia and taking Seattle to their first championship playoff series in ten years. Now, with five seasons behind him, his star was still rising.

Not only did his height stand out, his easy grace and charm caused people to flock toward him and not want to leave. It was the same everywhere they went. Vince was used to it. He and his boys stood to the side of the walkway chatting about regular everyday life, giving Rhashad time to sign a couple of autographs.

"Sorry about that, fellas," Rhashad said when the four finally resumed walking down the left hall toward the clubhouse section of the establishment. The right hall led to the dining area and a bar, both complete with dance floors and music. The dining area usually played jazz and old school music, while the bar blasted hip-hop, R & B, and reggae.

"No sweat, man. You'll be doing that all night. I'm used to it." Vince patted him on the back.

Vince enjoyed his cousin's company. When Rhashad first joined the league, it was Vince he turned to when he needed to stay grounded. He didn't want to make the mistakes he saw other young players making. Getting a large ego and becoming cocky and conceited only caused problems with you and your teammates. Rhashad didn't join the NBA to just make money and not have any friends.

And Vince was more than happy to visit his cousin whenever possible, riding in the fast lane for just a little before returning to the normal pace of things. If anything, Rhashad's celebrity went to Vince's head faster than it did his own. Vince loved hob-knobbing with the rich and famous and enjoying the perks of Rhashad's lifestyle, especially the women.

Another perk of Rhashad's celebrity was getting the best seats in the house, just as they were getting tonight. But tonight, Vince wasn't thinking about the women who would grace the stage for the next couple of hours. He was here to see only one woman. Dominique.

As they were greeted by the club's maitre'd and were escorted past the heavy velour curtains tied back by thick ropes through a maze of tables toward the front of the room, the lighting dimmed considerably. The room became dark except for the long built-in wall aquarium and the round columns of water that were displayed in various positions around the room. The floor-to-ceiling columns were filled with water that was constantly in motion. The wall aquarium was full of numerous exotic fish, causing a rainbow of color to leap from behind the glass shield.

They took their seats and were immediately approached by a waitress who seemed very eager to take their orders. She deliberately reached across Rhashad, nearly dripping her large breasts into his lap.

"If you need anything at all, Mr. Burton, just call on me," she seductively said before prancing away. Rhashad wasn't the least bit phased by her comment.

"Yo, man," Sean laughed. "Is it like that all the time?"

"All the time," Rhashad answered, sounding withdrawn and disinterested.

"You could have had your way with her right here on the table," Nairobi commented, grinning.

"Yeah, but you get tired of that after a while. I'm content now with married life."

"Aw, hell no. I don't want to hear it." Sean put his hands over his ears. "Just keep all that to yourself. I'm trying to live vicariously through you. You'll ruin it for me if you tell me the truth."

"All right, then, I'll keep it to myself."

When the waitress came back, she introduced herself as Amber and asked for his autograph for her son, Steven. Rhashad graciously signed a napkin and thanked her for her services as she placed their drinks down.

The music was a steady mix of R & B and soft rock and roll, combining just as the diversity of the crowd had. The club was filled with businessmen, hustlers, local celebrities, and regular, hard-working Joes, patiently awaiting the entertainment and fantasies that the night had to offer.

A tall, thin, pecan-colored goddess dressed in a flowing white gown wrapped with golden ropes crossed the stage and immediately eyed Rhashad. Just as every dancer before her, she focused on him before giving her attention to the other men in the room. Slowly, one by one, the golden ropes fell to the stage floor as she twisted and twirled to the beat of the music.

The applause and cheers of the audience grew louder when she began to peel the pieces of her garment away. Turning her hips in circles, she glided to the pole in the middle of the stage and lifted herself off the ground, climbing to the top. Then, wrapping her legs around the steel rod, she flipped herself upside down, and slowly, using only her legs, lowered herself to the floor with her arms spread apart. The sheer white thong she was wearing didn't leave anything to the imagination.

Sean, completely devoid of inhibitions, walked up to the stage to run his hands along the legs of the dancer, burying a crisp ten-dollar bill in the string by her hip and running his finger down the center of the thin piece of fabric. She smiled as she stuck his finger in her mouth and began to suck it.

When Sean sat back down, he laughed, "I think I'm taking that one home with me tonight. I can't wait to get her between my sheets."

"Man, please," Nairobi interrupted. "You don't have a shot in hell. Plus, I think she thinks she's going home with big man over here." He pointed towards Rhashad, who shook his head and laughed.

Vince took a sip from his Corona bottle and watched honey-dip move to the end of the stage closest to Rhashad. He smiled when the girl dropped down in front of his cousin with her legs spread-eagled, trying to entice him into giving up a couple of dollars. Vince knew better than the dancer that she was barking up the wrong tree. Even with NBA money, Rhashad was tighter than a Vlasic pickle jar with his funds.

"Go 'head, man," Nairobi urged. "She's waiting for you."

"Then she's got a long wait." Rhashad shook his head again. He laughed and picked up another barbecue chicken wing. "See, I know somebody that she doesn't—

my wife. Tell them, Vince. Regina doesn't play that shit. She'll run through my pockets so fast, that she'll have that girl's address and social security number. I won't even know her name."

"Aw, damn, man, there you go again. You're really fuckin' with my dreams," Sean said, disgusted. "I thought y'all ballplayers had it goin' on."

"And we do, but you got to know how far to take it. If my wife pops me tomorrow, you got my back. I can come to your house and moan and complain while I fall into a slump on the court?"

He looked at Sean, then at Nairobi. They looked back.

"I didn't think so. What's the rule, gee?"

"Look, but don't touch. Fantasize, then forget," Vince answered quickly, having stated the rules countless times over the years.

"That's right. Makes my life very pleasant. Besides, I did as much playing around as any man could while I was single. Ain't nothing changed."

"But don't you get that itch every now and then? Look at her." Sean pointed to the girl on stage. "Man, you're crazy." Both men turned to honey-dip, who was bent over shaking her fat ass at the crowd, anticipating Rhashad's answer.

"She's a nice looking girl, but no. My wife handles all my itches. And she can trust me. You think I would let go of four years of happiness for four hours of physical pleasure? Now, that's crazy. And the sad part is I see weak men doing it all the time."

The conversation went on for a few more minutes, but Vince was bored with the topic. He already knew all about Rhashad's unrelenting faithfulness to his wife. And to be honest, he envied him for it. He couldn't wait to have somebody he felt compelled to be faithful to.

Vince was only there because he told her that he would be. Now, looking around the room, he wondered where she was. It had been a week since he had seen her. The night of the party she had showed up unexpectedly and left after she saw him dancing with Marcia. His phone calls had gone unanswered until Wednesday night, when he told her he was sorry if he had hurt her feelings and explained the situation to her.

He and Marcia were friends just like they were. They didn't have an exclusive relationship. He didn't want one. Being completely honest with both ladies usually kept things in perspective, but every once in a while you came across one who didn't like sharing. In this case, neither of them did.

Marcia realized that the only way to keep him was to let him go when he wanted to, but she didn't like it. But Dominique seemed determined to make him hers. Would he mind it? Probably not, if he knew more about her. But she kept her business to herself. He was surprised she even told him about this club.

When he asked her why she managed a place like this, she told him that a girl had to keep an eye on her money. Said it rather nonchalantly, too. Apparently, her former boss had passed away and left it to her in his will. Now, who would do a thing like that? Admittedly, her mysteriousness had him captivated. Her family and past, what she did on a daily basis, were things he needed to find out.

Totally Dominique's opposite, Marcia was the silent, strong type. She seemed to get pleasure from making sure he was always satisfied. When he was at her house, she gave him the utmost attention, making sure that his every need was met. She had one child, a teenage daughter, who adored Vince and saw him as the father figure she hadn't had since her own father had passed away five years earlier of prostate cancer. Marcia was totally devoted to her daughter, and Vince liked that. So why wasn't he completely happy with her?

Giving more attention to his half-empty beer bottle than the petite dancer who was now on stage, Vince exhaled as Tonya's face flashed through his mind. He saw her smile and the sparkle in her eye that had appeared when she took her first step outside. The pride that pumped through his heart had to be similar to that of a father watching his newborn walking for the first time. Jaimer, he noticed, had a look in his eyes, too. One that made Vince wonder just how far their relationship had gone. He truly hoped whatever was developing between them was a success. It seemed to be good for both of them.

"You all right, cuz," Rhashad said, pulling him back into the conversation.

"Yo, man," Sean whispered to the whole table. "Look at that Reese's Pieces standing over there by the bar."

All four men turned their heads simultaneously in the indicated direction. Vince hid his smile from the others as he turned back to his original position and took another swallow from his beer bottle.

"Damn, she's sharp as hell," Nairobi commented.

"She can't be a dancer. Look at her; all sophisticated like she owns the spot." Sean's cockiness came to life as he continued. "I should go over and holla at her."

"Man, please," Nairobi laughed. "She's way out of your league. That chick would have you running around in circles trying to figure out what the hell just happened after she took you for all your shit."

"I'll have that honey wrapped around my finger begging me to marry her ass and keep her barefoot and pregnant."

Rhashad sat back, shaking his head, listening to the two fools dispense different outcomes to a situation both were dreaming up and neither had a chance in hell of fulfilling. From what he could tell by just looking at the beauty, whom he recognized as the same woman his cousin had introduced him to at the party last weekend, these fools wouldn't be able to handle a two-sentence conversation with her.

The impression Rhashad got from Dominique was that she was tough lady, a sharp businesswoman, and someone used to getting what she wanted. She had jumped down Vince's throat when she saw him dancing with Marcia at the party. He and his wife had been standing on the porch when she stormed out the door with Vince following closely behind her.

"Boy, that girl wouldn't let you lick the bottom of her shoe," Nairobi laughed.

Joining in on the banter, Rhashad added, "If you were the last man standing, she'd become a lesbian."

"Oh, now, you got jokes, too," Sean replied. "I bet you I'll have her digits before the end of the night."

"Please, she don't want you," Rhashad egged Sean on. "As a matter of fact, I bet she won't give you the time of day. She'll holla at one of us first."

"What? Oh, I know you're crazy." Sean found that hard to believe. All through life, his bluish-green eyes, smooth, almond complexion, and naturally pitch-black curly hair, all compliments of his Caucasian father, had enabled him to catch the attention of many high-profile ladies. His past conquests included celebrities, beauty queens, models, and currently the anchorwoman of a local newscast. Tangled throughout this list was also a mixture of local yokels he used to entertain himself when he couldn't find a mate that fit into his usual high standards.

"Let me get this straight," Rhashad said. "You believe that if she comes this way, you will be the one she will want. As soon as she sees *you*, she won't look at another soul at the table."

"That's what I'm saying, yeah." Shaking his head repeatedly, Sean looked around the table confidently. Then unknowingly putting his foot in his mouth, he continued, "I'll bet you she will try to holla at me first for a pair of tickets to your next game against the Sixers, court-side seats."

"It's a bet," Rhashad agreed immediately, shaking hands with his friend. "And, if you lose, you have to buy all our drinks for the rest of the night."

"It's a deal. Nairobi, I'm about to get a two for one. I'm going to hook up with honey-dip *and* make Cynthia happy when I take her to the game." Cynthia was one of his latest chicks. She was a big basketball fan after having dated several of the league's less famous players.

"Don't count your chips too fast. You got to win the bet first." Nairobi didn't like Cynthia's snobbish attitude and condescending ways. He saw her for what she was— a money hungry gold-digger willing to use anybody to get to the next level. Why didn't his boy see that?

Vince remained quiet during the exchange. He knew what Rhashad was up to. Sean's conceit had often gotten on his last nerve. As far as Vince was concerned, Sean was a pretty boy, which was cool, but Sean knew it and let it go to his head . . . and his mouth, on most occasions. For all Sean's good looks and large bank account, he still pulled the same number of women as Vince and Nairobi did.

As they tried to tell him time and time again, it all depended on what the women wanted. If they wanted jokes and a good time with lots of laughter, they tended to gravitate towards Nairobi. He was the clown of the group, and laughter was the way to a lot of ladies' hearts.

For purely physical attraction, Sean was the man on the job. He was deeper than that, but his devotion to bachelorhood only allowed him to let a woman get so close. Sean was a love 'em and leave 'em type of guy. When it was over he usually pledged to keep a platonic friendship with whomever, but more often than not, he was never heard from again. That led to some ugly situations for him, but he seemed to take breaking hearts in stride.

Vince was the most honest in the group. He was straightforward with his wants, needs, and desires, which proved to be a tremendous turn-on to some women. In his boldness, his actions sometimes came off as a bit hard. Women just ate up that thug mentality. They couldn't get enough of his roughneck persona. It also led to difficult situations, but he even handled those with a no-nonsense sort of attitude that kept them coming back for more.

CHAPTER 10

Dominique moved slowly through the club, ever on the alert for anything amiss, making sure her clients lacked for nothing—liquor, food, entertainment. Her clientele was her meal ticket, and she made sure that every visitor to the club felt welcome and received first-class attention from her ladies.

Her ladies were clean, wholesome, educated, and goal-oriented. Many had college degrees and were using their extracurricular activities for the sole purpose of fattening their bank accounts. That is what Dominique demanded of her girls: Dancing was not to be their main ticket; it was just a meal ticket, just a way to stay one step ahead in a world dominated by men.

She herself had started out on the stage, but thanks to her quick mind and ambition she was ready when opportunity knocked. Once she showed Meltdown what she could do for him and his businesses, her dancing days were over. He encouraged her strengths and helped her overcome her weaknesses. He loved her determination to succeed. That is why he had so willingly left her in charge of his interests.

He never saw past her deceptive persona, and was totally taken in by her charm and business strategies. And the wild and uninhibited sex she provided him didn't hurt either. Although it turned her stomach, she gave herself to him willingly because it was a means to her ultimate goal. Before he knew what hit him, Dominique's supple body and sexual skills had the older gentleman's eyes wide open.

After talking with the bartender to make sure everything was running smoothly, she looked around the club at the usual crowd. Through the pulsing red and blue lights, Dominique thought she saw a familiar face in the far corner.

Her heart rate increased at the prospect of a glorious ending to an otherwise stressful day. She imagined herself in his arms between her satin bedclothes, enjoying his expertise. It had been so long since she had wanted a man so much; lately, she had found herself daydreaming about him more than usual. For once in her life, she was tempted to actually have a sexual relationship just for the pleasure of it. For once, she wanted to have sex with someone without having a goal attached to it. For once, it could be for love instead of a car, money, or a business advantage. For once, she wanted to make love, not have sex.

Her startling self-discovery shocked her enough to pull her out of her reverie, but her smile remained. Was it possible? Was she finally beginning to fall for a man, for Vincent Perkins?

But now wasn't a good time for that. She had other things that she had to do. First, she had to get her overbearing cousin off her back so that she could begin to live her own life. There was a time she was truly interested in helping him get his revenge on Meltdown and his other enemies, but this was his fight, not hers.

Dominique had been around this criminal environment all her life, and she was ready to get away from it. Her mother, Rosie Lee, had been a madam in Louisiana before she gave up the life after making thousands of dollars. Ironically, Rosie Lee fell in love with a suave, fast-talking mulatto who had greasy hair and a greasier tongue. He ended up stealing her money and leaving her penniless.

By the time Dominique's uncles caught up with him, the money was long gone. His death was Rosie Lee's only consolation. But Dominique's mother was inventive and determined. Instead of returning to her old life, she used the little money she had left to open a legitimate gentlemen's club, complete with masseuses, dancers, and certain extras. In no time at all, she was back on top, without ever again having to lie on her own back. Though they rarely saw eye-to-eye on most things, Dominique had to admit that her mother was her best teacher.

"Hello, fellas," she said, standing beside Vince's chair and greeting the table in general.

They all returned the greeting before each pair of eyes slowly moved from her face down to her low-cut, form-fitting double-breasted button-up dress. With the help of a padded Victoria's Secret bra, her breasts sat up proud and prominent. Her small waist helped draw attention to her flat stomach and wide hips.

"I take it you're enjoying the evening," she added, making eye contact with everyone except Vince.

"Yes, we are. Thank you for asking," one man replied, standing and offering his hand. "Sean Thomas."

"Nice to meet you, Sean." She smiled at his weak game. "My name is Dominique."

"Hi, Dominique. Why don't you pull up a seat next to me and join us?"

"No, thank you. I can't allow myself that pleasure, I'm afraid. I have to run the place."

"Oh, you're the manager?" he asked, obviously surprised.

"No, dear, I'm the owner," she said, turning to Rhashad. "I heard that we had a celebrity in the house tonight. Thank you for coming, Mr. Burton."

"Rhashad, please. I'm glad I came. This is my boy Nairobi . . . and my cousin Vince." Rhashad looked at her, waiting for a reaction.

"Hello, Nairobi, nice to meet you." She extended her hand, and Nairobi eagerly accepted it, thinking that he had been her choice of the men. Then she pulled it back and turned to face Vince. "I'm glad you could make it out tonight."

"Yeah, I really wanted to come," he said, peering up into her eyes so as to make his double meaning plain.

The rest of the table was forgotten when she saw the sparkle in his eye.

"Do you allow yourself the pleasure of getting to know your patrons better?" Sean asked, still trying to capture her for himself.

"Only the ones who truly interest me," she replied, still focused on Vince. "So, Vince, will you be staying until closing?"

"I'll stay as long as you want me to, Dominique." He looked away from her long enough to see the smile on Sean's face turn into a stern frown.

"Good. We usually close pretty late, but I'll see if I can get one of the managers to close up for me. Then are you all mine?"

"I'll be right here, waiting," Vince answered, sure to keep his smile in place. *Are you all mine?* For some reason, that question sent a tremor of fear rushing to his stomach. He watched her walk away and head for a dark corner off to the side of the room.

"Why do I get the feeling that I just got played?" Sean asked, trying to laugh, but finding it very difficult. "Rhashad, y'all know that shit ain't right."

"Man, shut up!" Nairobi said. "You know you would have done the same thing. Anyway, I think I'm about ready for another round, so pay up. How about you guys?"

"Yeah, man. I'm ready for another, too," Rhashad said, downing the rest of his beer.

Sean pulled out his gold American Express card and laid it on the table when the waitress came to take their orders. "You might as well start a tab," he told her, defeated.

Standing behind the one-way mirror, Howard watched men watching the ladies and offering them their hard-earned money. He was about to turn away from the mirror when he saw Dominique walk away from a table seating four men. Rhashad Burton he recognized immediately, basketball being his favorite sport. He didn't know two of the men at all. But the fourth man he would never forget.

He and Vince Perkins had been good friends at one time. The man had introduced him to the love of his life, hoping that the two would hit it off and build some kind of relationship. And they had. But it was not to last; much to his regret Howard had found himself in the middle of a huge criminal investigation.

When his own shady past caught up with him, he had no choice but to turn state's evidence against the crime boss. His only mistake was not insisting on being told exactly when and how the government planned to take him into custody. If he had known that he would have to feign death and lose Tonya at the same time, there was no way he would have gone along with their plans.

But why was Dominique so friendly with him, Howard wondered. How did she even know him? Not fully trusting anyone, he knew that he had better find out what she was up to. He was so deep in thought he didn't realize she was headed for the office until he heard the door opening.

"How do you know Vince Perkins?" he asked as soon as she closed the door.

Though he appeared relaxed, Dominique could tell that the fact that she knew Vince unnerved him. "Why? How do you know him?" she asked, walking past him to her desk.

"Answer the question," he said, stalking toward her.

She sat back in her seat, defiantly glaring up at him. This was her place of business. She didn't work for him or anyone else. Even though he was her cousin, he didn't run her show. She was doing him a favor.

"He's just a friend of mine, okay?" she replied, hiding her growing contempt for the man.

"How close a friend, Dominique?"

"How do you know him?" she asked curiously.

"We used to be pretty good friends."

"He must not have known about your shady dealings," she said half under her breath.

"Whether he knew of it or not is beside the point. The point is that you becoming involved with Vince Perkins is going to jeopardize the plan."

"What plan, Howard? You mean *your* plan to be the top dog of a crime syndicate. And I never said that I was involved with Vince or anyone else."

"Something is going on here. And I didn't sacrifice three years in that hellhole or ride on that dirty-ass bus, might I add, for you to blow it all because you want to fuck Vince Perkins."

"Go to hell, Howard." She stood up and faced him, nose-to-nose, ready to pounce.

"You can't beat me, Dominique," he seethed through clenched teeth, all but offering a challenge through his glittering eyes. "You need to calm down."

"No, you need to stay the hell out of my business," she yelled back, her hands firmly planted on the desktop as she leaned forward, wanting desperately to meet his challenge, even though she already knew what the end result would be.

"You are my business, little cousin. Fucking Vince Perkins is not on our agenda."

"Howard, get the hell outta here. I'm tired of your shit. I've done everything you've asked of me. All of us have. Poor Marion is sitting in jail because of you, and you haven't once asked about him since your ass got in town."

"What the hell are you talking about?" He moved around the desk to stand directly in front of her. "I care about all of you. But I can't do anything for Marion right now. Right now, we just have to wait it out. I gave Jimmy two hundred dollars today to put on Marion's commissary."

"Marion has plenty of money on his commissary already, from me."

"Well, that's good. What do you want me to do? I'm not supposed to be here, remember?"

"You know what? You're right. You're not supposed to be here. So why don't you leave? I got enough going on with this club."

"Oh, so now it's *your* club?"

"Damn right, it's my club. Meltdown left this and the plant to me in his will. There's nothing you or Darius can do about that."

"Oh?" he laughed. "Is that right?"

"That's right. You can have the plant, but I'm keeping this club. I don't care what you do or have planned, but don't fuck with my club, Howard. I'm warning you."

"You're warning me? You're warning *me*?"

Before she knew what was happening, Howard had pulled Dominique from the desk and had her up against the wall. He lifted her up until she was face to face with him. Even as she fought against his superior height and strong grip, she knew it was no use.

Wisely, she relaxed her body so that he would think she had given up her struggle. He was so close she could smell the cinnamon mint on his breath.

"Don't you ever threaten me, cousin. Do you hear me?" He didn't wait for her to answer. "Now, we started with a plan, and we're going to stick to it. Do you want to give Vince Perkins some that bad, so bad you would betray our family?"

"I'm not betraying my family. Now let me the hell down. I said let me down, motherfucker." Dominique kicked hard at his groin, but not fast enough for it to connect before Howard blocked her kick with his thigh.

"You know who he is?" Howard asked, trying to put his temper back under control as he slowly let her slide down the wall until her feet were once again on the floor.

"Of course, I know who he is. It's not my fault he's Tonya's brother. Look," she said, twisting out of his hands, "I like him, Howard. And I'm not going to stop seeing him just because he's her brother."

"Does he know who you are?"

"Of course not. I don't want him to know anything about my involvement with you."

"Just stay away from him until all this blows over." Moving away from her, he turned around and pulled on his lightweight jacket before heading for the back door.

"Just do what I tell you before you fuck up the whole deal. If not, we'll all end up in jail. You know they'll look at you as an accessory to Meltdown's murder."

Dominique leaned over her desk, breathing hard. Her hands shook from the look she saw pass through Howard's eyes. *That motherfucker is crazy.* She was going to have to be very careful dealing with him from here on out. Giving up Vince wasn't an option, but neither was staying involved in Howard's crazy plan. There was no way Vince would be with her if he knew how deep she was in this scheme, not to mention Meltdown's murder. But she had lied to him so many times already.

She picked up her metal letter opener and gripped it tightly.

That bitch, Marcia, thinks she's going to get him. Over my dead body.

In a rapid motion, she raised the letter opener above her head and then brought it down hard on the desktop. Leaving it there, she stalked toward the club door to get one of her managers to work late.

She was in serious need of an evening of tension-releasing sex.

CHAPTER 11

It was a clear Friday night. Looking up at the sky, she counted approximately as many planes as there were stars. The Philadelphia sky was always crowded with flights in and out of the Philadelphia International Airport. Howard and Tonya had just left Dave and Buster's on Delaware Avenue and were walking down a small one-way street heading to where they had parked the car. Holding hands, they smiled at each other, trying to decide whose house they would go to and put a perfect ending on a wonderful night.

Tonya shifted restlessly in her sleep.

Jaimer moved only slightly from where he rested on his side of the bed. In his sleep, he had already changed positions several times, moving from his back to his stomach until he finally ending up facing her back. Before finally drifting off to sleep, he had made sure that he wasn't touching her.

Howard was unlocking the car door when the shadows of other people cast by a single streetlight caught them by surprise. Just as fast as the shadows had appeared, her head was covered by some kind of thick cloth. She heard Howard shouting for her, heard some kind of struggle. Then there was complete silence. Frantic, she moved her head from side to side, instinctively raising her hands to pull the bag off her head, but someone behind her pulled her to him, holding her and whispering calming words in her ear.

Tonya mumbled incoherently as she continued to twist through her nightmare.

Her agitated mumbling awakened Jaimer slightly. Without thinking he automatically put an arm around Tonya to comfort her in her sleep, and then drifted back off into his own oasis of dreams, all involving her.

"Howard," she whimpered. "Howard, are you all right?" There was no answer. "Howard, answer me."

She pulled the bag off her head, looking around the alley for him, but he was gone. Just like that. His keys were still in the car door.

Tears fell and her shoulders shook violently. Hysterical, she stumbled around the darkened street and tripped over an empty bottle. She landed against the grimy concrete wall, where she sat for half an hour before calling her brother on her cellphone and telling him what had happened.

Vince arrived quickly, fearing that something might be seriously wrong with his sister. The blurry wetness of her swollen, red eyes made it hard for her to recognize him. When she heard footsteps, she feared they might have come back for her. She whimpered softly, drawing him toward her. She held her breath until he reached for her and took her hand.

As she moved, Jaimer's arm tightened around her waist.

Tonya sat up, screaming. Still half asleep, she began fighting the hand that held her captive.

Jaimer sprang up, instantly becoming fully awake and alert. Jumping from the bed, he rushed to her side.

"Tonya? Tonya, wake up, baby."

She continued to scream, not realizing her dream was not her reality.

"Tonya . . ." he said again, shaking her gently.

When she finally calmed down, tears were streaming down her face. "Oh, God . . . I'm sorry," she said, pushing past him and running into the bathroom. Her embarrassment was huge.

He followed her and stood outside to the door. "Are you okay?"

"I'm fine," she said, sitting on the closed toilet seat with her hands over her eyes. "I'm sorry. I just had a bad dream."

"Are you sure? I can leave and go on home if you want. I wasn't sure if you were going to make it through the night with me here. Look, I'll just leave. I don't want to be the cause of you not being able to sleep. I can just come back to check on you in the morning."

"No!" she yelled, rushing to the bathroom door. Taking a deep breath, she opened the door slowly. She wasn't going to let him leave. He had brought her so much joy, made her see so many things again. "Jay," she whispered. "Please don't leave me. It wasn't you. I just had a bad dream, the same dream that has been haunting me for the past three years. It's something that I have to deal with, that's all. Besides, the night is over. The sun is coming up."

"I just don't want to cause you any problems, Tonya," he said, pulling her out of the bathroom and into his arms. As he held her, he smiled. "Well, since we're up, we might as well watch the sunrise."

"I've seen more sunrises than I can count." Her embarrassment having passed, she asked, "Can't you think of something else to do?"

"Hah . . . lady, you know what? I think I could probably think of a thing or two to take your mind off things."

Tonya screamed out in ecstasy as Jaimer's mouth covered hers. Like flashes from a camera's bulb, colorful explosions danced behind her tightly closed eyelids. Completely consumed by the power he wielded over her, totally lost in the waves of orgasmic release that assaulted her body, she held tightly onto the bedsheets as the heels of her feet dug deeper into the soft mattress.

"Oh, Jaimer," she called out repeatedly, as she felt another strong convulsion jerk her body. She gripped his shoulders, determined to pull him to her. "Now, Jaimer, please," she begged as he expertly continued to caress her inner thigh.

Hearing her pleas only made him want to hear more. Jaimer relished the cries coming from Tonya, enjoying the fact that he could bring her so much pleasure, but when she started groping for him, his enjoyment was quickly replaced by a thirsty desire.

Eagerly, he moved back up her body, leaving a sloppy trail of wet kisses in his wake. He stopped to take one nipple between his teeth as he slipped a hand between her open thighs. The wetness he felt made him aware of her readiness to receive him.

"Now," she whispered in his ear when he moved from her shoulder to her neck. "Now."

Jaimer captured her lips seconds before he plunged deep into her. He hesitated briefly once his shaft was fully embedded. The hard gasp she expelled caught him off guard. He wasn't sure whether he had hurt her until he felt her hands on his back urging him on, telling him that she was pleased.

Keeping his strokes deep and slow, Jaimer tried to concentrate on other things, anything except for the tightness that had his head spinning and the wetness that made his stomach constrict. But he managed it as he raised her hips higher off the bed, dove deeper into her core.

"Aghh . . . shit, Tonya," he yelled in a strangled tone. His moans mixed with hers as he quickened his pace, blindly chasing nearly unattainable heights.

Tonya was beside herself, fulfilled to the point of near-completeness. The painstaking pleasure of his love-making lifted her as he continued to move wildly inside her. She moved with him, contracting and releasing her vaginal muscles, bringing them both closer to the glorious pinnacle.

Suddenly, he tightened his hold on her hips, driving deep into her, and she knew he was very close. Tonya stopped thinking about her own pleasure. All she wanted was for Jaimer's experience to be long-lasting, forever on his mind.

She worked her hips faster, helping him to complete his journey. She wrapped her legs around his waist, opening herself up wider to him as he plunged into her body repeatedly. In giving him more access to her, she had also allowed him to push her closer and closer to her own brink, until before long they were both on the open field racing toward an imaginary finish line.

Jaimer grabbed the sheets on the edge of the bed, then the mattress itself when the sheets gave way. He gritted his teeth but continued, knowing that they were both close to the end.

"Come with me, baby," he whispered in her ear, feeling himself on the verge of release. "Come with me, Tonya, oh God, baby."

Tonya held onto him, the pressure of his manhood buried deep within her quickly pushing her into release. "Jay, I am," she managed before screaming out her own release. She tightened her hold on him as he continued to grind into her.

"Baby? Baby?" Jay stirred gently, weakly turning his head into her shoulder.

"Huh?" she replied, catching her breath.

"Girl," he breathed heavily, "all I can say is that you got some good stuff. Your mother definitely blessed you."

"Jaimer!" she cried, shocked.

"No, baby. I'm for real. That shit was good. Makes me want to go back to sleep."

"It's almost six-thirty. It's Sunday. If you don't have anything to do, then go on back to sleep. Do you have someplace you got to go?"

"No. Do I have to get off you?"

"Of course. Come on now, it wasn't so good that you can't move. Now get off me and let me up. I got to go to the bathroom."

"Huh? Oh, I was almost asleep."

"Jaimer, get off me." She pushed at his chest, but he didn't budge. Instead, she felt him move inside of her. "Jaimer?"

"Yes," he smiled, wiggling his eyebrows and bending down to kiss her. "Maybe I'm not as tired as I thought I was."

"Oh, yes, you are," she replied, pushing him over far enough for him to slip out of her. Smoothly, she escaped and ran to the bathroom, leaving him on the bed smiling after her.

Jaimer felt his heart swell as he watched her running from him. Collapsing back onto the bed, he sighed with both contentment and regret. How was he going to get himself out of this mess? He knew he wouldn't be able to let her go, but at the same time, could he keep the fact that he knew her before a secret? And if it ever came out, how would he be able to go on without her?

In the shower, Tonya became revitalized. She should be tired and worn out, but she was miraculously full of energy, a giddy kind of energy. Instead of wanting to lie in bed, she wanted to go outside and plant flowers. She wanted to take a walk around the block. Well, maybe not the block, but surely the yard.

The morning sun was bright and inviting, and she wasn't ready to be locked up in her office for the whole day. She had deadlines to meet, but she could take a little time for herself. And she was full of ideas as to how to spend that time. Of course, she tossed out the ones that entailed leaving her home, but they sounded good, anyway. These were things that she hadn't done in years. Getting a manicure, a pedicure, a facial, and a massage were at the top of her list. Mentally, she put stars by them, because even though today was out, one day soon she would be opening the door and going on all kinds of adventures.

Today, she could pull the weeds in her garden, sit in the swing out back, and maybe even go out the front door and sit on the porch for a little while. The cars going by didn't unnerve her as long as they weren't loud. It was the people who walked by the house that she would watch.

After drying herself off, she wrapped the towel around herself and went back to the bedroom. True to his word, Jaimer was stretched out on his back sound asleep, the sheet covering his lower body. *Damn, he looks so good.* She was tempted to join him. Instead, she moved closer to the bed, lifted the blanket and briefly glanced at his body. That would have to be enough for now, she thought, deciding to let him rest while she made herself a cup of coffee before going out in the back yard.

Before she could start the coffee, her doorbell rang. Thinking that it was probably Vince, Tonya went to the front door trying to think of an excuse to get her brother out of her house as fast as possible. As soon as she pulled the door open, Jordan rushed into the house with her arms opened wide.

"Is it true?" she asked excitedly. "Is it true, Tonya?"

"Girl, calm the hell down. Is what true?" Her cousin was in her work uniform, a printed nurses' shirt covered with lollipops and licorice and matching mint green nurses' pants. She wore thick rubber-soled white clogs. "And shouldn't you be at work?"

"I'm on my way, thank you very much. Is it true that you went outside yesterday?"

"News sure does travel fast."

"So, it is true?" Jordan asked, moving into the room and reaching behind her to close the front door out of habit.

"Leave it open," Tonya told her.

"Oh, all kind of changes happening around here, huh?"

"You could say that. Anyway, don't you need to be on your way to work?"

"Yeah, I'm going. I'm goin'."

Jaimer sat up in the bed with a start, the morning sun shining directly in his face through the bedroom window. His hand moved to his side, searching for Tonya as the blanket fell off his body, revealing his aroused manhood.

"Tonya?" he called softly, looking around the room.

"Tonya?" he called again, moving off the bed, wrapping the discarded sheet from the night before around his waist, and then walking to the bedroom door.

He wasn't immediately worried about her whereabouts, just curious, but with the news of Howard Douglass possibly being in the vicinity, he didn't want to take any chances.

Without thinking, he took the stairs two at a time until he reached the bottom.

≈

Tonya closed her eyes against the inevitable when she heard the noise on her stairs.

Jordan's eyes opened wide as Jaimer came hurtling down the stairs. His chiseled chest was bare, showing off a combination of toned muscles, ebony skin, and smooth chest hair that tapered in a downward spiral, which unconsciously she followed until it stopped short around the edge of the sheet. He had those neck things like football players had, and his legs—

The look in Tonya's eyes warned Jordan to cease and desist the full assessment.

Jaimer paused at the bottom of the steps, uncomfortable with her thorough appraisal.

"Uh, I'm sorry. Excuse me," he said, backing up the stairs with a tight hold on the sheet. "Tonya, I just didn't know where you had disappeared to." Spinning around, he began making his way up the stairs, very quickly.

Jordan was smiling when Tonya turned back to her.

"You were on your way to work, weren't you?" Tonya asked impatiently.

"Girl, this time, I don't blame you for kicking my ass out. If I had something like that lying around, I would kick my ass out, too," she said as Tonya led her, none too gently, to the door.

"I know it's useless to ask you to keep this to yourself?"

"You know it is. Cindy will be calling you in about ten minutes. Just give me time to get to the car and on my cellphone."

"Well, since my secret is out, tell my sister to give me two hours before she calls. I might as well enjoy myself some more first. And it would be useless to tell her not to tell Cecilia, but tell her that I said I want to tell Vince myself."

"Will do, cousin. Enjoy yourself," she said, walking out the door and toward her Nissan Pathfinder.

Tonya stood by the door until she drove off. As she waved good-bye, a man standing on the other side of the road caught her attention. He wore a dark hoodie sweatshirt as if he had been jogging. Though he was far away, he appeared to be light-skinned and tall, a thin man with eyes—

Tonya quickly shut her front door. For the first time in a long time, she thought the unbelievable, that Howard Douglass was alive.

Opening the door again, she looked back at the same spot where she could have sworn the man had been standing. But he was gone. *I must be losing my mind. Now I'm starting to see things.*

CHAPTER 12

As Cecilia peeled the shells off hard-boiled eggs, she glanced out the kitchen window and watched Tonya playing chase in the backyard with her children. The sound of her sister's laughter made her heart swell, but she controlled her tears as a sob caught in her throat.

"Hey, big sis," Vince said, walking in and placing a bag of sodas on the table and a bag of ice in the freezer. Noticing that something had Cecilia's total attention, he followed her glance into the backyard. "It's a hell of a sight, isn't it?"

"Hey, babe. Yeah, it's breathtaking just to see her out there. I never thought we'd see the day."

"Come on, now. You didn't doubt her, did you?"

"I guess seeing so many depressing and horrifying things in my line of work might be turning me into a cynic. I'd hoped that I would never get used to all the bad in the world."

He came up behind her and put a hand on each of her shoulders. "Nah, I don't believe that. You've just learned not to be overly optimistic."

"Well, I knew she was trying, beginning to fight it, but I had no idea that it was happening so quickly." She looked at him thoughtfully as if she were running something through her mind.

"I see that look in your eye, Cecilia. Don't start!" Vince warned her. "Can't you just leave well enough alone and be happy with the results?"

"How did it happen so quickly?" she asked.

"Does it really matter?" he countered.

"Your friend have something to do with it?" she asked, beginning to cut the eggs in half.

"Jaimer is a good guy, Cecilia. I trust him completely with her."

"Okay, brother. Just remember you said that." Cecilia was tempted to mention Jaimer and Tonya's intimate relationship. But it wasn't her place to tell him, so she decided to keep it to herself for now.

"What's that supposed to mean?"

"Nothing—nothing at all." She turned away from him and went back to her task.

"Hey, y'all." Cindy walked slowly into the room with Dayton close behind. Her cheeks were rosy, and her skin glowed.

"Hey, girl. How you feeling?" Cecilia asked, bending to kiss her on the cheek.

"I'm fine," she sighed, rubbing her belly in a circular motion.

"Hey, Dayton. How you feeling?" Vince reached over to shake his hand.

"Just tired, man. Between the concerts and the ball games, I'm running myself ragged trying to make sure everything is covered." Dayton was the head event coordinator for the Wachovia Center. He was in charge of securing dates for a multiple events—concerts and bas-

blame her. In her place, if he looked at the limited knowledge she had, he, too, would have to make the same assessment. Adding weight to her suspicions, she believed she had seen him at a law enforcement workshop going by the name of Dallas. And she had.

"Is Tonya around?" he asked wearily.

"You know she is," Cecilia snapped harshly. "Where the hell else would she be? You think she walked down to the corner store or something?"

"Oh-kay," he responded, treading lightly. He was in a good mood, and humoring Cecilia's hostile interrogation wasn't on his agenda. She was too good at her job. "Can you tell me where she is?"

"Can you tell me what the hell is going on between you and my sister?" Her anger quickly surfaced when she thought she saw a smug grin cross his face.

Cindy stood between the two forces, fully expecting a volcano to erupt. Cecilia was never good at minding her own business. Cindy didn't want her sister's day ruined by Cecilia's tendency to be overbearing.

"As I told you before, Cecilia, your sister and I are good friends. I don't understand why you have a problem with that."

"It would seem to me that you're more than that *now*. Didn't you stay here last night, sleep with my sister, and take advantage of her loneliness? Did you think that once you had your way with her, she'd be at your beck and call?"

"Whoa. Cecilia, I don't think that is really any of our business," Cindy said, trying to intervene. She was totally ignored.

"For your information, Cecilia—if you really must know, and I'm sure you already do—yes, I did stay here last night. Do you want to know why? Because your sister asked me to."

"You could have said no."

"Why in the hell would I tell her no? She wanted me here, and I wanted to be here."

"You slept with her knowing that she was vulnerable."

"Maybe she's not as vulnerable as you think. She's not stupid, Cecilia. Tonya knows what she wants, and she also knows how to go after it. I don't think you give her enough credit."

"I give my sister all the credit in the world for getting her damn self out of this house, but it's you that I don't trust. And I'm not going to let you take advantage of her."

"Oh, is that what you think? I'm trying to take advantage of your sister? Cecilia, you don't know me at all. You don't know how I feel about your sister or how she feels about me. Have you asked her? Have you asked either of us? No. You'd rather make your own assumptions."

"Okay, okay, you two need to stop this right now," Cindy said forcefully, raising her hand high, and then rubbing her forehead to soothe the beginning of a massive headache. "Look, we all care for Tonya. That's the reason we're here. Y'all are going to have to put your differences and mistrusts aside because I'm not going to let you ruin her day."

"Whose day?" Tonya asked, walking into the kitchen and looking questionably at the tense little group.

"Hey, baby," Jaimer said, sidestepping her question by pulling her into his strong arms. His heart fluttered when he saw her eyes gleaming, telling him she was thinking of their night, and morning, together. He did love her. There was no denying it. He had just defended himself to Cecilia, but the guilt of his deception still weighed heavily on his mind.

Tonya openly accepted his affectionate embrace. It felt so good being in his arms again, just being near him. She held on, allowing herself to revel in the feel of it.

"Hello," she finally said, releasing him. There was a hint of a blush on her cheeks. Her embarrassment was understandable, what with her sisters gawking at them, one in approving amazement, the other clearly disapproving and shooting darts of disappointment. "Did you get everything done?"

"Yeah, I pulled all the files that I will need for tomorrow and even set up appointments for two interviews. The office should be in full swing by tomorrow afternoon."

"Good. Vince is outside."

"Yeah, I saw his truck out front. Let me go holla at my boy." Jaimer held his hand out, waiting for Tonya to grab onto it.

"I'll be back in a minute to help you," she told her sisters as she walked out with Jaimer.

"I still don't trust him," Cecilia insisted, slamming the last deviled egg onto the oblong tray. She covered the tray with foil and slid it into the refrigerator.

"Cecilia, he's right, you know. You need to back off and mind your business."

"What?" Cecilia stammered, unsure of what she had just heard.

"What I said was that you need to mind your own business," Cindy said smartly. "Take a good look at her, Cecilia. The girl is happy. For the first time in a long time, she's really happy. Why can't you just let her be that?"

"I don't trust him, Cindy. And I don't want to see her hurt again."

"But you're not the one to decide her happiness. She's happy right now, so just let her be. She is not a child. Damn, between you and Vince, I'm surprised she can breathe straight."

"Fuck you, Cindy." Cecilia pulled a bowl out of the cabinet and began cutting up lettuce for a tossed salad just as Jordan walked in carrying two bags of groceries. "Oh, here comes your partner in crime. I know it's time for me to get outta here."

"Hey, ladies," Jordan said, placing her bags on the counter. "Okay, what's left to do?"

"Nothing. Thanks for the help," Cecilia said acidly.

"Cecilia, you're so anal. I'm beginning to think that being a cop doesn't agree with you anymore."

"Go to hell, Jordan," Cecilia hissed and walked outside.

⌇

"What's up man?" Jaimer greeted Vince. "What's new?" He nodded at Curtis and Dayton, who were keeping watch over the grill.

"You tell me. I'm starting to get the feeling that there is something going on around here that I don't know about."

"What gives you that idea?" Jaimer asked innocently. He looked around the yard at Cecilia's three young kids playing on the nicely manicured lawn. Tonya was sitting in the swing chair, watching him and Vince talk. She seemed so happy and content, so beautiful, so everything that he wanted. The sun was hot and heavy on his back, and he felt a little like the meat on the grill as Vince pressed further.

"Man, let's keep it real. We've known each other for a long damn time. We cool. I think you need to talk to me about some shit. I mean, I know how it is with you and my sister. And maybe, just maybe, in the beginning, when I first saw you and found out you were still single, a thought did go through my head that made me want to introduce you. When you needed a bigger office, hey, that was even better. I've watched you work your way into her good graces, maybe even her heart, but now I think we need to talk about where this is leading."

"Yo, man, damn. Take it easy. You all uptight and shit. Vince, as you said, you know me. I don't want anything but the best for your sister. I really like her a lot, but this is between her and me. She's a grown woman, man. I'm not talking about what's going on between us, because it's all good. I don't want to betray her trust. Now if she wants to tell you something, that's up to her."

Vince looked at him closely before nodding his head in agreement. Although he was uncomfortable with the speed in which their relationship was moving, he couldn't find one single reason he shouldn't want his sister to be with Jaimer. The guy wasn't a criminal; in fact, he was working very hard to make his business even more of a success. Jaimer was well respected in his field, had money in the bank, and appeared to have genuine feelings for Tonya.

Maybe Cecilia was rubbing off on him. It was no big secret that his sister didn't feel the same way about Jaimer as he did.

"We cool, man?" Jaimer asked. "All I can say is that I honestly do care for her."

"And I believe that. Yeah, man, we good." Vince led him to the grill and introduced him to his present and future brothers-in-law. "Please, help these knuckleheads with the fire. They're cooking the outside of the food and leaving the insides raw as hell. And I ain't eating no bloody chicken. I'm gonna talk to my sister."

Jaimer watched him walk toward Tonya, feeling the knife of guilt bury itself in his heart, but he didn't show concern on his face. Instead, he focused his attention on Dayton and Curtis and the mess they were making at the grill.

"Vince, don't you think they need your help over there?" Tonya asked as soon as he sat next to her in the swing. She wasn't in the mood for one of his lectures.

"They got it. I wanted to talk to you for a minute."

"I'm not surprised," she said, turning to look into his handsome face. "So they told you, huh? I should have known. I don't know why Cecilia is making such a big deal out of the fact that he stayed the night. I'm grown."

"Do what?" Vince asked, astonished by her declaration. "He stayed the night?"

"Don't you start, too." Tonya looked at him, her eyes pleading with him not to make a scene. Vince was known to have a quick temper like their father. "You know what, Vince," she quickly continued, "I owe you all an apology. For the past three years, I've allowed you to shelter me like I was some kind of invalid or something. I've been locked up in this house feeling sorry for myself."

"But we wanted to do that because you needed us."

"And I did need you, I still do, but I'm not a little kid, Vince. I'm a grown woman. Before I got sick, y'all didn't mind me going out, hanging, or having relationships. We all did our own thing, even though we had each other's backs. But now it seems that I'm the only one not doing my own thing. It's like I have to get permission from either you or Cecilia to do what I want to do, and that's got to change. Just as my being stuck in this house had to change, so does my whole life."

"But, Tonya, this is all just too fast."

"For who? You and Cecilia. Vince, for the past three years, my life has been moving in extra-slow motion. Right now, right here, is where I feel I need to be. I'm making a lot of progress mentally and physically. I'm not afraid anymore of what might be out there, and I owe a lot of it to Jaimer for helping me get over the final hump."

"You really like him, huh?" Vince sat back and blew out a breath of air as he watched Jaimer work his magic at the grill.

Tonya's smile brightened when she, too, looked at him. "Yeah, I do. But I'm still me, Vince. I know what I'm doing. I'm not blindly jumping into the first thing that comes along. But I am enjoying myself."

"Well, if he stayed, where did he sleep? Never mind, don't answer that question. I don't think that I really want to know the answer."

"No, you don't," she laughed, giving her brother a quick hug. "Enough about me. How are things with Miss Crazy and Miss Homemaker?" She didn't like Dominique that much, but that was based solely on her performance the night of the party. Marcia was more Vince's type, or her opinion of what Vince's type should be.

"Stop calling that girl crazy."

"Well, all I can talk about is what I've seen, and I saw how crazy she went when she saw you dancing with Marcia at the party."

"She's just a little jealous and a little domineering. Used to having things her way."

"And you're okay with that. I thought you and Marcia were getting along pretty well. Haven't you and her daughter become close, too?"

"We are doing good. Her daughter is cool. She's a normal teenager. Although she's pretty and everything, she still has peer-pressure problems, feeling she needs to stay popular, with the athlete for a boyfriend, hair and stuff."

"It's good that she has you to talk to. Her father has been dead for a long time. Vince, when are you going to learn that you have to take the good with the bad in any relationship? When Marcia pisses you off, you can't just up and run to the other chick because you don't want to hear it."

"That's not what I do."

"That's exactly what you do," she retorted.

"Look, I'm honest with them both."

"About everything?"

"Yeah."

"So who were you with last night?"

"Dominique," he stated flatly, watching Tonya frown her distaste. "You don't like her, do you?"

"I don't know her, but I don't think she's for you. Anyway, so when you see Marcia, you'll be telling her that you stayed with Dominique last night, right?"

"Tonya, don't be smart."

"I mean you tell them everything. You have an open relationship with them both, right? How about this, did you tell Dominique that you stayed the night with Marcia on Friday?"

"Whatever."

"That's what I thought, Mr. 'I Tell Them Both Everything'. Speak of the devil . . ." Marcia, her daughter Shardei, and a young man were walking toward them.

Before standing, Vince leaned over and kissed her on the cheek. "We can finish this conversation later on. I love you, sis."

"I love you, too, you big dummy." She swatted his arm and sat back on the swing, enjoying the feel of the light breeze passing through. *Her family loved her so much it was suffocating*. She was grateful for their love, but sent up a silent prayer that one day soon they would give her a little more room.

CHAPTER 13

"Jordan, did you see the man standing across the street when you left this morning?" Tonya asked as soon as Curtis finished blessing their food.

"No, I didn't see any man outside. Hell, I was still thinking about the one I saw in here." Snickers from Cindy and Shawnique followed Jordan's laughter.

Jaimer stopped eating momentarily, embarrassment shooting through him. As for Vince, he moved his face closer to his plate.

"Ha, ha, very funny. Anyway, there was a man outside standing across the street looking over here."

"Who was it?" Vince asked, becoming intensely interested. He wasn't going to have anybody scaring his sister half to death.

"I don't know, but for a split second . . . you know I'm not crazy, right? But for a minute, I could have sworn it was Howard."

Everybody stopped eating and looked at her, even Jaimer, before he caught himself. Realizing he had almost made a big mistake right under Cecilia's astute nose, he quickly recovered.

"Who's Howard?" he asked her, careful to keep his tone even and his face free of any sign of guilt.

"Howard is her ex-boyfriend," Vince explained, the tension in his voice letting Jaimer know that he wasn't too pleased with him at the moment.

"Oh. You think your ex-boyfriend is spying on you?" he asked Tonya, hoping she'd tell him what he wanted to know without having to ask.

"Well, at first, I thought it, but I couldn't see his face because it was hidden by a dark hoodie he was wearing. I looked away for a second, looked back, and he was gone."

"Why didn't you say anything about it this morning?" he asked, concern showing on his face. Only he knew the true reason for it. Out of the corner of his eye, he saw Cecilia whisper something to her husband. She then got up and went into the house.

He followed her into the kitchen, closing the back door securely behind him. He was totally focused on his goal. Although he knew what he wanted to say, he fumbled for words when she looked up at him.

"What do you want?" she asked hotly, snapping her eyes and going to the refrigerator and pretending to be rearranging its contents.

Ignoring her hostile question, he walked over to the island and leaned against it, waiting for her to turn around.

"Well?" she spat out, turning with her hand on her hip.

"When are you going to tell her?"

"Tell her what?"

"Whatever it is you know about this Howard Douglass person."

"What makes you think I know anything?" *How does he know I'm keeping something from Tonya? He's up to something. I knew it.*

"Cecilia, I'm in security, surveillance. My job is to watch people and their actions. And from your reaction to her thinking she saw Howard, I could tell you know something."

"Even if I did, what makes you think I would tell you?"

"Look, I plan to keeping eye out myself. I think he's around here, and I think you know that he is."

"Tonya thinks he's dead, and that's exactly how he is going to stay. I don't know exactly what went on that night, but I do know that my sister came out of it a mess. If it's all the same to you, I'd like to never mention him again."

"That is not going to fix this problem, and you know it. What do you think you're going to do, hunt him down? Make him wish he had never come into your sister's life?"

"If I have to. He's not going to hurt her again. I don't even know why I'm having this conversation with you. I don't know you, remember? You could be in on this with him."

"Look, Cecilia, you need to let that go. Vince and I have known each other since school. He's like a brother to me. I live right next door," he continued, trying to ignore the smirk on her face. "And I like your sister very much. That should be enough for you, but it's not, is it? The cop inside you won't let it be enough."

"Jaimer, I know that was you I saw in Washington, DC. The names might be different, but it was you. No two people look that much alike. You got a twin brother or something?"

"Cecilia, why can't you just leave good enough alone?" he asked, frustrated by her bulldog determination.

"For some reason, you feel that you need to keep that part of your life a secret. And that's fine, but I'm a police detective, and you have gotten yourself all tangled up in my family. I think you need to come clean, at least to me."

Jaimer silently contemplated his next move. He knew that he needed to confess, especially now that Howard had made his presence known, even if it was only to Tonya, who still believed he was dead. Sooner or later, he would not be satisfied with just watching her from afar.

But could he trust Cecilia with information that he was there that night? Would she be able to work with him if she learned that he was the one who had held Tonya with his hand over her mouth, covering her head with a pillowcase, telling her not to move? Scaring her to death? He could barely live with that truth himself.

Cecilia stood across from him, patiently watching his shifting expressions. He was obviously weighing his options very carefully; something was running through his head. But, when he put his head down and tilted it to the side, she realized he was going to be as mum about his past as she intended to be about what she knew.

"I guess I have to respect your decision and the reasoning behind it, but I'm telling you, Jaimer, you're only making it harder on yourself."

"Right now, all I'm worried about is Tonya. Is this Howard Douglass really dead or not?" he asked, knowing the truth but wanting to find out what she knew.

"I think I'm going to have to take a page out of your book, Jaimer. I'll keep my secrets, you keep yours."

Jaimer watched her walk out the door. He had hoped that she would reconsider telling him something, but he should have known she wouldn't. Cecilia wasn't going to give an inch.

When Jaimer got home that night, he was uptight and tense, sensing that his plans to woo Tonya were about to be put to a serious test. To release some of the pressure he felt building up in him, he went to the back of the house and onto his closed-in porch, where his weight equipment had been stored.

In a matter of minutes, he had worked up a sweat by repeatedly lifting the iron bar holding eighty pounds of weight on either side. Over and over, he raised the bar high in a pumping frenzy as he debated the pros and cons of his decision. Before he acted, Jaimer liked to look at the known scenarios from every angle and try to predict possible outcomes.

Three years ago, he had gone through the same process before deciding that kidnapping Howard was the best way to get him into the witness protection program. The only time he was vulnerable was when he was with Tonya. It was the only time Howard wouldn't have a posse of his henchmen following close behind him. Jaimer hadn't thought that Tonya would assume Howard had been killed, or that local authorities would be informed to make that the official story. And he definitely didn't know his actions would lead to her becoming a recluse.

"Damn!" he blurted, slamming the bar into its resting place. He was thoroughly disgusted with the whole predicament. "Ugh, man, you've done it this time," he said, shaking his head from side to side and then holding it in his hands.

He finally got up from the weight bench and went into the living room, where three desks were set up for his secretary and two assistants. He picked up the black desk phone and dialed a number long burned into his brain.

"Agent Dallas," he said firmly into the mouthpiece. "257671, code word razorblade." While waiting, he walked to the front of the house and peered out the front window. *I think I should put a camera up out front. One facing the door, another the street.* "Um, yes, Director Johnson, please. Thank you."

"Dallas, my good man," Johnson said cordially. "I didn't expect to hear from you so soon."

"Yeah, well, I didn't expect your case to come into my life, either."

"So you've seen our Mr. Douglass?"

"No, not exactly. Listen, I've kinda got a small problem going on here. It is possible you might already be aware of my situation."

"Well, I've had reports from our field agents that Mr. Douglass might have been seen standing in front of your residence on an occasion or two."

"Or two?"

"Yes," he said simply.

"Why wasn't he apprehended?" The irritation in his voice was unmistakable.

"Both times there were innocent bystanders in the vicinity. Knowing that he is desperate to remain out of the program, the agents didn't want to provoke Mr. Douglass. I think they made a wise decision. Mr. Douglass has been classified as a high-risk capture."

"Why is he even in protective custody anymore? Why hasn't he been released? Melbourne is dead." Although Jaimer preferred him in the program, the question was a valid one.

"Yes, Melbourne is dead, but he was only part of the problem. Douglass has more information than he has let on. We would like to make him another deal. I haven't been obliged to tell you this, but there is a price on Douglass's head as we speak. An unknown assailant is tracking him. We believe that it may be Melbourne's son, Darius, who issued the hit, but our information also shows that numerous others want him dead. Some of his own people suspect him of being responsible for Melbourne's death."

"So what you're telling me is that Howard Douglass has been seen near my house, and there may soon be an attempt on his life."

"Yes."

"That's putting my life and the lives of everyone around me in danger. You didn't think that I needed to know that?"

"Listen, Dallas, I'm not exactly sure of everything that's going on over there, but I have reports—"

"You and those damn reports!" Jaimer exclaimed, straining to keep his temper under control. "Director, this is not a good time for the kind of things that you're allowing to happen. You need to apprehend Howard Douglass right away before someone gets hurt. I have people living next door to me who are in possible danger. I can't have that."

"Ah, a Ms. Tonya Perkins, yes. My reports say that she is a recluse. She never comes outside."

"Do you know that she is the sister of a very good friend of mine? Do you know that she is working on her illness and attempting to overcome her fear? She is already walking out the back door. Before long, she will be going out front." Jaimer's anger became scalding fury. How in the world was he going to help her get better with Howard lurking around freely? Even if there was a hit out on him, he wasn't letting that deter him from trying to step back into her life. Jaimer couldn't let that happen.

"My reports tell me a lot of things, but the sound of your voice is telling me more," Director Johnson said knowingly. "I think there is something that you're not telling me about your next-door neighbor. So tell me, son, tell me what I need to know to help you." Director Johnson was seriously willing to do whatever he could for his friend. Dallas had always been a good man as far as he was concerned. Very intelligent, fiercely loyal.

"I need Howard Douglass to be apprehended as soon as possible." He hesitated before continuing, hoping that what little he told the man would convince him to expedite Howard's apprehension. "Director, the girl is Douglass's old girlfriend. She was with him the night we took him three years ago. I didn't know who she was," he lied, his stomach knotting. "I didn't know she was my friend's sister then. But when I met up with him here, I realized who she was. The night we took Howard, we left her there, damn near scared to death. That's the reason for her sickness. She believes that he was killed that night, never to be seen again. Now she is finally over the trauma and is getting herself back together. Can you imagine what it will do to her if she sees him again?"

"Calm down. Calm down, Dallas. Listen, I wish I could help you in this matter, but it's out of my hands. Director Jamison is over this one. I can speak to a few people, but I think I'm going to need more than a girl with a sickness to persuade him."

"What more do you need? He's already stalking her."

"But he hasn't harmed anyone. Tell me he has harmed someone, and I'll call Jamison right now myself."

Jaimer remained quiet, trying to think of something, anything, to make him reconsider. But he couldn't think of a single plausible reason to have Howard detained.

"Dallas, is something going on between you and the lady next door?"

"No, sir," he lied again, knowing that the truth was in one of Director Johnson's reports.

"Well, I wish that I could do more for you, Dallas. But what I can do is try to keep you as informed as possible."

"Thank you, sir," Jaimer replied, deflated by his failure to get the bureau to move in on Howard. He realized his position had changed—for the worst. He figured that Howard was probably more anxious than ever to get reacquainted with Tonya. If he knew about the contract on his life, he was taking an awful risk trying to see her, which meant that he was close to desperate. If he didn't know about the contract, he would be a dead man any day now if he kept walking around unprotected.

Maybe he didn't care; maybe he wanted to be with Tonya that badly. Could Howard still love her after all these years? Jaimer imagined every possible reason for Howard trying to resume his relationship with Tonya. And he believed that each reason was a valid one, because he would probably be doing the same thing. In fact, he *was*. Three years later, he was still in love with Tonya himself. But what Howard probably didn't know was that Tonya believed him to be dead. How could he use that to his advantage?

"What to do, what to do?" he asked aloud, going to the front door and peering out, just to make sure, before he went up to his bedroom.

CHAPTER 14

Howard sat in a secured office in the back of the warehouse used to store the heavy equipment of the Melbourne Construction Company. The office, completely furnished in black wrought iron and glass, looked more like one belonging to a Wall Street executive than to the head of a crime syndicate.

He hated this office. This was where he had been hired as a young teenager, too eager to get his hands on some fast action and faster money. His enthusiasm was so great and noticeable that before long Jackson Melbourne had taken him under his wing and had begun showing him the inner workings of the business, the seedy side, the side where the truly powerful played. And as if it were crack, Howard had become instantly addicted to it.

Meltdown spent more time with him than he did with his own son, who, it seemed, could do nothing to please his father. Before long, the hatred that sprang up between the two youths was hard to ignore. Finally, Darius Melbourne was sent away to handle his father's affairs in another state. He found a niche for himself in Atlanta and stayed away for long stretches of time, only returning home on special occasions, such as the death of his father.

The muscle-bound guard standing beside the office door went unnoticed as Howard remained deep in thought, pondering his next move. He focused on the jet black wall-to-wall carpet that lined the room, but only saw Tonya's face whenever he stared at one spot too long. He rested his head against his clasped hands as a wave of anxiety hit him. He forced the tense lines on his face to relax when a knock sounded at the door.

He nodded to let the guard know it was okay to admit the person on the other side into the room.

"The car is ready, boss," his driver said quickly, fear absent from his voice but more than evident in his eyes.

Howard shook his head. *Where did this kid come from? He shouldn't be working for me, scared out of his wits to even say a simple sentence. All that pretend confidence is going to get him, or even worse, me killed.* "Well, let's go," he said, getting up. He paused in front of the ceiling-to-floor mirror and did a quick self-appraisal.

The olive double-breasted suit had been tailored to his slender, tall form. He liked the suit because it made him appear just as big and powerful as he felt. His well-groomed facial hair and closely-cut curls gave him an air of authority, but it was his large, light- brown eyes that gave him the appearance of one who demanded instant obedience. Pleased, very pleased, with himself, Howard walked out the door accompanied by his bodyguard, a man twice his size with half his mental capacity, and his driver, who was smart enough to be afraid of the company he kept and stupid enough to want to impress a criminal.

"Where to, boss?" Jimmy asked, moving ahead of Howard as soon as they reached the bottom step and reaching for the back door handle of the Lincoln Town Car.

"Gallery Mall, parking garage, third level. You'll know what you're looking for when you see it." As the car pulled away from the curb, Howard's phone rang. "Talk to me."

"Howard?"

"Dominique."

"Listen, Howard, are you on your way out?"

"Yes, I've got a meeting."

"I'm starting to hear a lot of things that I don't like. There are some rumors about a hit being put out on you. Did you know about that?" she asked.

"Not to worry, Dominique. I've got it covered. I'm on my way right now to talk to some men about protection."

"Well, who is it? Who put a hit out on you?" Dominique asked, her voice edged with frustration. If he knew about the hit, why hadn't he told her about it?

"I don't know. If I did, they wouldn't be after me; I'd be after them."

"Howard, this is getting way too deep for me. Okay, yeah, I did go along with Meltdown's murder—"

"Um . . . this line isn't secure. Stop talking like that. Meltdown's murder was not your fault," he said, certain wandering ears were listening in on his cellular line. Even getting the phone using another person's name wasn't a guarantee. The government was too good. He knew that from experience.

"We need to talk, Howard."

"In due time—"

"I heard you went by the house. Why?"

He got her meaning right away. But that was something no one was supposed to know about.

"Are you having me followed or something? How did you know about that?"

"No, I'm not having you followed. I heard that she saw someone outside her house and said that it looked like you, her old boyfriend."

"This is something that we need to talk about later, not over the phone. I'll be back right after the meeting." He heard the anger in her voice, but wasn't willing to deal with it right at the moment.

"Howard, you lied to me."

"I did not lie," he replied. "Look, I don't have time for this."

"Well, you better damn well make time. All this, everything that you put this family through, me and Marion, even the others, it wasn't for us all to become wealthy. It was all for a girl."

"Not now, Dominique. I said that I would call you after the meeting."

"Howard—"

He snapped the phone shut and held it tightly before slamming his hand down against his leg.

"Damn," he muttered. The last thing he needed was Dominique giving him a hard time. Time was running close enough as it was. Not only had he been unable to get a good look at her that day because she had remained inside the door, but the other two days he had spent staking her house had been a complete waste of time, too.

From what little he did see, she looked as good as he remembered. If Jordan hadn't come rushing out, he would have stayed there all day.

But now he had to deal with his life being threatened. He didn't know who his would-be assassin was, but Darius Melbourne was at the top of his list. There was no doubt in his mind that, by now, Darius had been told that he was back in town. After he testified against Meltdown, the family knew that he wasn't dead; they just didn't know where to find him.

That was one thing the government was good for. They knew how to hide you. *Uh, the government.* They had to be after him, too. He was surprised that he hadn't crossed paths with any of them. Then again, if he had, they wouldn't be good, would they?

The last time, they had caught him off guard, even after he had signed the papers and agreed to be their witness. He could only imagine what they had in store for him this time. The plan was to keep him in protective custody so that he could testify against other family members. But that was a little too risky for him. Wind of that might have gotten out. Maybe that was why someone wanted him dead.

The car made a sharp left-hand turn into the parking garage at the Gallery Mall, bringing his attention back into focus.

"Jimmy, slow down. On the third level, you'll see a white Cadillac Escalade parked beside a black Ford Excursion. Pull in next to the Escalade. Stay in the car, but keep it running. Stink, move with me."

Stink got out and opened the back door for Howard and followed him to the elevators, where three men were standing, one of whom turned toward them as they walked up.

"Craven?" Howard approached a tall, beefy white man, dressed in dingy black jeans and a T-shirt, with his hand outstretched. The man's thick arms were bare save for the multiple tattoos covering over eighty percent of his skin.

"Mr. Douglass," he responded, taking Howard's hand. "This is Dragoon and Parch," he said, pointing to his two look-alikes.

At first sight of his new employees, Howard wasn't quite sure he had made the right decision. He had hired them mainly because they weren't from Philadelphia. He didn't know who he could trust, including Stink, who was small compared to these goliaths. But these three men looked like maybe they were members of the Hell's Angels bike club.

"I can tell by the look on your face that you're not sure you made the right choice in hiring us. I can assure you that our company is very reputable. If you prefer that we shave or dress in suits, that can be accommodated."

"No, it's not that. I, um—"

"We're white. Is that it?"

"Honestly, yeah. I'm supposed to be keeping a low profile, but this is just going to draw more attention to me. Damn, I'm between a rock and a hard place."

"Well, the decision is up to you, sir, but you do understand that your deposit is nonrefundable. However,

I assure you that you couldn't be in better hands. We guarantee your safety."

"Wait, just wait a minute. Let me think," Howard said, walking a short distance away.

⤙⤚

"Come on, girl," Cindy yelled to Shawnique from the passenger side of Jordan's silver Nissan Pathfinder. "You need to hurry up."

"I'm coming, hold your horses," Shawnique yelled back from the third-story bedroom window of her townhouse.

"Damn, she's always late," Cindy said to Jordan. "We should leave her ass."

"Calm down, Cindy, she's not late. Remember, we told her the wrong time."

"Yeah, but what if we hadn't? I'm trying to get to the mall early, before all those kids get in there."

"It's always young kids in there," Jordan said as Shawnique opened the back door and got in. "Maybe we shouldn't go out today. Somebody seems to be in a bad mood."

"It was your idea to go shopping today. Got me out here in this hot-ass sun. I don't like this. Damn, it's hot out here," Cindy complained, feeling her mood darken.

"The damn air conditioner is on, Cindy. I just wanted to buy my godbaby some clothes and sneakers. Is that too much to ask?"

"Your godbaby?" Shawnique asked. "When was this decided?"

"Look, don't you start," Cindy said, rubbing her swollen stomach under her sheer silk multicolored capelet. She pulled the top of her elastic-banded blue jeans down until it rested under her bulging belly. "All I want to do today is go and get these pictures taken so that we can stop at Red Lobster. I want some seafood."

"Okay, I'll let it go for now," Shawnique said, settling back in her seat. "These pictures were a good idea. They should come out real nice. I know Dayton is going to want a large one right in the living room behind the sofa."

"Yeah," Jordan agreed, "a nice black and white one would match the furniture. That would be nice, Cindy."

"I just hope your girl knows what she's doing," Cindy replied, agitated and moody. Jordan's girl had been her roommate at Delaware State University. They roomed together for the first two years of college and shared an apartment in their junior year. Danielle Davis had majored in mass communications. Now she owned her own studio in the Gallery Mall, which she opened to the public when she wasn't away on assignments. The girl was one of the best photographers in the area. Black celebrities in the city flocked to her to have their portraits done.

"Don't worry, you know she's going to do a great job. We're lucky she is able to do them. You know how busy she is? She actually shuffled her clients around for this. And you can't ask for too much more than that, considering the price she's giving us. We still going half, right, Shawnique?" Jordan asked, peering into the rear-view mirror. The pictures were a baby-shower gift from them both.

"That's what I said. I got you," Shawnique replied, feeling her pockets to make sure she hadn't forgotten her credit cards and identification. Purses had never been her thing; names like Gucci, Prada, or Liz Claiborne did not excite her. Preferring to be comfortable rather than fashionable, Shawnique sported a two-piece navy Nike tracksuit with stripes down the sides, a white T-shirt underneath, and white Nike Air Force Ones.

"Well, I just hope Dayton appreciates everything I'm going through for these. I'm not too comfortable being half-nude, belly hanging all out."

"They'll be great," Shawnique assured her. "But, I still think you should wait a little longer and maybe even have Dayton in the pictures with you."

"Thanks for your two cents, Shawnique, but after the baby is born, we will get photographs taken. Why the hell would I wait? I'm fat enough as it is. You want me to wait until I have stretch marks showing? Look, just let us get there."

"What the hell is wrong with you? With all that damn cocoa butter you've been using, I doubt you will end up with any stretch marks. Jordan, just take her ass home."

"I can't do that, Shawnique, as tempting as it sounds." Jordan glanced at Cindy, who was looking increasingly sullen and resentful. "You are so damn evil. Don't get the fuck pregnant again."

"Go to hell, Jordan," Cindy said, trying to contain the beginning of a smile. She didn't feel like being in a good mood, not with this bowling ball of a baby pressed against her bladder. It was awful—the swollen feet, the weight gain. Just plain awful.

The truck came to an abrupt stop when Jordan slammed on the brakes to avoid hitting the car in front of her, which itself had stopped suddenly so as to not miss the turn into the parking garage connected to the Gallery Mall.

Flinging her hand up, Jordan yelled, "Come the hell on."

"Go around them. Look, Delaware tags," Cindy said, quickly sitting up. Instead of going around, Jordan calmly waited for the vehicle to correct itself, and then she followed it into the entrance and up the ramp into the garage. She hated driving in here. It always seemed so small and congested. She stopped to retrieve the ticket, and then continued up to the next level. There was never a parking space available on the lower levels, so she just followed the other cars.

"Oh, they are moving so slow," Jordan complained, wanting to be out of the car.

On the third level, they saw a group of five men standing near the elevator exit—three white, two black. One of the white men was extremely attractive. The hair on his face was well groomed, giving him the rough look of a young Sam Elliot.

"Girl, look at that guy over there," Jordan said, slowing down. Her fondness for white men was well known.

"Jordan, this damn tint is too dark," Shawnique complained as she pushed the window's automatic button so she could see.

Cindy sat up in the seat trying to get a better view. "Oh, shit, drive. Drive!" she screamed, sliding down in her seat as far as she could, hitting Jordan repeatedly on the arm.

"What the—?" Jordan pushed her foot on the gas pedal, causing the truck to leap forward with a squeal. "Cindy," she yelled, "what the hell is wrong with you?"

"Shhh. You know there's an echo in here. Be quiet, he'll hear you. Just drive. Hurry."

Jordan did as she was told, taking the truck to the next level.

"Keep driving until we can't see them anymore. Hurry."

Jordan glanced into the rearview mirror at Shawnique, who clearly was as much in the dark as Jordan was. After parking the truck, Jordan turned to Cindy and demanded, "Now, would you mind telling us what the hell is going on?"

"Didn't you see him?" Cindy asked, struggling up in her seat, panting slightly. "You saw him, right, Shawnique?" She asked hopefully.

"Saw who?" Shawnique asked, moving forward and looking dumbfounded.

"Howard," Cindy answered. She had to have seen him, too.

"Howard? Howard who?"

"Howard, Tonya's Howard. Howard Douglass."

"The guy Tonya used to go with? The dead guy?" Jordan asked, disbelievingly. "You can't be serious about this, Cindy. I think you and Tonya are both coming down with something."

"It was him," Cindy said defiantly. "Go look, Jordan."

"You must be out of your damn mind," Jordan answered, turning her head away. "I'm not going to look for some damn ghost. And wasn't he some kind of criminal or something?"

"Yeah, he worked for Meltdown," Shawnique said. "That can't be good. I say if it was him, and he wants to be dead, let's leave him that way."

"You didn't see him, Shawnique?" Cindy asked again, still seeking confirmation of what she was positive she had seen.

"I didn't see him. I was busy trying to check out the white boy Jordan was pointing out."

"Well, look, I'm not crazy. I know what I saw." Cindy tried to open the car door, but Jordan grabbed her hand.

"What are you doing?"

"I'm going to go see if it was him. And if it is, I'm going to give that bastard a piece of my mind. For the past three years, my sister has been locked in that damn house, thinking he had been killed in front of her. And here he is walking around all this time like nothing ever happened. And at the damn mall? What the hell is he doing here?"

"Cindy, you can't do that," Jordan pleaded.

"Like hell I can't," she said, snatching her hand from Jordan's grasp. She then opened the car door and slid out. Jordan and Shawnique scrambled out of the car and caught up with her before she reached the next car. They stood in front of her, blocking her path. But both noted the determination on her face.

"Okay, look," Shawnique said, "let's think about this. You can't go down there ready to confront that man, Cindy. You're seven months pregnant. Or did you forget that?"

"I don't really want to confront him. I just want to make sure that was him. All we got to do is get a good look around the corner or something. Hell, crawl across the ground and see if they're still down there."

"I'm not crawling along no ground," Jordan said, looking down at her seaweed-colored sateen cuffed capris and matching jacket. This was a new outfit worn specifically to draw attention to herself, and she was not getting it dirty. "Shawnique, you do it. You got on a track suit."

"A track suit that cost more than that hoochie set you're wearing."

"But you're the fastest, Shawnique," Cindy said, looking at her pitifully. "And this is for Tonya."

"Don't try that pity shit with me, Cindy. I would do anything for Tonya, but getting killed kind of crosses the line."

"Come on, we're wasting time. He's getting away," Cindy said. Her feet were starting to hurt, and they were swelling. Damn, she knew she shouldn't have worn the strappy sandals, but they matched her capelet so well.

"Shawnique, just scoot over to the edge of this level, look over, and see if he's there."

"That's easy for you to say. Just stay back here. Don't be crowding me. I might have to run or something." Shawnique walked down the ramp to the lower level, stooping down behind cars the closer she got to where the men were standing. *Hopefully, he won't be there. Damn Cindy. Always getting them in the middle of some dumb shit. Thinking she was a member of that damn TV CSI team she was always watching. FACSI, if you ask me. Fake-ass CSI.*

"Do you see anything?" Cindy asked, impatiently.

"Will you be quiet," Shawnique answered, sounding irritated. She squatted low, and tried to look down, but couldn't see. Moving like a crab, she inched closer to the spot.

"Well?" Cindy said, when Shawnique returned from her reluctant foray into spying.

"They're not there. None of them," she said.

"Good. Let's get out of here. We're already five minutes late for your appointment," Jordan said. "Why don't we just go on and enjoy the day? Maybe it was him, but maybe it wasn't. Maybe you were just thinking it was him because of what Tonya said at the picnic on Sunday."

"Maybe, but I thought for sure it was him," she said, reluctantly letting them pull her toward the elevator doors that would take them to the fifth-floor entrance. "We need to pick up a pair of slippers from Payless."

Howard didn't know who was in the Nissan Pathfinder as it slowed down in front of him and his associates, but he thought he heard someone say the name Cindy. He remembered that name easily enough. Cindy was Tonya's little sister; a handful, to say the least. The last thing he needed was for her, or any member of Tonya's family, to see him. He wasn't ready for that yet. And what if it wasn't her, but someone scoping him out to carry out a hit on him? He had to keep moving. Deciding to get out of there as fast as possible, he hired the three men despite their pigment deficiency and told them to follow him back to his office.

CHAPTER 15

"I love being with you so much, Jaimer," Tonya said, eagerly returning his kisses. Her arms were wrapped around his thick neck as he gently lowered her to the bed.

"I love being with you, too, baby," Jaimer replied, placing tender kisses along the side of her face and neck. He untied her robe, pushed it off her shoulders and then lengthened the path of his exploration. "You feel so good, love."

Tonya closed her eyes as he moved lower over her body, basking in the pleasure he created. He changed directions and began moving back toward her face. She opened her eyes and looked up into his eyes. Howard's eyes. Howard's face.

She sat up in bed, disoriented and frightened by the dream she had just had. Ever since she'd thought she had seen Howard across from her house, she hadn't been able to get him off her mind. But he was dead, had been dead for three years. Maybe it was because she had not had a chance to mourn his passing. His body had never been found, and she had been unable to go to the memorial service held for him in North Carolina, having been in no shape to travel.

Glad that it was morning, she pushed her melancholic thoughts aside and decided to get dressed. As she dressed, she thought about what she would work on that day. With only one article to write, she hoped to put in at least six hours of writing on her novel. It wasn't due for three more months, and she was close to the end, but she always liked to give herself a month to do an in-depth review and edit of her manuscripts herself.

She already had an idea for her next novel, and she couldn't wait to get started on it. That was the way it was every time she was nearly finished with a manuscript.

It was a bright, hot, and humid Thursday morning, and Tonya decided she would take another small step in her recovery and try venturing out to the front porch again. She was still not that comfortable with the idea, but this time she was more confident, more secure in her decision, and more determined. She was convinced the time was right.

Banishing thoughts of her other disastrous excursion outside, she armed herself with a cup of hazelnut coffee and the latest issue of *Essence* magazine and gingerly opened the heavy wooden door. The sun flooded her entryway as she peered outside, acutely aware of cars speeding past her house. Just her luck she lived on one of the busiest streets in the Germantown section of the city. But she didn't let that throw off her focus, which was firmly centered on the white wicker high-back rocking chair in the corner of the porch.

Okay, just open the damn door. You got this. It's no big deal. You've been outside before. Before she could second-guess herself, Tonya opened the screen door and stepped outside as if she had been doing it every day for her whole life. She stopped to check her breathing and watch her foot movement, paying no attention to cars passing or passersby going about their daily lives. She just kept walking until she was in front of the chair. She quickly turned and dropped down, letting out a deep breath.

Mrs. Sharon Tinsdale parked her car at the curb and walked up the path to the front door. On her way to work, she had stopped and picked up a dozen donuts and four coffees. The men she worked with might have been three of the most unruly, uncooperative, and foul-mouthed bunch she had ever known, but how she loved them. She treated them all as if they were her sons. Having lost her own son at an early age, she was thankful to have them to spoil. And what a handsome group of unmarried men they were.

Damon Reynolds, the youngest, reminded her of a sleek panther—dark, muscular, boyishly handsome. He wore his temper visibly on his shoulders, and it didn't take much to send him into overdrive. He was smart as the devil, knowing all about computers and other elec-tronic devices. Anything electrical could be easily taken apart, down to the last screw, and put back together. Unfortunately, he had been unable to find a gentle woman to soften his rough exterior.

Colin Reynolds, no relation to Damon, was tall and handsome, but an unrelenting health nut of a white man. He would have made her mouth water if she were twenty years younger, maybe thirty. Born in Boston, Massachusetts, to a wealthy family, he attended Brigham

Young University on a football scholarship and then joined the DEA. Several years back he was injured in his left eye and decided to leave the agency. Luckily, he had already met Jaimer by that time. Colin's problem wasn't attracting women, it was staying married to them. After two divorces, he decided that marriage wasn't for him.

Her favorite, Jaimer Lambert, could do no wrong in her eyes. She had fallen in love with him during her interview two years ago. He'd pulled out her chair for her and had walked her to her car. Jaimer was a gentleman at heart, and his eyes told her that he was looking for someone to share his heart with. Maybe he already had. He had filled her in on his next-door neighbor and her reclusiveness, explaining that she was part of the reason he had installed extra security cameras around the property. Something was going on there; he wouldn't have invested that much time and effort into the equipment except for a client.

The screen door opening caught her off-guard. That's weird, she thought; it's only seven-thirty in the morning. But she put on a friendly smile when she saw a tall, beautiful woman walk onto the porch.

"Hi," she said softly, not wanting to startle her.

"Oh, hello," Tonya replied, fighting the urge to run from this stranger. She made herself walk to the rocker. "It's a lovely morning, isn't it?" she asked, thinking polite conversation was a safe way to start. The lady looked nice enough, and she was walking toward Jaimer's house.

"Oh, at my age, every day is lovely, dear," Mrs. Tinsdale answered. "I'm Sharon, Mr. Lambert's secretary. You must be Tonya. Jaimer has told us about you."

"He did?"

"Yes, he told the guys to keep the noise down just yesterday." Mrs. Tisdale paused before continuing. "Excuse me, but I thought you were supposed to be a recluse. You don't look like a recluse to me, sitting out here in this beautiful sunlight."

"Well, Miss Sharon, I've decided that I don't want to be a recluse anymore," Tonya said, feeling her confidence soaring. "Three years is long enough," she added, prouder of herself by the second.

"God bless you, dear. And please, call me Sharon," Mrs. Tisdale said. *Funny how one person's positive attitude had the effect of lifting another person's mood.*

"Oh, I couldn't do that. I'm sorry, but even though my mother passed away some time ago, I think if I went around calling my elders by their first names, she'd find a way to discipline me."

"And you're probably right, dear. That's how you can tell that someone was brought up right. You don't see enough of that nowadays. You have a good day now, sweetie. Maybe I'll see you later. I have to get in here to these men. They can't do a thing without me."

"You know what? I believe that, Miss Sharon."

"Mrs. T," Damon beamed, rounding his desk in the far corner and hurrying to help her with her bags. "Good morning. You're just in time for the staff meeting."

"I knew I would be. Jaimer wouldn't start without me. I do have to take the notes," she answered, thankful for his help. "Colin," she said, acknowledging a wave from Jaimer's other assistant. "Where's the boss?"

"He ran upstairs for a second," Damon answered. "I think something might be wrong with him today; he seems a little bit on edge. You know how he gets. Either we have another big case or someone has complained about our services."

"First of all, we don't get cases, we get clients. You're not a cop anymore. Secondly, you guys are too good at what you do to get complaints. Now this is just a regular staff meeting, and he has nothing but praise for you." Putting her hands on either side of his face, she lifted his frown into a smile and then patted his cheeks gently.

"That's why you're here, Mrs. T. You brighten up the place."

"Well, not completely yet. We need to open up these windows and let the sunshine in. It's a beautiful day, and we need to let some of that good air in. Why he likes this secluded atmosphere, I'll never know."

"Because it keeps me out of the open," Jaimer said, coming down the stairs with a folder in his hands. "I'm used to being in the shadows, Mrs. T."

"That was the old you, dear. It's time for a change. For all of you." With that, Mrs. T went to her desk and began reorganizing her space. She did it every day. Her desk had to fit her mood. Stapler on the left side, phone on the right with her message pad next to it. Flip the calendar, and it's the start of a brand-new day. "What y'all need are some women in your lives."

The three men let out a collective sigh, each suddenly assuming an attitude of total absorption in work. Every day, three times a day, the subject of their bachelorhood was raised.

"Don't try to ignore me. I might be old, but I know what you need. Maybe then this place would seem a whole lot more cheery, and you wouldn't need me to brighten up tha spot."

"Tha spot?" Damon ventured. "You been listening to your nephews again, haven't you, Mrs. T?"

"No. For your information, I have not. You might think I'm old, but I'm hipper than the three of you tight booties put together. I, at least, have a love life."

"How do you know we don't have love lives, Mrs. T?" Colin asked, risking a weak attempt at defending their manhood.

"Please, if any of you were treating a woman the way you should, there would be lunches being dropped off, telephone calls during the day, something." She looked at the three chastened men, each head slightly lowered. "That's what I thought," she finished with a dismissive wave of her hand.

"Well, for one thing, we're too busy working to have that kind of commitment," Damon said defensively.

"Of course, you are, dear," she said, picking up her telephone and dialing a number on her message pad. Having had the last word, she added, "Oh, there are donuts and coffee."

"Staff meeting in ten minutes," Jaimer announced after finding his voice. Fifteen minutes later, he had explained the Howard Douglass situation to them completely, omitting his involvement with Tonya.

"So, the agency contacted you and asked you to keep an eye out for him?" Colin asked. "Isn't it ironic that your office just happens to be next door to the woman who went with Douglass, your last assignment?"

"Honestly, it's not. During the assignment, I discovered that Tonya was the sister of an old school friend of mine. I didn't want to be pulled off the case, so I didn't report it. Besides, I had never met her. She never came on campus while I was there."

"Okay, then after you retired, you and Vince Perkins ran into each accidentally?" Damon asked.

"Well, while I was with the agency, I kind of lost touch with a lot of people I went to school with. At first, it's a year that you haven't talked, and then the next thing you know, it's ten years. I was so busy that I just didn't have time to stay in contact with anyone but my sister. I used to get invitations to different fraternity events all the time, but it's hard to fly in from Dallas or Florida or anywhere when you don't know how soon you'll have another assignment. It seemed like all my assignments ran back to back. But I was finally able to go to an event once I left the agency, and there he was. We started talking, or rather I started complaining about the size of the apartment I was renting, and he told me his family had a place for rent. So here we are."

"And what are we to do about this?" Colin asked.

"I'm going to take the job, for free."

"Do what? The government is not going to pay you to help them locate this guy?"

"Well, they didn't exactly ask me to work for them. The director just wanted me to know that Douglass was around because of my involvement with the family."

"What exactly is your involvement with the family, Jay?" Mrs. T asked. "Seems to me you're more interested than you let on."

"Please, not now. These people are my friends. Of course, I'm not going to let any harm come to them if possible."

"Uh-huh," she said cryptically, pointedly tapping her notepad with her pen.

"What is she talkin' about, Jay?"

"Who knows, Damon," Jaimer quickly answered. "At any rate, this is the reason for the additional cameras around the premises. Here is a picture of Howard Douglass for each of you. All I ask is that you keep an eye out."

"Will do, boss," Colin said. "Hey, I gotta run. One of the cameras went down over at the Temple gym. I promised I would be there first thing this morning to investigate."

"Do you need some help?"

"No, I'm good. It shouldn't take that long, unless the women's team is practicing. Then it might take me a minute or two." He walked past Mrs. T, winking flirtatiously.

"Boy, you're a mess. Instead of gawking at them, you need to be trying to tie one down."

"You know me better than that, Mrs. T," Colin laughed, pushing the front door open.

"So what you got for me today, boss?"

"Stop calling me 'boss'. Do me a favor and check out that new equipment that just came in. It's in the back, next to the table with the transmitters."

"I'm on it," Damon smiled, walking toward the back.

"We need to talk," Jaimer said, walking over to Mrs. T's desk. "Look, you're—"

A knock at the door interrupted him. He paused as Damon went to the door. When her returned, he was carrying a bouquet of flowers and a smile. Jaimer moved away as he put them down.

Good Lord, this is all we need. We won't be able to live through the day. Mrs. T was sure to make them watch her bask in the glow of her love life.

Jaimer was surprised when Damon handed the flowers to him. "What?"

"They're for you, man," Damon said. "Who are they from?"

"How am I supposed to know?"

"I think you're keeping secrets from me. I thought we were closer than that," Damon laughed.

"Whatever." Jaimer turned toward his office, leaving the flowers on Mrs. T's desk.

"Oh, no, you don't," she said.

"Come on, Mrs. T, keep them out here," he pleaded, lowering his voice.

"No. Somebody took the time to send you flowers. The least you could do is appreciate the thought."

"They're probably from a client, in which case they're for the whole office."

"Read the card."

He hesitated.

"Read the card!"

Feeling cornered, he snatched the card from of its holder and read it. "Oh, they're from Tonya, thanking me for my help. She asked me to lunch," he lied, nonchalantly placing the card in his back pocket. It actually said she was remembering their night together and wanted to spend lunchtime with him.

"That's a nice girl. I was talking to her this morning."

On his way to taking the flowers into his office, Jaimer stopped short. "Talking to her?"

"Yeah, she's been sitting on the front porch all morning."

"Do what?" Astonished, he quickly moved towards the door, shoving the flowers into her hands as he passed. He pushed open the screen door and rushed outside. Mrs. T was hot on his trail after placing the flowers on her desk.

Tonya saw him run out of the house. He didn't touch the two bottom steps, and ran across the yard to her. She stood when he approached her, aware that Miss Sharon was taking it all in from his porch.

"Hey, baby," he whispered. He, too, was aware that they had an audience. But he couldn't escape her open arms or her waiting lips. Nor did he want to. Mrs. T would be expecting an explanation, and he was ready for her. But right now, he was holding Tonya in his arms and accepting her tongue's warm caress before moving back from her and looking into her face.

"Where's the fire?" she asked, her face aglow.

"Why didn't you tell me? You shouldn't have done this alone."

"I needed to. I've been out here all morning. Isn't it wonderful? Maybe I'll take a walk around the block later." Her excitement and enthusiasm were contagious.

He picked her up in his arms and swung her around. "Baby, I'm so proud of you. This is a big step. We need to celebrate." His excitement mounting, he wasn't even whispering anymore.

"Tonight?" she smiled at him.

"Lunchtime," he corrected, smiling, kissing on her again before lowering her to the flower. "I'll be back in a couple of hours. You just sit right here and enjoy your day."

"I will," Tonya promised, knowing that as soon as he went back inside she was going inside to get ready for lunchtime.

By this time Mrs. T was gone. Jaimer wondered what her first question would be. But when he entered into the office, she wasn't there waiting to pounce on him. She was sitting at her desk with the phone to her ear. Hoping that she wasn't blabbing his business to one of her nosy friends, he continued on to his office. His hopes were dashed when he heard her next words.

"Oh, Martha, it was beautiful. They make such an adorable couple. I think this is the one."

He shut his office door. *That woman's mouth is like a sieve. Everything passes right through it.* He decided to ignore it because, before long, he would be celebrating.

CHAPTER 16

As soon as she heard the knock on the front door, Tonya rushed down the stairs. It was precisely two hours later, and Jaimer was always on time. To her surprise, it was Cecilia waiting at the front door.

After having stood at the door for a few minutes trying to decide exactly how she would approach her sister with the truth about Howard's disappearance, Cecilia decided she would handle it just as she would every other police case. She would go right in there and flatly state the truth. Even though it wasn't proper protocol to have her sister privy to the information, she felt that it was necessary, especially after Cindy's phone call last night.

With Howard back and apparently moving about freely she had no choice but to come clean to her sister, even if it meant having to deal with the turmoil that was sure to follow. For starters, Tonya was sure to be furious when she found out that Cecilia knew Howard was still alive, that he hadn't been murdered. She would be devastated to learn that she had gone through three years of terror, aggravation, worry, pain, and mourning for nothing. And the fact that Cecilia could have prevented it, should have prevented it, would weigh heavily on her heart.

~~~~

Instantly, a shiver of foreboding passed through Tonya as her mind struggled to fathom a reason for Cecilia being at her house dressed in her detective uniform, a navy blue pantsuit with a white blouse and black flat loafers. It was such a drab outfit. And the somber look on her face didn't help matters any.

"What is it? Cindy? Vince?"

"No, calm down," Cecilia said, moving further into the house. "It's nothing like that."

"Well, what are you doing here then?" Tonya asked, releasing the breath she had been holding. "You can't stay, either. I'm expecting company."

"Let me guess? Tall, dark, and hard-to-get-rid-of from next door. You still seeing him, I presume? I thought you would have gotten tired of him by now."

"Really? What gave you that idea?"

"Forget it. Look, I really need to talk to you. It's, um, important." Cecilia went into the living room, motioning for her to follow. "Have a seat."

Tonya did as she was told, but worry was beginning to crowd her mind.

"Listen, I got to tell you something. And you might hate me for it, but I did it for your benefit. No matter what you say or what you think, you got to believe that."

"What did you do?" Tonya asked. "How many times do I have to tell you to stay out of my life? Damn, Jaimer and me are just fine. Let me handle my own life."

"It's not about him," Cecilia replied, fighting the guilt that was causing her stomach to do flip-flops. "Look, back when—" Just then, she saw Jaimer's tall frame cross the front yard. Seconds later, a knock sounded at the door just before it squealed from the pressure of being opened. The sound of his heavy footsteps grew louder as he moved toward them.

"Hey, baby," he said, walking into the room, stopping in mid-stride when he saw Cecilia sitting next to her. "Oh, hello, Detective. If I'm interrupting something, I can just come back later."

"Jaimer," Cecilia said curtly, before she stood. She was half-relieved that her confession had been interrupted. "Tonya, I'll talk to you later."

"Are you sure? I thought you said it was important."

"It'll keep," Cecilia assured her as she stood up to leave, then she hesitated. "Um, Jaimer, may I speak to you for a moment?"

Both Tonya and Jaimer looked at her curiously. Tonya was the first to speak.

"Cecilia, I thought I just said that I didn't want you in my business."

"It's not that. I need to talk to him about another matter."

"Well, I, um—" He decided to just be quiet and followed her out the door.

Cecilia walked out the door and continued to walk until she reached her unmarked police car. Then she turned to him like a woman trying very hard to maintain her composure. Jaimer simply crossed his arms and waited for her to begin the argument he was sure to come. She looked over his shoulder to make sure she was out of earshot of the house. Her mouth opened slightly when she saw her sister standing on the front porch. Shutting her mouth tightly, she looked him in the eye.

"I see . . . . that more of your handiwork?"

He turned around, wondering what she was looking at and smiled at Tonya, who was standing against the porch rail, arms crossed, staring at them.

"Actually, I didn't have anything to do with it. I was just as surprised as you when I saw her out here this morning."

"So, you haven't been staying there?"

"Cecilia, you're starting to cross a line," he said.

"Okay. Look," said, quickly going into police mode. "Against my better judgment, I'm going to tell you something. In fact, I'm going to trust my own judgment. I know who you are. I know you were Archie Dallas, lead man for the DEA." She raised her hand to ward off his interruption. "You can deny it, you can keep quiet about it. I really don't care. But you know I'm a damn good detective. And I know I'm right." She walked around him so that her back was to Tonya. "Now to be honest with you, I didn't trust you one bit at first. But things have changed. You can be whoever you want to be, but I need your help. Last night, I got a call from Cindy. She said that she was riding to the Gallery Mall with Shawnique and Jordan yesterday. When they rode into the parking garage, she saw Howard standing with a black man and talking to three white men. She said the white men looked like they could have been in a bike gang, Hell's Angels or something."

Jaimer stood there with his hands crossed in front of him. Looking down at her, Jaimer realized she knew how to command respect. Granted, she was a tall woman, but in a world of men, she could have been invisible. But she was actually hard to ignore.

"I don't know what he's up to, but I know that he's not giving up without trying to see Tonya first. Jaimer, I'm telling you this from the heart. I love my sister, but I can't be here twenty-four hours a day. I need to know that I can trust you to protect her. I need to be able to do my job, catch this bastard, and know that Tonya is safe."

At that moment, something in Jaimer snapped him back to when he was a field agent. And now, he had another mission. He stood up straighter, a steely determination in his eyes; even his tone changed.

"Detective, I feel that I have misjudged you and your ability to handle this situation. I assure you that Tonya will be constantly under surveillance. As we speak, the perimeter is being watched and recorded. Additional equipment will be mounted in the backyards of both dwellings for your sister's safety. Sensors have been placed along the back fences and along the entrances."

Cecilia looked at him in amused amazement as he described each of his electronic devices.

"You really love your job, don't you?"

"Yes."

"But I wonder, is it the job or my sister that has you in such a state?"

"Both. Regardless of what you believe, your sister has come to mean a great deal to me."

"Yes, I'm starting to believe that."

"But about Howard Douglass, I have a close source that tells me that there is a contract out on his life."

"Really? Now that's interesting. Maybe the men he was meeting with don't have anything to do with drugs. Maybe they're bodyguards."

"That's possible, but why would he hire three white men to protect him in this environment? That won't do anything but draw more attention to him."

"True. This source of yours, would he by chance be a federal agent?"

"You know I could never reveal my sources. All in due time, all in due time."

"Okay, okay . . . Just keep that sister of mine safe."

"Don't worry about that. She'll be safe and happy," he said. "So I guess this is a truce."

"For now, Jaimer Lambert. For now." She stuck her hand out, and he gladly accepted.

Tonya stood on the porch expecting something to start flying at any moment. Whatever they had to talk about was very important; the look on their faces said as much. She was eager for Jaimer to return so she could ask him what it was all about.

"Well?" she asked as he walked past her and reached for the handle of the screen door.

"Well, what?" he called behind him, hearing her following him inside. Her sandaled heels clicked against the hardwood floor.

"Well, what were y'all talking about?"

"Oh, the police department wants me to supply them with some samples of a line of, um, new equipment that I'm working on." He lied so easily he surprised himself.

"What kind of new equipment?" she asked persistently.

"Um." *Think, think.* He turned and pulled her into his arms. "Hey, are we going to celebrate or what?" Bending down, he lightly licked the side of her neck before taking a bite.

"I hate to tell you this, but you spent all of your celebration time talking to my sister," she whispered.

"I'm the boss. I set my own time," he said between kissing her face and neck. "And right now, I want to celebrate." Moving toward the stairs, he grabbed her around her waist and pulled her with him.

"But we don't have enough time," she said through gasps.

"How much time do you need?" He lifted her off the floor, and she wrapped her legs around his waist. Then he ground into her as he pressed her back against the wall. "I'm ready now. Can't you feel it?"

"Right here?"

"Right now."

CHAPTER 17

"Are you out of your fucking mind?" Dominique asked Howard as soon as the door to the office was closed. "Are you trying to get yourself killed? Are you trying to draw attention to yourself? Why in the hell would you hire three burly white men to protect you when there are more than enough qualified brothas right here?"

Howard spun and pointed his finger in her face. "First of all, don't you ever talk to me like that. And don't ever question my fucking decisions. Damn it, I know what I'm doing. I need protection, and I don't know who in the hell I can trust around here. These guys may be white, but they get the job done and they don't ask questions."

"Why do you even need additional protection? All you have to do is lay low. Where are you planning to go?" she asked, ignoring his menacing stance. If it was a fight he wanted, she was going to give him one. He wasn't only putting his life in danger, but hers as well, and she'd be damned if she'd let her chance at finally being happy pass her by. It was time for her to have a little happiness in her life. She was getting out of this situation, this relationship with her cousin, if it was the last thing she did. "It has something to do with her, doesn't it? Tonya Perkins? Vince's sister? You're going to see her, aren't you?"

Howard turned his back on her, not willing to let her see his intention on his face. Of course he was going to see her. He hadn't come all this way, planned the death of a man and outwitted the law to come up empty-handed. He wanted control of this organization badly, but he wanted Tonya Perkins even more.

"Look, Dominique, you don't need to worry yourself with my business. You said the club was yours, take it, and continue making it a success. I'm letting you out of our plans. I know that you don't want to be a part of this life anymore. Maybe Vince will finally be willing to let his other lady friend go and be dedicated to only you."

"What are you talking about?" she asked, pretending to be shocked by his revelation. Howard knowing that she already knew about Marcia wasn't good. He would use it against her.

"I'm talking about the other woman that he spends his time with. Surely he's told you about her?" Howard continued, wanting to break down Dominique's suddenly high confidence level.

Dominique remained quiet.

"You know that he has another girlfriend, don't you?" Howard couldn't let her get too full of herself. Before you knew it, she'd be turning on him if he didn't find a way to keep her in check.

She stayed quiet.

"Oh, you didn't? So I guess that wonderful life you're looking for with him is a little further off than you thought."

"What's your point, Howard? Why are you telling me this?" she demanded, trying not to show her anger.

"I just thought you should know what you want to give up your family for."

"What did you do, have him followed or something?"

"Of course I did. I can't have the man my little cousin's falling for just running around without knowing what he's up to," he confessed.

"He's not up to anything."

"So I see. Aside from the girlfriend and her daughter, he seems to be pretty straight. It's that older sister of his that's going to be a pain in my ass."

"The cop?"

"Yeah, but she's more than a cop. She is so relentless, she should be working for the feds."

"Why isn't she?"

"Her family is more important to her than being a hotshot. I guess that's commendable."

"So what are you going to do about her?"

"Nothing. If I was a different kind of guy it would be easy for me to have her kids taken or her husband, but that's not my style. So I'll just pray that I accomplish my goals before she gets too close to me. They've connected me to Meltdown's murder."

"You thought they wouldn't find out that you and Marion are related?"

"We do have different last names," Howard retorted.

"Please, Howard, you were fooling yourself. But I'm not. I'm going to take you up on your offer and get out of this before all hell breaks loose. But if you need anything outside of this, anything, call me. We're still family." Pausing briefly at the door, Dominique turned to him before walking out.

His back was to her.

Howard turned around when he heard the door shut firmly. *Bitch. He wasn't going to let her leave the family just like that. Nobody left the family that easily.*

Under the blazing sun, Vince stood up in the bleachers, dressed in a white T-shirt and dark blue jeans, clapping ecstatically after Shardei made the last of her four three-point shots. He was as proud as the fathers in the stands as the teenage girls jumped around in a circle celebrating their final summer league victory. Next to him, Marcia smiled and cheered on her daughter's team as the crowd began to disperse from their seats and head onto the court.

Vince felt his cell phone vibrate on his hip. He unsnapped the phone, briefly glancing at the picture that appeared and identified the caller. It was Dominique dressed in a long black negligee. Quickly, he shut it and replaced it on his hip, ignoring the beep that came shortly afterward indicating a voice message had been left.

"Well," Marcia said, still smiling and watching with joy the happiness on her daughter's face, "aren't you going to answer it?"

He turned to her, knowing she had seen the picture. If Marcia was anything, she was quick with her mind and her eyes. "No, I'm not going to answer it," he replied, hoping the matter was dropped.

"You and Dominique having problems?" She wanted to know for purely honest reasons, she told herself. But that was a lie.

"No. No problems. Why?" he replied with a more important question.

"I just wanted to know."

"Why?"

"Because I did," she said, stomping down the bleachers toward Shardei. "Forget it. It's none of my business anyway."

"That didn't stop you from asking," he said, following closely behind her.

"You're right, and I apologize for asking about you and your girlfriend."

"She's not my girlfriend, and you know it."

"Whatever . . . Hey, baby," she said as Shardei approached, giving her a big hug. "Good game."

"Thanks."

Vince held his hand up in the air for their routine high-five. "How many points?"

"Twenty-one."

"Not bad. Keep this up, and you'll be playing in the WNBA."

"I hope so. I can't wait for school to start back up. Two more years, and its college ball."

"Hey, and I'll be right there," Vince replied, never foreseeing himself absent from Shardei's life.

Out of the corner of his eye, he saw Isiah, Shardei's friend from the picnic, approaching them. He had a tall, pretty girl on his arm. He walked up to the group and spoke, told Shardei that she looked good out there, and then walked off, his arm draped around the girl as he whispered something in her ear.

"Um, that was Isiah, right?" Vince said, dumb-founded.

"Yeah," Shardei replied, showing only the slightest hint of her misery.

"I thought he was going with you." Vince stood waiting for a sign that he should go after the kid and whip his ass for hurting his baby's heart. *His baby.*

"He does, I guess. Me and her," she said, walking toward his white Durango.

Vince looked at Marcia for an answer. Getting none, he silently followed Shardei to the truck. On the way to Marcia's house, his eyes continuously searched for Shardei in the rearview mirror. The ride to the house was silent as Vince wondered what he should do. If he were her real father, how would he handle the situation? What should he say to her?

Marcia looked straight ahead, offering no help. *Obviously, she knew this was going on in her daughter's life. Maybe they had already talked about it, and I shouldn't be concerned.*

But as he watched Shardei walk from the car to the house with her head held low when she should be feeling triumph after her win, he couldn't keep quiet about the situation.

"Baby girl," he addressed her, "you shouldn't let him treat you like that. You know you're worth more than that."

Shardei stood there quietly, listening to him with her arms crossed. The average teenager, her eyes never set on him as her agitation began to show. She didn't want to hear it because he didn't understand.

"Why are you letting him treat you this way?"

"Well, he's popular and nice looking. All the girls want to date him."

"You have to let even the most popular guys know that you deserve to be treated with respect."

"He respects me," she protested. *Why is he all up in my business, anyway? As much as I wish he were, he's not my father.*

"How do you know that? From his kisses. He makes you feel special from his kisses?" Vince grabbed her hands, trying to get through to her as Marcia stood in the background watching. "Shardei, it doesn't matter what he thinks about you. It's what you think about yourself that is important. Regardless of how popular he is, regardless how he makes you feel. When he leaves, how do you feel about yourself? Before you can expect him to put you on a pedestal, you have to make sure he knows you've already put yourself on one."

"He treats me good when we're together!" Tears fell as she realized that he was right.

"So if he's with you, then he shouldn't be with anyone else."

I think that staying with you in the mindset that I've been in all this time is unfair to both of us." Vince wrapped his arms around her. With his head close to hers, he whispered in her ear, "I do love you, Marcia. I want you to know that. And we are friends. I just need to get my mind straight."

"I'm sorry you feel that way, but maybe it is for the best. You go work on yourself. I love you, too."

She watched him walk to his car and wondered if that would be the last time she ever saw him. *Is he going to Dominique? Maybe she is a better woman for him.* All her doubts flooded her mind as he pulled off, but when he turned the corner and his taillights disappeared, she wished him the best.

CHAPTER 18

This is it, Howard told himself as the black Cadillac Escalade inched closer and closer to Tonya's house. He thought that he had control of the situation, that when the time came, he would handle it just as calmly and with as much finesse as he handled everything else in his life. In the end, it would be his way. But as the moment drew near, he began to have serious doubts about what he was doing. Still, it seemed as if he had no other choice but to confront Tonya and get their first meeting over with.

I know she probably thought I was dead along with everyone else, but surely her cop sister had told her that I was away in the witness-protection-program.

He sat quietly in the back seat contemplating his next move. Beside him was one of his newly hired bodyguards, Craven, while the other two occupied the front seats. He held his hand to his mouth as his resolve slowly began to unravel.

All too soon, the house came into view; it was time for him to spring into action. As the truck came to a halt at the curb across the street from her house, Howard hesitated for a split second, almost rethinking his plan, and then he opened the door and jumped to the ground.

The sun was merciless on this hot Friday afternoon, and he wasn't sure if the sweat on his forehead was caused by its rays or by his frazzled state. But he quickly refocused, determined to see this through. He heard the doors on the other side of the car close as Craven and Dragoon, who was driving, got out and looked up and down the street. As he rounded the front of the car, he heard the front passenger-side door closing when the third guard, Parch, emerged.

"At least we got to actually have lunch this time," Tonya laughed, holding Jaimer's hand as they walked to the front door.

"Yeah, it was good, too," he smiled, pulling her close to him in the doorway and bending to nuzzle her neck. "But not as good as yesterday's lunch was."

"You're so nasty," she replied, blushing under his steady gaze, which told her what he was thinking. Today, he had roast beef on wheat. Yesterday, he had her.

"I know, and you love it." He moved out the door with his arm around her shoulders, pulling her with him onto the porch. In an instant, his arm tensed, but he relaxed it immediately, not wanting her to see what he was seeing.

He turned her around so that her back was to the road and wrapped his arms around her, keeping an eye on the men on the other side of the street. *Two white men . . . Howard Douglass . . . three white men. Damn.* He stroked her back as she lightly kissed the side of his face and his neck, then rested her head against his chest.

The white men wore hats, making it hard to see their faces.

⌒⌒

Howard stopped cold in the middle of the street when he saw who she had her arms wrapped around. As soon as she came outside holding hands with the tall, extremely tall man, his determination grew stronger. Whoever the guy was, a very rude awakening was about to come his way. But then he saw that familiar face. A face he would remember for the rest of his life. The face responsible for taking him away from everything he had way before he was ready to leave it.

"Back to the car," he said, forcing his legs in the opposite direction. "Back!" he repeated sharply. His guards followed his movements and returned to the vehicle.

"Everything all right, boss?" Craven asked once they were all back in the car.

"Yeah, everything is cool. Take me back to the office."

"Whatever you say," Dragoon responded, looking through the rearview mirror at Howard, wondering what had just happened and what had made his boss run away like that.

Howard was lost in his thought, ignoring the landscape, the sounds from the radio, and the three bodyguards talking across the truck's cabin. *So this motherfucker planned it from the start. He grabbed me so that he could be with her. For the last three years, while I've been stuck in that damn desert, he's been here in a relation-ship with my woman. Touching her, talking to her, making her laugh, fucking her.* The more he thought about it, the more his temper rose and the madder he became. He imagined Jaimer with his arms around her, kissing her, lying between her legs, making her squeal with ecstasy. *I'm going to kill him. Nobody, nobody takes what's mine. Nobody steals from me.*

Jaimer sighed with relief when he saw the men retreat and the truck pull off. He didn't release Tonya until they were out of sight, watching the vehicle until it turned onto another street.

"I'll talk to you later, baby. Okay?" he said, thinking only of his next move.

"All right. You know where I'll be." As she watched him cross the lawn, it dawned on her that he hadn't wasted any time getting away from her. But instead of dwelling on it, she went inside, locked the front door, and went into her office to resume editing her novel.

As soon as Jaimer got into his office, he picked up the phone and dialed Cecilia's cellphone.

"Hey, Cecilia, it's Jaimer."

"What's up, Jaimer? Something wrong?"

"Yeah, very wrong."

"What is it?" she asked, tension and excitement filling her voice.

"Look, I was leaving Tonya's a minute ago, and Howard pulled up with his three bodyguards."

"What?" she asked in disbelief.

"He was on his way, crossing the street, until he saw me. I know he recognized—"

"Recognized you?" She finished his statement for him and then fell quiet, giving him a chance to confess fully.

He didn't answer right away. "Look, Cecilia, there's a lot of explaining that I need to do. I don't want you to think that what's between me and Tonya is something I did on a whim."

"Jaimer, I told you earlier that I knew a lot more than you were willing to tell me. I almost know the whole story, but I'm not the one you're going to have to explain things to. Hell, I'm gonna have to do some explaining myself. Look, I'm on my way over. Maybe we should both tell her the whole truth before he gets a chance to approach her again."

"I guess that might be the best thing. I'm at the office," he said, hanging up the phone and turning to Colin, who was at his desk in deep thought. "What's going on, man?"

"Uh, oh, nothing," he said, after giving his head a quick shake.

"Something is on your mind."

"It's nothing," Colin replied, leaning back to take a quick look at Mrs. T. Sure enough, she was listening.

"We can talk about it later," Jaimer said as he walked toward the back. "Is Damon in yet?"

"Yeah, he's back there tinkering with that new equipment again."

"With one hand?"

"Yep, he's not going to let that stop him. You know better."

"Yeah, I guess I do. Mrs. T, let me know when Detective Summers arrives."

"Will do, Jay," Mrs. T replied.

CHAPTER 19

The black Escalade turned off Delaware Avenue and continued moving down the block until it came to a stop in front of the tall brick-face building. Howard had to get into his office so that he could sit down, clear his head, and figure out the best way to go about seeing Tonya again. After all three bodyguards had gotten out, Craven opened the door for Howard.

POP! POP! A bullet ripped through the leather interior of the back passenger-side door, missing Howard by inches.

"Get down! Get down!" Craven yelled, reaching for his gun. Two more bullets pierced the air. "Shooter on the roof!" he screamed at Parch, grabbing Howard by the neck and pushing him further down into a crouching position. He intentionally fired two shots into the air as Parch went in search of the gunman and Dragoon came up beside him to stand in front of Howard. Together, they hustled Howard toward the door just as the tinted back window of the truck crashed to the ground.

Another round of gunfire rang out, hitting Dragoon in the shoulder blade. "Agh . . ." he yelled, managing to remain standing as they pushed Howard through the front doors of the building, making sure he was safe. Then Craven went back out to help Parch.

Blood was quickly spreading across the back of Dragoon's shirt as Howard assisted him over to a chair in the front office of the building. There was no way he could make it up to Howard's office in his weakened condition, but he remained focused. In any case, Howard didn't want him up there bleeding all over the place. He ordered one of his two secretaries to get towels and another to call for an ambulance.

"How you doing, Dragoon?" Craven asked, rushing to his partner's side with Parch close behind.

"It went straight through," Dragoon answered, wincing as he moved his shoulder to give them a better view of his injury.

"Just hang on," Howard was saying. "He's lost a lot of blood. Did you get whoever was out there?"

"No, by the time I got up there, he was gone. All I found were some shell casings," Parch replied. "Want me to call the cops?"

Howard glanced at him, realizing they didn't know the whole story. He hadn't told them anything about his past. All they knew was he needed protection. "No." He didn't want to see the police. He was supposed to be dead or in protective custody. Either way, there would be a lot of questions. "No, just get him to the hospital." Ignoring their obvious curiosity, he headed to his office as if nothing had just happened. "Call me with his status. I'll be right here."

"Parch, you stay here," Craven commanded. "I'll get him squared away and be right back."

As soon as his door was closed, Howard moved the large framed portrait of Jackson Melbourne, revealing a wall safe. He opened the safe and reached inside, removing a shiny, silver-handled .45. He carefully checked to make sure it was loaded before sitting down at his desk.

He tried to formulate a plan of action, but the walls seemed to be closing in on him and he was not thinking clearly. The discovery of Tonya in the arms of Dallas, his agency contact, had taken him for a loop. Why was Dallas around here, anyway, if not investigating his disappearance? And what in the hell were he and Tonya doing? How and when did they become so intimate? Unwanted thoughts crept into his mind, bad thoughts that he didn't want to even consider. Had Tonya been in on it from the beginning? Had Dallas put him away just to take his girl?

He didn't see how Tonya could have anything to do with him going into the witness protection program. She hadn't even known that he had talked to the government. He did that on his own after he had been arrested on some serious drug charges, which, again, she knew nothing about.

So here he was trying to figure out the best way to approach the woman he loved and win her back from the man who had put him away. Howard had thought that he could walk up to her door, tell her a lie or two about being put away, even in jail, if necessary, and she would welcome him back into her life with open arms. Apparently, she had moved on without giving a thought to his whereabouts. That hurt. The whole time he was away, he thought of her. He dreamed of her, of the day they would reunite. Even when he had lain between the legs of those wrinkled-skin antiques at the spa, he was with her, making love to her. That was what got him through, that and the money they willingly gave him.

Damn, I've been such a fool. And being made a fool of was something for which he had zero tolerance. He resolved that this was going to come to an end, either for good or for bad. He was going to go back over to Tonya's house, talk to her and make damn sure he got the answers to all of his questions, Dallas be damned.

Cecilia was at her desk at the police station putting on her jacket. She didn't want to keep Jaimer waiting too long. Now that he had come clean a little bit more, she was glad to have an ally in her mission to keep Howard Douglass away from her sister. It would have been easy enough for her to pick him up, but on what charges? He had left the witness protection program, but the feds hadn't given them the okay to arrest him. In fact, they were pretty adamant about keeping the local authorities out of their case. And when it came to her investigation of Meltdown's murder, they wanted to know everything she had found out. It was all a bunch of red tape bullshit as far as she was concerned. But if Howard was indeed involved in Meltdown's murder, she was going to haul his ass in quicker than a mongoose attacking a snake.

Although she had never particularly liked Jackson Melbourne, she had foolishly been in love with his son for a long time. Even after all the fighting, he still held a special place in her heart—after all, he was the father of her twins. Nobody other than her husband knew. Nobody needed to know–not Darius Melbourne, and especially not her twins.

She met Curtis when she was two months pregnant, and when she told him of her predicament, he had sworn to her that he would take that knowledge to his grave. So far, he had kept that promise. His support and love for her was what made it easier and easier to ward off Darius's advances.

Darius didn't love her anymore. He just wanted to see if he could still get her under his thumb—he could still pull her strings, as he did to every other puppet he had ever had. When she had miscarried their first pregnancy shortly after graduating from high school, he had been truly devastated. It was the only time she had ever seen him break down and cry, but he had left when his father suggested that he take over several of the businesses in Atlanta. Left without offering to take her with him or promising to keep in contact. He was gone.

He came back for his mother's funeral, and that was the last time she saw him. He had stayed around long enough and had pulled her strings well enough to leave her pregnant with twins. But this time was different. He was home for his father's funeral, and surprise flashed in his eyes when she told him that she loved her husband and would remain faithful to him. For the first time, she saw the doubt in his eyes hinting that maybe he couldn't have anything he wanted, whenever he wanted it.

Looking up, she saw her partner, Detective Carl Williams, hurriedly coming toward her. He grabbed his blue suit jacket from the back of his chair and barked at her without slowing.

"Let's go. We got shots fired over at the old paper factory."

"Meltdown's warehouse?" she asked, jumping up and racing to catch up.

"That's the place."

"Damn. The drama never ends, does it?"

"Never. Word is that the construction company and warehouse are being run by a Dominique Thibodaux. She was Meltdown's assistant before he got sent up. The majority of his businesses were transferred to her."

"Interesting. Sounds like more than an assistant to me," she declared, sliding into the passenger seat of their unmarked car. "Must have been something going on between them for him to do something like that. Why wouldn't he leave it to his son?"

"You're right. So what do you think? Mistress? She doesn't have a record."

"Is she from out of town?"

"I think that's our safest bet. None of the other detectives have ever heard of her. But before Meltdown was locked up, word is that he had a very attractive woman beside him most of the time." The detective smoothly drove the car through traffic as he continued to brief Cecilia on all he knew. When they pulled in front of the warehouse, two patrol cars were already parked in front.

Cecilia approached one of the officers, surveying the scene. "Anything?"

"Nothing," she replied. "Thompson collected a few shell casings from that roof over there after we figured out that it's where the bullet that hit this car must have come from," she said, pointing up at the roof across the street. "But until forensics analyzes them, we won't know if they are from this shooting."

Cecilia scanned the roof across the street, thankful for her sunglasses because the sun was still high and bright at two o'clock in the afternoon. "No victims?"

"No one was out here when we arrived, which was only three minutes ago."

"Have you been inside?"

"Two officers are inside now."

"Okay, officer," Cecilia said, patting the cop on her shoulder. "Radio for their location, and let them know we're coming."

The officers stated that they were on the first level in the back of the building and hadn't found anyone there.

"Tell them that we will check the second floor."

She removed her sunglasses as they approached the front door of the building. Their guns were drawn. She opened the tinted glass door slowly, peeking into the reception area and then easing in.

Except for the sound of large machinery coming from the back, the place was quiet and appeared to be empty. Suddenly, Cecilia pointed to a chair in one corner of the room with a huge bloodstain on its back. They cautiously moved further.

"Police," Cecilia announced. No answer. They opened a door labeled OFFICES and climbed the stairs to the upper level.

"Police," Cecilia called out again.

"Yes?" a male voice behind the closed door answered. "Can I help you with something?"

The voice grew closer, indicating that someone was walking toward the door. As the knob turned Williams quickly moved to the other side of the door. Howard opened the door, expecting to answer a few quick questions and intending to easily play off the shooting, but he was definitely not prepared to come face to face with Cecilia Perkins Summers.

Seeing his startled expression, Cecilia reacted fast to take advantage of the element of surprise. She didn't want to give him time to think up a lie.

"Howard Douglass, I heard you were back in town. I'm glad to see you. We've been looking for you, you know. And look where we find you—right in Meltdown's very own establishment. You know, Meltdown, the guy you testified against in a court of law."

"Look, I don't know what you've heard," he began, putting his hands up in a gesture of innocence and backing into the room, "but I didn't have anything to do with anything. My hands are clean."

"How do you know we think you've done anything?" Cecilia asked suspiciously. "Who got shot downstairs?"

Howard decided against lying. "My bodyguard."

"Bodyguard?" Williams asked. "Why do you need a bodyguard?"

"Because somebody is trying to kill my black ass! That's who you need to be looking for." He was happy to redirect the conversation to something other than himself. Anything that would shield him from Cecilia's suspicions for a second.

"Who would want you dead, Howard?" Cecilia asked, walking around the office and looking for any clues as to what he was up to. She found nothing. The office was spotless. No papers on the desk, no cabinet drawers open. Just a picture of Tonya sitting on the swing in the backyard of her house. *The picnic. What the hell?*

"Where the hell did you get this picture?" Cecilia asked, lifting it off the desk.

"It was given to me."

"By whom?"

Instead of answering, Howard simply stood there watching her.

"Motherfucker." Cecilia lunged forward and stuck her finger into Howard's face. "If I find out that you've been stalking my sister . . ."

"Easy, Detective," Detective Williams said, moving forward and pushing Howard away from her. The subtle taunt was all it took to light Cecilia's fuse.

Howard turned the subject back to the danger he was in, ignoring her threat. "As you know, a lot of people want me dead," he said, looking at Detective Williams. "Darius Melbourne for starters."

Cecilia moved to a far corner of the office. "So you think that Darius is behind this shooting? Why didn't you call the police?"

"Because you know that I left the program, and they're trying to pull me back into it."

"Why? Melbourne is dead. They don't need you anymore. You've already testified."

"Cecilia, you think Meltdown was the big fish? He might have been one of the sharks they were after, but he's not the whale. He's not the biggest fish in the ocean, and that is who they want now."

"And they want you to testify again?"

"Yeah, but I'm not doing it." He walked over to the windows, which took up an entire wall and looked out. "I've lost enough time being stuck out in the desert. I want my life back." He turned and faced her, his hands stuck deep into his pockets. "And I plan to get it back. All of it."

She heard the challenge in his voice, saw it in his eyes as she followed them to her sister's picture. Her anger was instant—and explosive.

Before her partner could stop her, Cecilia had rushed Howard, pushing him up against the window with her arm tucked snugly against his neck. She put pressure on his windpipe to weaken his strength, rendering him less than equal to her. Then she leaned forward and whispered a warning in his ear. "Howard Douglass, I would suggest that you think twice before you try to slither back into my sister's life. You have no idea what you would have to go through to make that happen."

"Easy, Cecilia," Williams was saying behind her.

"I will see you dead first, you sorry bastard. Do you hear me?"

"Detective!" Williams yelled, grabbing Cecilia's forearm when he saw Howard gasping for air. "Fall back, Detective," he said, repeating it twice before Cecilia finally let Howard go.

"I . . . I, um, want to . . . to file charges," Howard stammered, bent over and rubbing his neck, barely able to speak.

"For what, sir? I didn't see anything," Williams replied. "Sir, do you want to tell us where your body-guard is now?"

"He's . . . at the hospital."

"And he will corroborate your story?" Keeping one eye on Cecilia as she paced furiously on the other side of the room, Detective Williams moved closer to Howard so that he could better hear what he was saying.

"Yes."

"Well, since we don't have any reason to haul you in, I guess we're done here. But sir, you need to be more careful, especially when—" Detective Williams stopped and drew his gun when the office door flew open. He didn't know who to expect to see when he turned around.

Standing behind the door, Cecilia also had her gun in hand.

"Wait . . . wait," Howard creaked, his voice raspy and sore from Cecilia's assault.

Dominique rushed into the room with Parch on her heels. Unsure as to why she was there, she quietly decided that concern for Howard should be her main reason.

Parch tried to stop her, but she was too quick. Once they were in the room, he sized up the situation fast and pushed her behind him, not knowing whether the badges being displayed were real.

Cecilia saw the action-ready look on his face. Despite being a big man, he was obviously fast, because the gun he was now holding hadn't been there two seconds ago. She had to defuse the situation.

"Sir, put the gun down," she said, holding her badge out far enough for him to see it. "Sir," she said, "I'm Detective Summers with the Philadelphia Police Department. That's Detective Williams. You need to lower your weapon."

Parch didn't move.

"Howard, you better tell him something before this shit gets ugly."

Howard nodded. The last thing he needed was more attention. A gunfight with police was not on his to-do list.

"Put the damn gun down, man," Howard managed, his voice still hoarse. "They're the police, here to investigate the shooting."

Parch lowered his gun and tucked it into the band of his pants behind his back.

"You," Cecilia yelled, "take the gun out and place it on the desk. Come sit your ass down over here," she ordered, indicating the black leather sofa. She pointed at Dominique, saying, "Sit down over there behind the desk."

"I thought you said your bodyguard was shot?" Williams asked Howard.

"I got three bodyguards," Howard explained.

"Three? Why do you need so many?"

"Because, like I said, somebody is trying to kill me." Howard's temper was getting the best of him. "So are you done?" He was ready for them to go on about their business. But Cecilia had just gotten started.

"You," she said, pointing at Dominique. "I know you. What is your name?"

Dominique realized that Cecilia remembered her from the party two weeks ago, and she was thankful that Vince had never formally introduced them. In fact, he hadn't introduced her to any of his sisters, had just pointed them out.

"I'm, um, Howard's cousin." *Damn, I shouldn't have said that.*

"Howard's cousin, huh? Weren't you just at my sister's house a few weeks ago? With Vince? What's your name?"

Dominique thought fast before the lie spilled out of her mouth. She couldn't tell them her real name because they could then trace her back to Meltdown's businesses and Meltdown himself. She couldn't say that she was Vince's girlfriend—at least in her mind, she was. And she wasn't about to take the chance of Vince finding out that she was related to Howard. "No, I'm Tiffany," she said.

"Tiffany what?" Cecilia persisted, looking at the woman closely. *I know it's the same girl.*

"Tiffany Brittingham," she said, smoothly using her half-sister's name. She didn't see Howard's eyes grow wide. Her only concern was that she had gotten away with her little white lie and that Cecilia was about to leave. "I just came over here to see if Howard was all right. I heard about the shooting."

"How did you hear about it?"

"Off the street," she said smartly. "You know we get the news first."

"And you weren't at my sister's house? You don't know a Vince Perkins?"

"No."

Cecilia eyed the beauty one last time. She didn't look like a streetwalker; she was too high class for that. Maybe she was one of the high-priced prostitutes that Meltdown was known to have kept hanging around. Maybe she really was Howard's cousin. Or maybe she was lying. Now was not the time to worry about it. She still had to get to the hospital to interview the shooting victim before going to Tonya's house.

"We done here, Williams?" she asked her partner.

"We're done," he replied, keeping his eye on the mammoth of a man sitting on the leather sofa.

"Good." Stopping in front of Howard, she said, "Remember, I will have my eyes on you." Then she snatched Tonya's picture off his desk and turned and walked away, her head held high.

Howard's expression darkened the minute she left the room. Disgusted that he had accomplished nothing that day, he opened his top drawer and pulled out a framed picture, placing it in the exact same spot as the last one. That was the second time something of his had been taken.

"Parch, would you please make sure they've left and lock the front door?" Once Parch was gone, he calmly turned to Dominique. "Now why did you tell her that lie?"

"What else was I supposed to say? She's Vince's sister, for God's sake."

"So?"

"So? I shouldn't have come over here to check on you. You don't give a damn about anybody but yourself. I don't even think you really give a damn about Tonya Perkins."

His swift response surprised her. In seconds she was pinned against the wall, his hands wrapped around her throat. She grasped at his hands, trying to break his hold.

"Don't . . . you . . . *ever* speak to me like that. You still think that you have a chance with Vince Perkins? You're just as dumb as your mother was, thinking that every man who crosses your path will fall at your feet. Vince Perkins will never be yours."

"Get . . . off . . . me," she groaned, trying to preserve as much of her breath as she could. She fought against him, but Howard wasn't budging.

"She'll remember you, or she'll pull up Tiffany's name. She's not a dummy."

"Let . . . me . . . go."

"You've just made the situation worse, not to mention the fact that you gave her the Brittingham name in the process. How long do you think it will take her to put together the fact that Tiffany and Marion are related?" Repulsed by her stupidity, he abruptly let her go. Gasping for air, she slid down the wall.

"But, I . . ." She held her throat, feeling the welts he'd left.

"But nothing. I'm going to get Tonya Perkins. If I have to face that damn Agent Dallas, then I will. I already knew this wouldn't be easy. All you had to do was listen to me and do what I said, but now they're going to be waiting for us. I should have made sure she saw me today."

"You can't just walk up to her door," Dominique protested.

"Watch me."

CHAPTER 20

Jaimer nervously paced the length of the patio at the side of his house. By six that morning, he had already exercised away much of his frustrations and fears. The slim hope that everything would turn out okay was all that kept him together. That and his love for Tonya. And he knew it was true love. Although she had wanted him to stay with her last night, he had declined, feeling increasingly uncomfortable with his deceitfulness. How could he say he loved her, make love to her, and not confess the guilt he harbored over his past actions? That's not the type of man he was. He couldn't do it.

Cecilia had never made it over to the house for their talk with Tonya. She had called to explain that she had been called on another case and then had to rush home. They planned to talk to her today and come clean about everything.

As the sun peeked through the opened blinds, sweat dripped from Jaimer's body as he repeatedly pushed off the floor with his hands. His body board-straight, his concentration unshaken, he let his mind drift back to another time.

"It's time to pull him in, Dallas," the director said *through the wireless earpiece.*

"No problem, sir. We just have to wait until they make their way back to the car."

"*The least amount of violence as possible.*"

"*No problem, sir. Douglass already agreed to come in tonight after his date.*"

"*No. We need to get him now, as soon as possible.*"

"*But sir, he's with the girl,*" *Dallas said worriedly.*

"*They want him here now. Do your job, Dallas.*"

"*But, sir—*"

"*No buts. Have him at the office within the hour.*" *With that, the director was gone. In minutes, one of his men signaled him that the subject was approaching.*

Sweat poured down him, forming a small puddle on the mat beneath him. Heedlessly, he increased the speed of his repetitions.

He soundlessly crept up behind Tonya, holding a white pillowcase. Three of his associates stood in front of the couple and blocked their path as if they were about to rob them. As soon as the men approached, Jaimer put the bag over her head and pulled her away from the four-man unit. He held her until Howard was securely locked away in a waiting van. He then released he and quickly moved down the dark alley behind a parked car.

Jaimer silently watched as she removed the bag and looked around in confused terror. She called Howard's name repeatedly until her predicament overwhelmed her. She tripped over an empty beer bottle before cowering behind a parked car. He instinctively started to help her before coming to his senses. In the silence, he watched as she slid to the ground against the car and cried.

He waited while she called Vince on her cell and asked him to come get her, her words slurred and filled with fear.

And he stayed on the scene until Vince came rushing to her side.

The brutally strenuous workout finally caused him to collapse on the mat, cutting his self-punishment short.

"Vince called me this morning," Tonya cheerfully confided to Cindy. They had been on the phone for the last hour talking about the baby shower, which Cindy insisted not be a surprise, and the delivery.

Tonya knew how badly Cindy wanted her to be in the delivery room with her, but she wasn't going to raise false hope by saying she would be there. Hell, she had just started going out on the front porch, and she still hadn't gotten up the nerve to take the first step off it.

"Oh, yeah," Cindy replied. "What's up with him?" she asked curiously.

"I don't really know. He just said that he had to get away for a minute to think about some things."

"Things like what?"

"I don't know," Tonya said.

"Well, who did he leave in charge of the company?"

"I don't know."

"Well, where did—"

"Cindy, I said I don't know. Damn." Impatient with the persistent questions, she moved the phone away from her ear and stared at it for a moment. She was going to have to give Cecilia the same answers later.

"I just want to know what's wrong."

"So do I, but he didn't tell me all that. He was just calling to let us know that he's all right, and he'll be home soon."

"Well, what are you doing today?"

"I don't know. I'll probably just work on the book. I had an idea this morning that I want to work on. I plan on sitting on the—hold on. Somebody is at the door."

"Who is it?"

"I don't know," Tonya replied, scooting off the living-room sofa and walking briskly to the door. "Who is it?" she asked.

"Tonya, it's me," she heard Cecilia say. She opened the door and was surprised to see Jaimer standing behind her sister, both looking as if something was wrong.

"Cindy, let me call you back," she said, hearing her sister ask why just before she pushed the 'end' button.

Moving aside, she gave Cecilia room to pass. She lifted her head and waited for Jaimer's kiss, but was taken aback when he simply grazed her chin.

"What's going on, you two?" she asked, following them into the living room.

"We need to have a talk," Cecilia replied. "Have a seat. This is something serious."

Worry lines instantly appeared on Tonya's forehead as she noted the serious expressions on each of their faces. What could Cecilia and Jaimer have to talk to her about together? They didn't even like each other. And the only thing they had in common was Vince. Vince. Was something wrong with him? She had just talked to him not more than two hours ago.

Cecilia could see Tonya was allowing her imagination to roam free. She was good at doing that, and Cecilia did not want her sister to slip back into her old routine. She had fought so hard and had come so far.

"Nothing is wrong with anybody. It doesn't have anything to do with the family."

"Oh, good," she said, allowing herself to breathe normally again. "Well, what is it?" She noticed that Jaimer was avoiding eye contact with her.

"Tonya, sit down here," Jaimer said. He didn't know where to start, his guilt was strong and his deception was unforgivable.

"Tonya, listen," Cecilia began, "I know you're going to be upset after I tell you this, and you might even hate me. You probably won't understand my reasoning for not telling you this, but just know that what I did was done for your sake." For the first time, Cecilia realized she was afraid to death of her sister's reaction. She was actually afraid to tell Tonya the one thing she needed to know the most.

"Okay." Tonya said, unsure of what was going on, but more than a little anxious to know what this was all about.

Cecilia was about to continue when the doorbell chimed.

"Hold that thought," Tonya said, jumping up. "Jordan is supposed to stop by this morning on her way into work. She picked up some things for me last night at the drug store."

"Okay," Cecilia said nervously to Jaimer, rubbing her hands down the side of her pants. *Damn, I'm nervous.*

"You scared about how she's going to handle this, too?" Jaimer asked.

"Hell yeah," Cecilia replied, walking over to the sofa. "This is not going to be good."

A horrifying scream pierced the air right after they heard the door opening. Then there was complete silence.

"Baby, don't be scared," they heard Howard saying as they both scrambled off the couch and ran to the front door. "It's really me."

After Tonya's frightened reaction, Howard wasn't so sure he had made the right move by appearing on her doorstep first thing in the morning.

Scrunched up against the wall with her hand covering her mouth, her eyes wide with shock, Tonya looked as if she were shielding herself from a mighty blow. She wasn't sure if she had finally gone crazy, or if it was truly Howard standing before her. She saw his lips moving, but couldn't hear a word he said.

"What did I tell you, you bastard?" Cecilia rushed to Howard, prepared to do battle. "I told you to stay the hell away from her."

"I couldn't do it," Howard confessed, fighting against the hand Cecilia was pushing into his chest as he tried to go to Tonya, who was now sliding to the floor.

A moment from long ago flashed before him and Jaimer rushed to her side, determined not to let her hit the ground again. He lifted her, holding her against him with one arm. "Cecilia, take her. I'll handle him," Jaimer yelled.

"Tonya," Howard pleaded, still trying to move further into the house. Now that he was near her, now that she knew the truth, nothing was going to stop him from getting her back. "Don't let them keep me from you any longer. Don't let Agent Dallas come between us. He's the one who took me away from you in the first place."

Cecilia had Tonya in her arms, but now Tonya was fighting to hear what Howard had to say. Howard was really alive? Howard was alive! She couldn't overpower her sister and was eventually pulled back into the living room.

"Shut the fuck up!" Jaimer growled at Howard, easily sidestepping the first punch thrown. He smiled inwardly; this was just the way he wanted it to play out. With all the anger and guilt built up inside, he was going to enjoy letting loose on Howard.

"You shut the fuck up, Agent Dallas. This was your plan in the first place, wasn't it? You wanted me out of the picture so that you could be with Tonya. That's sick."

"I said *shut up!*" Jaimer shouted, throwing a punch that landed on the left side of Howard's jaw.

"What were you doing, huh? Lusting after her the whole time you were following us with your little camera?" Although the side of his face ached like hell from Jaimer's blow, Howard determinedly kept screaming accusations at his nemesis. Then he turned to Cecilia. "Why didn't you tell your sister that I was alive, Detective? You knew the whole time that I was in the witness protection program."

Tonya slowly began to regain her sanity as the full impact of Howard's words sank in. Her heartbeat slowed

Stressed out by the whole scene, Tonya rushed through the door just as Howard turned back toward the house and yelled her name.

"Tonya! Tonya! I came back for you. I still love you. Please, you have to remember that."

In tears, she dashed off the porch, determined to make her way to Howard one last time before he was out of her life again. At one time, she had loved him more than anything. She didn't think about what she was doing—even as she felt grass under her bare feet. At one time. Moving just out of reach of Cecilia's long arms, she managed to get closer to her goal, but then Jaimer grabbed her from behind and held her immobile.

Shocked and stunned, she watched Howard roughly being taken away. Cursing, he struggled against the tight hold that the two big men had on him. With growing horror, she watched a large black van pull up just as the trio reached the sidewalk. The van's side door slid open, and four huge arms reached out and grabbed Howard. The van then sped down the street. It looked like something she had seen in a movie. But this was not a movie.

Soon she felt the warm hands that still held her arms. She felt the warm body pressed against her back and was snapped back into reality. Those hands, the ones she had earlier been craving to have touch her. That body, the one she had daydreamed about all morning. This man, who had betrayed her trust and love.

Jaimer felt her body begin to vibrate in his grasp. And he knew what was coming. She turned around and faced him with eyes filled with hurt and the knowledge of betrayal. It was agonizing for him to face the damage that he had done to her, but he knew that he had no choice but to weather her fury as best he could.

"Get your hands the hell off me," Tonya yelled, shaking loose and moving a step back. She looked straight into eyes that were full of regret, but she chose to ignore it. All she felt was her own hurt, her own regret—and her anger as she looked from him to Cecilia. "Why?" she asked simply. "Why would you do this to me?"

Cecilia spoke first, stepping forward and trying to defuse the situation. The fact that Tonya was standing outside her house in the front yard hadn't escaped her notice. "Tonya, you don't know the whole story."

"I know enough." Tonya walked away from Jaimer and moved toward Cecilia, animatedly using her hands to convey her anger. "You knew all along that Howard was still alive, and you didn't tell me. How long have you been trying to keep him from me?"

"I haven't been keeping him from you, Tonya. Howard has . . ."

Jaimer stepped forward to further explain. "Howard has been in the federal witness protection program for the past three years. Cecilia wasn't keeping him from you." Shrinking from the flash of hatred he thought he saw in Tonya's eyes, Jaimer plowed on. "Tonya, you have to know that no one planned for you to get hurt. Howard Douglass was involved in some extremely dangerous illegal activities. When the two of you first started dating, Howard was one of the biggest drug dealers in the tri-state area. He was facing drug and weapons charges, so he decided to become a federal witness in order to avoid imprisonment."

"So he was right, wasn't he? You did know him back then. You worked for the government." The hurt in her eyes seemed to magnify as she began to slowly comprehend the full scope of the betrayal.

"Back then, I was an agent and Howard was my assignment. I was to bring him into the program so he could help the government build a case against the leaders of numerous crime syndicates." He chanced facing her directly. "Look, Tonya, I know it looks bad, but you gotta believe that I never thought you would be affected by the way we took him in.".

"*You* took him in?" Then it struck her. "You were there that night?" Then it struck her. "It *was* you, wasn't it? You were the one who put the bag over my head and held me still. That was you, Jaimer?"

Jaimer dropped his head, finding it hard to look her in the face; his guilt was too naked. How could he explain to her that he was just doing his job? How could he make her see that he had begun to fall in love with her way back then, but he had to do his job? He couldn't have imagined she would become an innocent victim in the government's undercover scheme.

"Tonya, I—"

"It was you," Tonya stated flatly, her eyes brimming with tears. She didn't turn and run into her house as she was tempted to do. It was time to stop running and start facing all her problems head on. He had helped her learn that lesson.

"Baby—"

"Don't call me baby. What was it, Jaimer? What was the purpose of coming back around me? Why would you make yourself a fixture in my life after all that happened?"

"Tonya, please, let me explain." In desperation, Jaimer reached for her, but she drew back, clearly revolted. "Tonya, I spent nearly three months watching you through those damn surveillance cameras. And I know it might sound crazy, but Howard is right. I wanted you back then. I absolutely fell in love with you three years ago." He threw up his hands helplessly. "Maybe I am crazy, but I've thought about you every day since that day, wondering what you were doing. I knew you were Vince's sister. That is one of the reasons I stayed away as long as I could. But when I saw Vince at that party, and he offered me the house, I couldn't turn it down. I had no idea of your illness until he told me. And then—"

"And then you felt guilty enough to invade my space with more lies. The only reason you made a point of meeting me and helping me get better is because you felt responsible for my being in that condition. You never cared about me." Her heart broke anew when each new piece fell into place.

"You don't believe that. I helped you because I cared for you, and I wanted to help you get better. I was going to tell you the truth, Tonya. But it was more important to get you better first. I would never hurt you."

"Well, never must be a mighty short time." She began to walk away from him.

Instinct made him grab her arm. He couldn't let it end like this. "Tonya, please don't walk away from me. You know me better than this. You know how I feel about you."

She snatched her arm away and walked toward the porch without so much as a backward glance. As she took the second step leading to her porch, it suddenly dawned on her that she had been in the front yard, practically to the sidewalk, for the first time in three years. But she just kept walking until she was back in her house.

Jaimer just stood and watched her walk away from him for the second time in his life. This time, the stabbing pain in his chest was tenfold. A familiar loneliness was creeping up on him. It took the feel of Cecilia's comforting arm on his heavy shoulders to bring him out of his trance-like state.

"Damn," he muttered, feeling utterly defeated. All energy seemed to have been drained from his body.

"Jaimer, give her some time. She has got a lot to take in right now. She'll come around." Then they heard the sound of the heavy wooden front door being slammed shut.

Cecilia's expression told Jaimer that she wasn't too sure of her own words, but he thanked her anyway.

"Let me go and have a talk with her. I know my sister. She'll steam over it for a couple of days, but it will get better. Don't worry too much about it."

"That's easy for you to say. I knew that I should have told her right away, especially when I found out Howard was back in town. And I knew it was going to come back and bite me in the ass. I'm too used to keeping secrets."

"Give her a couple of days, then just start at the beginning. Hopefully, she will be ready to listen."

Depressed, he walked across the lawn toward his house. He paused briefly and glanced in the direction of the house, knowing that she was probably watching him through the slightly closed miniblinds. As badly as he wanted to turn and burst through the front door and make her listen to him, Jaimer knew it was time to back off.

Upon finding the front door locked, Cecilia shook her head and simply took out her spare key and calmly opened the front door. "You done with the hissy fit?"

"Hissy fit? Why are you even in here? I don't have anything to say to you, either."

"Oh, please, Tonya. Stop acting like a little kid. I can understand you being upset, but that man loves you. I can't believe you're going to let that go."

"Go to hell, Cecilia. You knew all about this shit, and you didn't tell me."

"Whoa. Hold up, sister. You can be mad at me for keeping the fact that Howard wasn't dead from you, but I was given direct orders not to talk about that case. And believe me, there were plenty of times I was willing to break that rule for you. But I also knew that it was best for you not to know."

"Did you think that maybe, just maybe, if I had known I could have been cured?"

Cecilia looked her dead in the eyes. "Yes, I did think of that. Tonya, thinking Howard was dead didn't get you locked up in here. You being scared did that."

"Me thinking of Howard being killed did it," Tonya screeched at her.

"Tonya, you really think that? The only person that kept you in this house is you. Jaimer helped you get out of it."

"Jaimer? Jaimer helped me out of guilt."

"You know what? I give up. I'm not going to apologize for not telling you that Howard was alive. He was a dangerous person who pulled the wool over your eyes. You never wondered how he was able to afford all the expensive gifts, the shopping sprees, the meals? He's a bad man, Tonya."

"He loved me."

"Sure he did, because it made him feel good to know that he could get a real woman, a professional, higher-class woman than he was used to getting. But you don't think you were his only woman, do you?"

Tonya turned and looked at her sharply.

"You know what? Never mind. Believe what you want to about Howard Douglass. And believe the worst about Jaimer just because he cared enough to keep something from you until you were ready to hear it." Cecilia was tired of beating a dead horse. Obviously, Tonya's mind was already made up.

"Cecilia, just leave, please," Tonya finally pleaded.

"Okay, if you're not going to listen to me, there's no use in me wasting my breath. I love you," she said, turning to leave.

Tonya didn't respond. She stood in the living room and listened for the front door to close. She didn't sit down until she heard Cecilia leave. Then she felt the tears roll down her cheeks. God, what was she going to do?

The shock of seeing Howard again left her exhilarated but befuddled. When she saw him, the past came rushing back, but nowhere in those memories had her feelings for him been nearly as strong as her feelings for Jaimer. She was glad to hear Howard profess his love for her after all this time, but her excitement ended there. But when Jaimer said he cared for her, her bruised heart still skipped a beat—even through her anger. How could that be?

Could she, should she, still want to be in any kind of relationship with him? Could she trust that he wouldn't keep more secrets? He had watched her with Howard and had fallen in love with her. He had come into her life with set plans to meet her. So when they'd met at the family party, Jaimer already knew who she was.

She finally lay down for the night after answering all Cindy's questions. Her day had been a total waste. Even when Shawnique stopped by to make sure she was all right and Jordan called to check on her, she did not realize the day was passing so quickly. And she still hadn't come to any final conclusions. Her confusion multiplied just as the pain in her heart had.

CHAPTER 21

The following Monday morning, Jaimer was sitting on the side of his bed holding his pounding head in his hands. The alarm clock on his nightstand read ten-thirty. *Oh, God, how am I going to make it through this?*

Rubbing his eyes, he ventured a quick look at himself in the mirror. Bloodshot eyes stared back at him, evidence of his sleeplessness.

"Jaimer?" Colin called, knocking on the locked bedroom door. "Man, you in there?"

"Yeah," Jaimer replied, slowly moving to the door and unlocking it.

"Oh, man," Colin blurted when he saw Jaimer's condition. "Man, you all right? I, uh, kinda heard about what happened yesterday."

"I'm all right," Jaimer said listlessly.

"Man, don't lie to me. You're not all right, and you don't look all right, either."

Jaimer looked at him, his friend, his boy, and knew that he didn't have to put up a strong front. "Man, I fucked up," he confessed pitifully.

"Ease up off yourself, man," Colin said. "All of us have done one thing or another that we're not so proud of to get a woman we really wanted. You loved her, and you saw your opportunity to get closer to her."

"Man, I lied to my friend. I lied to Tonya. Hell, I was even lying to myself at one point. I should have just told Vince the truth from the door. I don't think I can even face him after the way I played him."

"Vince is not the one you really should be worrying about right now, anyway. He'll come around once he hears your side of the story. He's your boy. He'll understand."

"Tonya hates me. She is not going to ever want to see me again. And I don't know how to make her understand. I don't think I'm going to be able to fix this."

"Man, look, just give her some time to think about things. She'll come around, too. She loves you. She's not going to be able to forget about you overnight. Hell, you live right next door."

"Hell, that might have to change. I'm going to have to find someplace else to live and move the office." He fell back onto the bed. "God, I didn't even think about all the consequences. All I was thinking about was having Tonya in my life."

"Don't worry, man. It'll all get better," Colin said. "Just stay up here for the day and rest your eyes. I don't think you're ready to deal with Damon or Mrs. T. Damon knows what went down, too, and Mrs. T is asking questions about why you haven't come down yet. I'll just tell her that you're not feeling well."

"Nah, man, then she'll be up here trying to take care of me. Just tell her that I have to be out tonight, so I'm taking the day off."

"Good enough. If you need anything, call my cell," he said, pounding Jaimer's leg as he rose to leave.

"Thanks, man." Jaimer stayed in his room for the rest of the day. He didn't move to do anything, including answering his phone when his sister called. He listened to her message around six that evening when he finally decided to get something to eat. She would be in town on Friday.

Cindy kicked hard at the bottom of Tonya's wooden door. She wasn't in the best of moods that morning, having had a miserable night herself what with the baby lying on her bladder and kicking her in what felt like her esophagus. To add insult to injury, Dayton spent the night snoring into her left ear. She'd had to wake him up twice to cuss him for being so rude. Now here she was banging on the front door and ringing the doorbell, and this damn girl was taking her sweet time answering the front door. She was madder at herself than at Tonya because she had forgotten to bring her own key.

"Tonya," she yelled, banging the door a third time. It opened a crack. "Tonya?" She entered the dark house and immediately became worried when she saw that the atmosphere in the house had radically changed. Again. Instead of being light and airy as it had been for the last week, the house was dark and stuffy. The windows, shutters and curtains were tightly closed, and her sister was still in her pajamas. She was disheveled, her hair unkempt, her eyes were red and swollen. It wasn't hard to tell that she had been crying, probably nonstop.

Tonya felt worse today than she had yesterday. She had awakened early but had stayed in bed, her mind on the day before and the man next door. She was feeling so sorry for herself, but she realized early in the day that it wasn't because of losing Howard. In fact, she had barely thought about Howard all day. It was Jaimer who was constantly on her mind. Trying to put up a brave front for Cindy, she sat up straight on the sofa with a silly grin pasted on her face.

"You can stop that, sister," Cindy said, seeing right through her facade. "That smile on your face isn't fooling me one bit. I know you're not that happy." Then she began opening curtains, ignoring Tonya's protests.

"Cindy, don't. I don't feel like all that sunlight."

"If you think for a second that I'm going to let you just sit here and float yourself back into a funk because you're feeling sorry for yourself, you've got another think coming."

"Look—"

"No, you look, Tonya," Cindy interrupted. "Don't do this to yourself. I'm begging you. You've come way too far to do this to yourself again."

"Cindy, for once, would you please just let me be? I don't feel like arguing with you about this right now. Just leave me alone."

"Sorry, I can't do that. I had Dayton drop me off. He's not coming back for two hours. So it looks like you're stuck with me for now."

"I'm tired of you and Cecilia being all up in my life."

"I'm tired of having to be all up in it," Cindy snapped back. "And Cecilia was only doing what she thought was best for you."

"What? You believe that?"

"Why else would she do it, Tonya? If you'd sit back and think for a minute instead of being mad at everybody, you'd see that Cecilia was only thinking of your best interests. You already thought Howard was dead. It was her job, and it's not as if he was a good person, anyway."

"Whether he was a good person or not, Cindy, he was the person I loved."

"You don't love him *now*," Cindy fired back. "Do you?" She watched Tonya closely. The answer was written all over her face. She didn't care about Howard in her heart. Had she ever?

Tonya turned from the question. Her love for Howard wasn't debatable; she didn't love him. It was that simple. She wasn't even sure if she had been in love with him back then. She did care for him, but the love she thought she felt had been implanted and magnified sometime within the last three years.

Somehow, she had made her feelings for him larger than life because of the tragic way she had lost him. But the reality of the matter was that she had fallen in love with Jaimer in the short of time they had spent together. And it hurt like hell to find out that he had lied to her.

"You need to talk to Cecilia and Jaimer and get whatever pent-up frustrations you have in you out into the open."

"I don't want to talk to Cecilia or Jaimer."

"You don't mean that. You know Cecilia loves you, and you should know that Jaimer loves you, too. But if you're willing to let a good man go that easily without a fight, there ain't nothing I can do. You must know a place where good men are a dime a dozen. I damn sure don't."

"A good man wouldn't have schemed and lied to me."

"No, but a good man just might scheme and lie to get with you."

"That doesn't even sound right. How can you make excuses for him?"

"I'm just calling it like I see it. He went through a lot of trouble to get to you. When I talked to Vince last night—"

"You told Vince already? He's not even here." Tonya was beyond anger; she was borderline disgusted with all her siblings being in her business.

"He's on his way home. And he's pissed. So expect another round of fireworks when he gets here this afternoon."

"That's just what I need. I don't know why you told him."

"Because he's our brother, and we tell him everything. And I didn't tell him, Cecilia did. He just called me to get my take on things. But he is pissed."

"What did he say?" Tonya asked, sincerely interested.

"He was just mad that his boy, one of his best friends, had played him like that to get to his sister, especially when he already knew who you were when Vince introduced the two of you at the party. And he never even knew that Jaimer worked for a government agency or that he was that high up in the FBI or DEA or whatever. He just thought that Jaimer used to be a cop. Just expect them to have words."

＝

Glancing at his watch, Vince saw that it was already after one o'clock. He turned his car in the direction of Tonya's house, hoping that at least some of the drama from the day before had subsided. Whatever the case, he planned to talk to Jaimer.

It didn't matter to Vince that Jaimer had played him to get to Tonya. Jaimer wasn't the first man to do that, but he did have a problem with Tonya being lied to and her heart being broken again. For hurting his little sister, Jaimer was going to have to pay.

＝

"Where is he?" Vince demanded, rushing into Jaimer's office as soon as Damon opened the door. He was halfway through the house before he realized Jaimer wasn't around. His anger, which he thought he had under control, had risen to the boiling point the minute he'd pulled in front of the two houses. How in the hell was Tonya supposed to live next door to the man who broke her heart? What if this caused her to be reclusive again? Damn it, this was all Jaimer's fault.

"Yo, man, you need to calm down," Damon said, instinctively trying to keep a bad situation from escalating.

"Don't tell me to calm down. Who the hell are you? Jaimer!" he yelled. "Get your ass down here!"

"Yo, man, I said calm down. My name is Damon, and I work for Jaimer. What's the problem?" Damon already knew what was going on, but he played dumb for Jaimer's sake. Plus, Mrs. T was sitting at her desk, mouth agape, taking in the unfolding drama.

Vince looked at the thickset man but refused to let logic dictate his actions, even though the threat of him enduring an ass whipping was definitely on the horizon. For his sister, he would take that ass whipping and much more.

"You tell Jaimer that I said to get his ass down here right now. I'm not leaving," Vince said, his teeth clenched. "Jaimer!"

"Young man, who are you?" Mrs. T respectfully asked.

"I'm Vince Perkins, Tonya's brother, and I want to see Jaimer right now." Out of respect, he lowered his tone considerably when he addressed her, but the fury was still ablaze in his eyes.

"Well, you can't see him " Damon was trying to come up with reasonably believable reason when he heard Jaimer's voice.

"It's okay, Damon," Jaimer said quietly, coming down the stairs. His head was still pounding, and his mood hadn't improved. After hearing the racket Vince was making downstairs, the man in him wouldn't allow him to stay locked in the bedroom like a scared punk, even though his brain was telling him otherwise. So he struggled up and left his room to face Tonya's enraged brother. "I've been expecting you, frat."

"Frat? Man, please, don't even start with that frat shit," Vince warned, advancing toward Jaimer even though he hadn't reached the bottom of the stairs.

Damon quickly stepped in front of Vince.

"That's some fucked up shit you did, man." He looked down at the hand firmly planted on his chest and wondered if he could get to Jaimer before Damon could stop him.

"I know. I know," Jaimer readily agreed. "There's no excuse for what I did, but you got to believe me, Vince. I didn't mean for Tonya to get hurt."

"You didn't?" Vince asked unbelievingly.

"Please, Vince, just let me explain, man. You know me. You know that I wouldn't intentionally hurt you or your sister."

"You played the hell out of me, man. But I could have gotten over that. I can't believe you played Tonya like that. That's unforgivable."

"Just let me explain my side of things. All I ask is that you listen to me. If we still ain't cool after that, then I'll understand."

"Yeah, whatever, man." Vince waited for Jaimer to descend the rest of the stairs.

Damon was still standing at the ready just in case Vince decided to make a move.

"We can talk out here," Jaimer said, walking out the front door. He sat on the steps, motioning for Vince to join him.

"Yo, man," Damon, who had followed them outside, asked, "do you want me to stay out here?"

"Nah, it's cool," Jaimer replied, as Vince sat down. He knew Vince wouldn't try to attack him from behind. And he had to act as though he didn't have anything to be afraid of. But he was afraid because once again he had to try to get Vince on his side, and this time with the truth.

"What's up, Jaimer?" Vince asked. "Talk to me."

Jaimer took a deep breath, his distress plainly showing on his face. "I messed up, man. Big time."

As badly as Vince wanted to interrupt him to agree with the sentiment, he thought better of it.

"I think that I was an agent for one assignment too many. 'Til the day I die, I will regret taking on Howard Douglass's case. I had been trying to break away from the agency for a while, but when I went to the director, he told me that if I did this last job for him he wouldn't give me a hard time about retiring early. I didn't know that it would be the worst move I ever made." He inhaled deeply. "I had been running surveillance on Howard for about two weeks before I saw Tonya. And man, as ashamed as I am to say it, I think I was mesmerized with her from that very first day. I swear, Vince, at first it was her beauty, so I tried to look at her as just another pretty face. I didn't know who she was. But the more I watched her, the more I began to see her in a different kind of light. I know it was wrong, but I couldn't stop myself from falling in love with another man's woman.

"I used to watch him wheel and deal, see with other women, commit all kinds of illegal acts during the day, then turn into a complete gentleman at night. And it used to piss me off. I believe that he did love her, although he wasn't exactly faithful. Then before I knew it, I hated Howard Douglass because I started thinking that she should be my woman. Vince, I've done so many things in the past in the line of duty that I wasn't proud off. I've had to watch things, watch Tonya and Howard together, and it drove me crazy. Honestly, I wanted that case to be over with. I didn't agree with the method we used to bring him in. I didn't want anyone to be around when we took him, but I was given my orders, and I had to follow them. Never in my wildest dreams did I think that the outcome would be Tonya's reclusiveness.

"I haven't told her this, but I was in the alleyway when you came and got her that night. I stayed after they took Howard. I stood watching her, just watching her fall apart, and it broke my heart, but I thought it would scare her more if I came out. I just wanted to make sure that she was safe. I found out she was your sister some time during the investigation, but I didn't tell anyone that I knew you because they would have taken me off the case. And as sick as it might sound, I didn't want to leave her.

"When I was finally able to retire, I came back here thinking that maybe, just maybe, I would see her around, but I never did. Instead, I saw you at the party. And I used you to get to know her better. I lied to you, schemed and connived so that I could be with her, but I didn't know about her sickness until you told me. And then I felt it was my responsibility to help her get better. But, man, when I saw her at that party, I fell in love all over again."

Vince listened to Jaimer's story and tried to keep his heart hard, but how could he judge a man for his actions when he himself had done close to the same thing and found that in the end he had still made the wrong decision. He was in love with Marcia, but was willing to overlook that for the small streak of excitement that Dominique gave him.

"You know what?" Vince began. "I think we're both a couple of dumbasses. I believe that you love my sister, but you made a lot of bad decisions, even if they were for a good reason. I listened to Cecilia's side of things, and she thinks that you have a good heart, which is saying a lot because I know she couldn't stand you at first. And you and me might be cool, but this between you and Tonya, I'm not getting into. I was ready to come over here and go to blows, but you know what? I'm going to let Tonya handle her own affairs. I got some other stuff I need to handle. But I will tell you this, I don't know if these living arrangements are going to be in either of your best interests if you guys can't come to terms with what's going on. I hate to say it, but you might have to move, dog."

"Yeah, I already got that feeling myself. I need to talk to her, but she's not in a receptive mood right now, and I understand that. Plus, I don't know what to say to her."

"Well, don't wait too long. Time tends to only make matters worse." Vince stood up and offered Jaimer his hand. "I'm going to make sure she's all right before I leave. I'll holla at you later."

"All right, man," Jaimer said. Watching Vince cross the lawn and walk into her house, he wished it was he strolling casually through the front door.

CHAPTER 22

"You, too?" Tonya asked disbelievingly, slamming a glass of ice water down on her kitchen counter, causing it to slosh onto the marble countertop. She ignored it and stared her brother down as he tried to reason with her.

"Tonya, I'm not saying that you shouldn't be a little upset. I'm just saying that maybe, maybe you're taking this a little bit out of perspective."

"Perspective? Vince, you sound right stupid. The man lied to you, too. He used you, Vince, to meet me."

"Hey, I would be lying if I said that I never did the same thing. Tonya," Vince paused and took a deep breath, trying to ease some of the tension the conversation was causing his sister. They'd been having this same conversation since he came into the house twenty minutes ago. "He loves you."

"Loves me? Yeah, right. Boy, you men will stick together through thick and thin, won't you?"

"Whoa, don't make this into a men-versus-women thing. This is about you and Jaimer, that's all. Now, I'll agree with you that what he did was messed up, and yeah, he did go about this the wrong way. But, Tonya, the man had a job to do, and he did it. He didn't know that you would end up a recluse. And when he found out about it through me, he felt guilty as hell. You just don't know the whole story, and it's not for me to tell you. You need to go over there and let him explain everything to you."

"I'm not going anywhere," she snapped.

"Well, then, I guess my job here is done." Vince got up and walked over to her with his arms outstretched. He gave her a long hug. "Tonya, you know that I love you. I would never advise you to do anything that would hurt you. I just want you to be happy, sis. And even in this short of time, I know you were happy with Jaimer. And I know he was happy with you. I . . . just don't let a really good thing slip through your fingers because you're too stubborn to follow your true feelings."

As he hugged her, Tonya began to feel more sorry for him than she did for herself. She didn't understand why, but his understanding tone made her aware of the anguish that was on his face.

"Is everything all right with you, Vince?"

"Yeah, I'm fine," he replied, lying to hide his unhappiness. "Look, just think about what I said. I'm going home to get some rest. I'll call you tomorrow."

"Okay. I love you." Tonya watched him leave, worried that he was going through something that he was unwilling to share with her at the moment.

"I love you, too," he replied.

As Vince pulled off his cellphone began to vibrate. Dominique's phone number was flashing in the caller ID box. Although she had been on his mind earlier, Jaimer decided not to answer her call. He was still preoccupied with what had transpired at Marcia's house and with the realization that he wanted her to remain a part of his life.

⟹

"I want to call off the hit," she hissed into the phone. "Didn't you understand me the first time I called you?"

"That's not an option," he replied.

"What? He's not even on the streets anymore. The feds have him."

"Do you think that will stop me? Once I'm paid to do a job, I follow through."

"Look, damn it, I want this stopped—now. How much will it cost?"

"Seventy-five thousand," he replied easily.

"That's more than I paid to have him assassinated!" she retorted.

"Look, lady, that's the price." He smiled, hoping that she wouldn't be able to cough up that much money.

Mario Renditio loved the power that coursed through him when he took a life. It was during those last moments that he felt the surge of energy and greatness that surely put him somewhere between God and Satan on the scale of power.

He had first felt it when he was seventeen. That is when he had finally stopped his father from sexually abusing him and his younger brother. He had broken off the back leg of their bunk bed and had sharpened it into a stake. When his father came for his brother that night, he jumped off the bed and stabbed the man repeatedly in the back. Then he went to his parents' bedroom and killed his mother, because she had known for twelve years what had been happening to him, and had never once tried to stop it.

In truth, he didn't have a set price for stopping a hit. He'd never had a need for one before. But if he had to set a price for being deprived of such a rush, it was going to be steep.

"Seventy-five thousand? Okay. Should I use the same drop-off spot?"

"Yeah, by noon tomorrow. If it's not there, everything will go as planned. I won't put a stop to it after that."

"It'll be there," she said with a long sigh. After hanging up, she checked her caller ID only to be disappointed to see that Vince hadn't returned her call yet. "Damn it." Instead of slamming down the phone, as was her impulse, she calmly dialed his number again, this time blocking her own number.

"Yes?" Tonya answered the phone drowsily, thinking it was Jaimer calling back. When he called earlier trying to apologize to her, she told him that she was sleeping and didn't want to talk to him at the moment. Glancing at the clock, she saw that it was 12:45 A.M. "What, now, Jaimer?"

"Tonya, it's Cecilia."

"Cecilia?" she repeated, immediately feeling the tremors of fear creeping up her spine. "What's going on? What's wrong?"

"First of all, I want you to calm down. Now, listen. Cindy is on her way to pick you up."

"What happened, Cecilia?" Tonya's breath seemed trapped in her throat as she scrambled off the bed and looked for the jeans she had tossed aside earlier.

"Calm down and go to the door. She should be there by now. She is going to bring you to the hospital. Do you think you can handle that?"

"I, um . . . I, ah . . . I don't know. Is the baby coming already?"

"No, it's Vince. He's been shot."

"Shot? Is he all right?"

"He's in surgery now, but they believe he's going to be fine. Can you come?"

"Yes, I'm coming. What happened? Who did it?" The doorbell interrupted her frantic stream of questions.

"I'll let Cindy explain everything to you. I have to go check on Marcia and Shardei. I'll see you when you get here."

"Marcia and Shardei?" Tonya asked, but Cecilia was gone. "Damn," she said, rushing to open the front door.

"Are you ready?" Dayton asked, catching the white Nike sneakers she threw at him.

"Yeah, let's go," she replied. Tonya barely gave a second thought to what she was doing as she moved down the front steps. "So what happened?"

"Well, as far as I know—"

"Hey, what's going on?" Jaimer asked loudly as he pushed open his screen door and leaned forward. He had been coming out of the kitchen when he heard the car pull up and instantly became curious as to who the late-night visitor was, especially when he saw Tonya actually leaving her house and preparing to go somewhere.

Caught by surprise, Tonya said, "Oh, it's Vince. He's been shot." She continued walking forward as Jaimer rushed through the doorway and followed.

"He was shot?" Jaimer asked, catching up with her and Dayton at the car. "By whom?"

"Dominique," Dayton offered, opening the back passenger-side door for Tonya.

"Dominique?" Jaimer and Tonya stopped in their tracks.

"Come on, Tonya, get in," Cindy yelled impatiently.

Tonya did as she was told, at first unaware that Jaimer was still behind her. When he slid in next to her and forced her to move over, she looked at him in wonder. "What are you doing?"

"I'm going to the hospital. Is that all right with you, Dayton?"

"No problem, mon," Dayton answered, pulling the car away from the curb.

"Hello, Cindy," Jaimer said. "When did this happen?"

"Not long ago," Cindy answered, glancing back at her sister. "Dominique went to Marcia's house to kill her. When she shot at Marcia, Vince jumped in front. Cecilia said that Dominique thought she had killed Vince, so she turned the gun on herself. Cecilia said she seemed to have snapped, kept talking about all she wanted was to be with Vince. When she thought that she had killed him, she said he was waiting for her to join him."

"I-I just can't believe it," Tonya said. "I only saw her once, the night of the party. She seemed so confident and independent. To me, it didn't appear she needed anyone but herself."

"Sometimes the ones who seem strongest on the outside are the weakest. They use their outside appearance as a shield," Jaimer offered absently.

"Well, I know a little something about weaknesses," Tonya said, sliding further away from him when she remembered she was still mad at him. "And there have been times that I wished I was dead because of it, but I'll be damned if I've ever wanted to kill myself. I don't know how much in love you have to be to want to kill yourself over a man, but as far as I knew, she and Vince weren't that close. They weren't together that long, were they?"

"Hell, no. Look, Dayton and I have been together for almost four years, and if he left my ass tomorrow, I still wouldn't consider that long enough to commit suicide. I don't love anybody more than I love myself, and I hope he feels the same way."

"I'm with you, baby," Dayton concurred, keeping his eyes on the road.

"I still don't understand. Who called Cecilia?" Tonya asked, wanting all the details.

"No, she was there. Vince had called her from his car when he suspected what Dominique was up to, but he got there first. I think he might have been trying to break things off with her or something."

"Dominique comes from a family of very dangerous people," Jaimer explained. "She was Howard Douglass's cousin. Cecilia suspected she had a hand in Meltdown's murder. The guy in jail claiming self-defense is a cousin, too. Cecilia said she was going to call Vince and tell him everything when she saw Dominique at Meltdown's warehouse."

"Well, Vince's been out of town for the last few days and hard to contact. She did tell me that if I heard from him to tell him to call her, but he didn't call until he was practically back home," Cindy explained.

"She said that Dominique tried to give her a fake name, but she remembered her from the party. And, as we know, Cecilia has a very good memory."

"How is it that you know so much about Howard's family?" Tonya cut her eyes at him.

"Your sister filled me in on some of the details of her case," he quickly explained. "Just because you're not speaking to me doesn't mean the rest of your family has stopped talking to me, too."

"Obviously," Tonya spat out, a bitter edge to her voice.

"Okay, you two, get over yourselves. If you're not making up, I really don't want to hear the conversation. Besides, we're here," Cindy interjected, putting an end to their little quarrel.

CHAPTER 23

Walking down the long halls of the hospital, Tonya felt small signs of her phobia growing stronger. Though she silently followed Dayton and Cindy, she counted her footsteps the whole way. Each time a passing orderly, nurse, or other hospital worker invaded the space around her, she physically cringed. *Oh, God, how am I going to get through this?* Tonya prayed that she would make it to the end of the hall, then the next hall, and so on until she made it to the waiting room.

Jaimer made sure that he stayed no more than two steps behind her as they walked through the hospital. At any minute, he expected Tonya to turn and run from the intense panic she was displaying. He noticed the sweat covering her brow, as well as the tight grimace on her face. When she seemingly stumbled when another orderly passed them, his hand automatically went to the small of her back to guide her the rest of the way.

"I got you," he whispered just behind her ear.

Tonya didn't respond to his reassurance or to the pressure of his hand, but inside she was grateful for his consideration and thoughtfulness. After snapping at him in the car, she couldn't turn to mush now, especially not when her heart made her want to turn around and let him shelter her from these strange surroundings. She fought against the familiarity of his touch. Fortunately, they finally reached the waiting room.

Jaimer's hand on her back urged Tonya forward when her footsteps slowed. The traffic and congestion of the waiting room caught her off guard. "Tonya, are you all right? Can you handle this? We—"

"I'll be fine," she replied in a voice that betrayed her inner struggle. "I need to be here for Vince." With determination in her eyes, she focused on Cecilia, who sat in a corner holding a box of Kleenex. Her face showed both agitation and exhaustion. Tonya walked over to her.

With the buzz of the waiting room close in her ear and policemen, nurses, and orderlies moving about, it was hard for her to keep her focus, but she tried hard to listen to Cecilia's words.

"He's still in surgery. It shouldn't be much longer. Could someone please take care of Marcia?" Cecilia asked, glancing at Marcia's crumbled body in the chair next to hers. "She has been like this since we came in, and I can't seem to get her together." Not waiting for a volunteer, Cecilia quickly moved out of the seat, leaving it vacant for Jaimer, who would have rather stayed close to Tonya. As Cecilia pulled Tonya and Cindy away, Dayton headed out of the waiting room to fetch water for Marcia and drinks for everyone else.

"Well, what are they saying, Cecilia?" Cindy asked as soon as they found a little privacy in a corner further down the hall.

"Honestly, I don't know," she replied, bending forward and placing a hand on the front of each leg, much like an athlete bending over for air. "I don't know."

Tonya and Cindy placed their hands on her back and began rubbing it. "Cecilia, don't worry, he'll come through this. We just have to pray that he will."

A single tear fell from her eyes onto her sky-blue dress shirt when Cecilia straightened up. "I felt so helpless when I got to that house and saw him lying there limp in Marcia's arms. I wanted to kill that girl myself, but I couldn't lose control. I just wanted to shoot her right there on the spot for what she had done to my little brother. God, I-I-thought—"

"It's all right, Cecilia," Cindy interrupted, wiping her own tears away. "We would have felt the same way."

"But I had the gun right in my hand, and I didn't—" She stopped herself, breathing heavily.

"Cecilia, you did the right thing. You're a cop, and if she hadn't killed herself, you would have taken her into custody as you should have. You did the right thing." Tonya embraced her as Cindy joined in the group hug. "You can't start second-guessing yourself. You know what you did was right."

"But I didn't want to do the right thing, Tonya. I swear, I didn't."

"Cecilia," Cindy added, "do you think everybody wants to do the right thing all the time? You got Vince to the hospital, and that's all that counts. God only knows how you managed to do that with Marcia in hysterics."

"Yeah, we need to keep a close eye on her. I asked the nurse to give her something to calm her down, but she refuses to take anything."

"I'll handle it," Cindy said, heading back to the waiting room. "Pregnancy seems to have made me more sensitive to the feelings of others."

Tonya and Cecilia looked at each other, and were about to follow when Curtis walked up the corridor.

"Baby," he called to Cecilia. His arms went around her in a bear hug. "How's he doing?"

Cecilia didn't hesitate to unload the overwhelming burden of her frustrations on him. As strong a woman as she was, she still needed the strength of her man. "Oh, honey, it was terrible," she said when she walked into his arms. As she went on to relate the details, Tonya eased away, feeling a little like a third wheel.

She hesitantly returned to the waiting room and tried to find a comfortable seat away from as many people as she could, but there were none in the overcrowded room. Cindy was talking to Marcia, who was making a solid effort at getting herself under control. Whatever Cindy had said seemed to be either just what Marcia needed to hear or at least enough to snap out of her desperate state.

"Tonya, here." Jaimer's voice almost caused her to jump clear out of her skin. "Sit here," he said, offering his own seat after noticing her dilemma.

She should have figured he would have the best seat in the house. It was in the corner at the back of the room, and he had a clear view of every exit, window, and person in the room. When she didn't move right away, he reached up and pulled on her arm.

"Don't . . . touch . . . me, Jaimer," she said quietly through clenched teeth. "I'm not kidding about that."

"I'm just trying to help you, Tonya," he replied, looking at her with exasperation. "Damn, you're determined to make this harder on both of us than it has to be, aren't you?" Walking past her, he muttered, "Just take the damn seat."

She finally sat down. Tonya caught Cindy's accusing glare narrow in on her.

"What did you do this time?"

"Mind your own business," she replied curtly before dismissing her completely. She simply did not have the fortitude to deal with Jaimer's guilt or Cindy's opinions. She had enough dealing with her own insecurities and mustering the strength to fight off the mounting discomfort and onrushing uncertainties her new surroundings were putting her through. But she was not leaving until she got some word on her brother's condition. She was not going to hear about her brother's outcome through a third person. The doctors were going to look her in the face, and she was going to hear what was happening for herself.

After three hours of sitting in the same position, her back rigid against the back of the chair, her eyes constantly moving from side to side, darting from one strange face to the next, Tonya began to pray that she could just hold on a little longer. Physically, she was a complete wreck.

The thin layer of moisture that had formed across her forehead two hours earlier had progressed to a virtual rivulet of sweat, which she constantly patted with a wad of napkins she had gladly accepted from Jaimer earlier. She didn't object when he sat next to her and handed her a bottle of water, nor did she snap when he patted her on the knee and told her how good she was doing. She was too weak.

"Jaimer, I think I need to leave," she finally whispered to him in defeat. "I don't think I can take much more of this."

"Vince will understand, Tonya," he assured her. "They'll all understand if you need to leave."

"I tried, but I didn't think it would take so long. I—" she stopped when yet another stranger rushed past them. "This isn't good for me."

"I'll take you home if you want, Tonya," he offered, rising and walking over to where Cecilia was sitting with her husband. He spoke quietly to Cecilia, and then they both walked back to Tonya.

"Hey, sis, are you okay?" Cecilia asked, squatting down in front of her, her voice full of concern.

"I don't think so, Cecilia," she replied, her hands shaking when she reached up to swab her brow.

"Okay, I'm going to get an officer to give you a ride home. And I'll call you as soon as I know something." She placed a hand on Tonya's knee and squeezed it.

"All right," Tonya consented weakly. "Thank you." She allowed Jaimer to help her up as Cindy walked toward them.

"What's going on?" she asked.

"I'm taking Tonya home. She's can't stay any longer," Jaimer answered so that Tonya could concentrate on her steps.

"Is she all right?"

"Yeah, she just needs to rest," Cecilia interjected. "This has taken too much out of her, but I told her we'd be sure to tell Vince that she was here."

"Of course we will. I'll call you later, Tonya," Cindy said, kissing her sister's cheek. The nod she got in return reassured Cindy that they were doing the right thing by getting her out of there.

Just after they cleared the waiting room, a doctor came down the hall. He was walking toward Cecilia and looking grim. Tonya stopped walking and motioned to Jaimer that she had to stay to hear what was happening to her brother. Already half carrying her, Jaimer stopped and turned her around.

"Detective Summers?" the doctor asked.

"Yes?" Cecilia replied.

"Your brother—"

"Is he all right?" Cindy asked.

"He's—"

"He's out of danger?" Cindy asked.

"Well—"

"Well, what?" Cindy asked.

"Cindy, would you please be quiet," Tonya said weakly. "Let the doctor say what he has to say. Please." She rested her head against Jaimer's shoulder, exhausted.

"Thank you. I'm happy to report that Mr. Perkins is going to be fine."

The family let out a collective sigh if relief.

"He's out of danger. The bullet didn't seem to damage any vital organs. He does have a lot of torn muscle, but no nerve damage. He will be sore for a while, but because he's in such remarkably good shape, his recovery will be quick and complete. Right now, he's resting comfortably, a little out of it but coming out of the sedation. He is asking for Marcia."

When she heard that, Marcia's sobs of joy increased. "I'm sorry," she said, accepting Cindy's offer of tissues.

"It's okay. I know how you feel," Cindy replied.

"I just can't believe this is happening. When can I see him?" Marcia asked, pulling herself together.

"Well," the doctor said, "I'm going to give him another hour to get reoriented then I'll let everyone have a quick visit. But after that, I'm going to have to ask you to come back tomorrow during visiting hours. He should be fully aware by then."

"That sounds fair," Cecilia said happily. "Thank you, doctor."

"You're very welcome," he replied. "I'll tell the nurse to come get you when they're ready."

"Tonya," Cecilia said, "you go on home and come back tomorrow for a visit. I think you're due a good rest yourself. But I'm proud of you. You did what you said you were going to do. You stayed until you found out how Vince was doing. I'll make sure to let him know that."

"Thanks. And tell him that I love him," Tonya answered, still leaning against Jaimer, still needing his support.

"I will."

CHAPTER 24

Tonya tiptoed down the steps in her stocking feet. Wearing her tightly tied cotton robe, she was trying to make it to the kitchen without waking Jaimer, who had spent the night on her living room sofa. The heavy rainfall and thunderclaps of an early morning storm had made it impossible for her to get a good night's sleep. The fact that Jaimer was lying below hadn't helped matters. Against her better judgment, and with his strenuous insistence, she had allowed him to stay at her house. She convinced herself that it was her weakened state that had actually made the decision. By the time the officer pulled up to the house, she was nearly too weak to stand on her own. Jaimer had to carry her into the house and up the stairs to bed. He could have simply gone home, but he said he would stay just in case she needed him during the night for something.

In all honesty, she wondered who had been fooling whom.

As soon as she smelled the aroma of coffee in the air, she knew that she was too late. Jaimer was already sitting at the island in her kitchen with a cup of coffee in his hand. He appeared relaxed and comfortable, but there was a line in the middle of his forehead that hinted at his deep thoughts.

"Didn't think you'd still be here, Jaimer," Tonya said, going to the cupboard to get her coffee mug.

"I said that I'd stay until you woke," he replied. "And I did."

"Yes, you did. Well, I'm awake now, and I'm feeling much better so you can leave," she said, trying to look boldly into his eyes, only to have to look away after experiencing a barrage of emotions she was not prepared to deal with. Jaimer didn't miss the confusion that she tried to hide; her eyes betrayed it all.

"What happened? Couldn't sleep?" he asked, ignoring her statement.

"If you must know, the storm was making it hard for me to sleep. But it's all right. I'm up, so you might as well go on home."

"If that's what you want, Tonya, I'll leave. You're right. I can see that you're feeling just fine this morning. I'll just rinse my cup and be on my way," he said, sliding off the stool.

Tonya didn't move. Her feet felt as though they had been nailed solid to the floor. And as he started toward her, she felt her heartbeat quickening, the blood rushing to her face. The pulse at the base of her neck was beating a hundred times a minute. Still, she didn't move. Even though well aware she was in his way, she held her ground.

Did she want him so close to her that she could feel the rough hairs of his unshaven face against her temple? Did she want to be able to smell his manly scent as it filled every pore of her being? Had she missed him that much?

She still desired him more than she wanted to admit. *Oh, God.* Could she love him more than she ever had?

Tonya put a hand to her forehead to stem the silent stream of questions, fearing the onset of a monster headache.

Jaimer lazily stepped over to her and leaned close in order to put his cup into the sink behind her. One of his legs was between her spread ones, and his hip brushed close to the apex of her secret triangle, causing her to moisten from that small amount of pressure. He could play that game, too. Backing down was definitely not in his plans.

She thought that her legs would buckle from his nearness. Instead, she found herself leaning forward, yearning to be closer to him. Her breasts seemed to rise of their own accord, as if the prolonged anticipation of his touch was too unbearable. She could feel his breath on her neck, felt him gazing at her, through her, as he stood waiting for her to make the next move. Waiting for her to feel the sexual magnetism that had already engulfed him.

Jaimer was holding himself in control by just a thread. His body was wound so tight and rigid that he knew she had to feel the evidence of his love for her, sense how much he wanted and needed her. But he didn't move away, deciding to wait patiently for her to want and need him just as badly. She had exactly five more seconds before he would take matters into his own hands.

She lifted her head upwards when she felt the hand on her waist caressing her gently. Searching his eyes, Tonya saw feelings that she was unwilling to deal with, but before she could lower her head, Jaimer started lowering his. She froze and waited for what she expected to be a light brush of his lips against hers, a soft caress that would cause her heart to flutter.

Instead, Tonya found herself defenseless in a tight embrace and fierce kiss that made her heart burn, melt, and yearn for more. In that instant, she forgot her insecurities, her fears, and the lies that he might have told. She struggled to put her coffee mug on the counter next to the sink, but it crashed to the floor. Ignoring the noise, Tonya wrapped her arms around his midsection, striving to quench the thirst she now felt for him.

Enjoying the feel of holding her once again, Jaimer deepened the kiss as he pulled at the tie that bound her robe. He inhaled deeply when he finally got the robe untied and flung it open. She stood before him completely naked. She was just as he remembered her: perfect. Pausing, he looked at her with desire and destiny swirling behind the surface of those chestnut eyes.

It was more than she could take. Tonya lifted his black T-shirt until it was nearly over his head. Her attention was now on his chest, which she lavished with kisses. She nibbled on each nipple greedily until he grabbed a handful of her braided locks and pulled her head back up to him for a slow, long deep kiss.

"I've missed you, Tonya," he said through the entanglement of lips.

"I've missed you, too," she said between breaths.

Wasting no more time, Jaimer used his lower arm to swipe aside the few items she had on her kitchen island.

In her lust, she could care less about a few bills, a letter opener, plastic salt and pepper shakers and a napkin holder, all of which flew off the island and landed loudly at their feet.

She was much more interested in Jaimer lifting her onto the island and lavishing her body with slow, mind-blowing kisses. She cared more about the wet trail he was leaving from her neck to the hollow of her breast and across each rigid nipple; down over and past her navel to the hairy nest that he was now nibbling on.

As he used his hands to hold her still, Tonya felt the pressure building inside her. She lay back against the wooden island, enjoying the feel of his lapping tongue against her.

Her cries of ecstasy kept him going, gave him strength as his determination to please her grew. He wanted to hear her sighs, her moans, and especially his name, which was now being called out repeatedly. Just as he felt her about to reach her climax, Jaimer pulled back, quickly peeled his pants down and filled her.

He needed to be closer to Tonya, connected to her. With all other thoughts pushed aside, Jaimer held her to him as he increased his speed.

Tonya moaned repeatedly as the pressure from his quick, hard strokes mounted.

Jaimer gritted his teeth to rein in his excitement as he watched Tonya totally give way to her emotions. Her face displayed all of the bliss and joy she was feeling. But before long, his own bliss matched hers. The wetness of her searing need, the tightness of her center, and his own passion made his release uncontrollably explosive.

In the afterglow of their lovemaking, while they stayed in the same position breathing heavy, too tired to move, Jaimer and Tonya realized that they were more confused than ever about everything except the fact that they loved each other.

Jaimer was the first to move. He stepped away from her, slowly pulling up his pants and looking down, pretending to adjust himself and his clothing. Tonya leaned up from the counter and gently slipped off. She put on her robe and looked down as she nervously retied it.

"Um, Tonya?" Jaimer finally tried.

"Don't, don't say anything, Jaimer," Tonya bent down and picked up the pieces of her coffee cup, and then walked to the closet to get the mop. "Let's just let it be what it was, okay?"

"I'm not quite sure what it was," he confessed, wanting to have a conversation.

"It was two grown people doing what grown people do," she replied, making sure to keep her gaze averted.

"That's it?" he asked, sure she didn't really believe that.

"That's it," she reiterated. "Um, look, I got a lot to do before I go to the hospital, so, um, I'll see you later, okay?"

Jaimer wasn't exactly shocked by her attitude. He could tell it was a front, but he was disappointed that she felt she had to be like that with him. What could he do? Nothing. So that's what he did.

"All right, Tonya. I guess I'll see you around." He tried to act as nonchalantly as she had, but he couldn't.

This thing between them wasn't nonchalant. If anything, they had just proved that in the kitchen.

Although the spill was already cleaned, Tonya didn't stop mopping until she heard the front door close. Then she slammed the mop to the floor and ran upstairs to her bedroom, flopping down on the bed just after the first tear fell.

When Jaimer walked into Vince's hospital room, he wasn't surprised to find a nurse in there going above and beyond the call of duty. The young brunette was massaging his temples. Vince was sitting in the raised bed with his eyes shut, talking to another man. As Jaimer moved further into the room, the man stood and introduced himself as Vince's friend Nairobi.

"Hey, man. I see they're taking pretty good care of you in here," Jaimer said, grasping Vince's left hand. His right one was wrapped snugly in a sling.

"What's up, frat? What you doing out this early in the morning?" Vince's speech was a little slow and lazy, but his spirits appeared good.

"On my way to the airport. Ebony is coming into town today. She was supposed to be coming Thursday or Friday, but decided to move it up a couple of days so she could visit. She's really coming to be nosy."

"Ebony is coming here? And you didn't tell me?" Vince joked. "Oh, hell no. I got to get out of this hospital. I look a mess. Is her husband coming with her?"

"What? Man, you better cut it out. I'd think you would have had enough women trouble to last you a lifetime."

"Yo, you know what? You're right. Excuse me, honey," he said to the nurse, giving her a polite smile. "Could you leave us for a minute, please?"

"Sure, but if you need anything at all, you just push the button," she said, sashaying out the room.

"Will do," he replied. Turning to his boys, he said, "Man, she ain't even my nurse."

"Well, who is she?" Jaimer asked. Nairobi, too, looked curious.

Vince gladly explained. "When Cecilia left earlier, she was walking past the room. She just came in and asked me if I was okay. I told her I was, but before I knew it, she was massaging my legs, then my head."

"Yeah, she's been in here ever since I got here," Nairobi laughed. "Man, old habits die hard."

"I guess, but last night . . . that shit was crazy. I'm done with all that womanizing shit. I had the perfect woman right in front of my face, and I knew it, but I still wanted excitement, something mysterious. Hell, I can't even explain it to myself. And I would have kept doing it if I hadn't seen Marcia yesterday with that man."

"What man?" Jaimer asked.

"Some joker was at her house visiting her yesterday. I guess it was supposed to be some sort of date. I got mad as hell about that shit. That's why I was in a bad mood when I came to see you, dog. And that's why I didn't go see Dominique. She was expecting me, and when I didn't show up, she called. I didn't really get a chance to tell her in so many words that I realized that I loved Marcia before she snapped the hell out. Next thing I know, we're all on Marcia porch, and she's got a gun pointed at Marcia. I couldn't let her hurt Marcia because of me. I couldn't let Marcia be hurt, period. So I jumped in front of her when Dominique fired the gun."

"My man," Nairobi said admiringly, wondering if he would have been so brave.

"Yeah, your dumb-ass man. That shit hurt," Vince laughed.

"Hey, sometimes we got to go through things to be with the ones we love," Jaimer said pensively.

"I heard that. I do love that damn woman. I probably already knew that and was trying to run from it, not being the settling-down kind. But I am willing to do that with Marcia."

"That's a good thing, dog," Jaimer said. "Did you tell her that?"

"Yeah, but she's not really trying to hear that right now. She said that she loves me and is willing to work things out with me, but I can't rush it."

"How do you feel about that?" Jaimer asked.

"I can wait for her. I still can't believe that Dominique tried to kill her. But then to kill herself. I keep blaming myself."

"You can't blame yourself," Nairobi said. "The girl obviously wasn't stable to start with."

"I did like Dominique. She excited me."

"That's how they trap us," Nairobi insisted. "Marcia will make you very happy."

"I know she will," Vince said.

"Well, I'm happy for you, man," Jaimer said. "Did Cecilia tell you that Tonya was here last night?"

"Tonya? She came out of the house?" Nairobi asked, surprised.

"Yep. Vince, she sat in that waiting room for nearly three hours. She was determined to stay until she heard *something* about your condition. But she was struggling. She finally couldn't take it anymore. I offered to take her home, and she didn't put up any resistance. As we were leaving, the doctor came in to tell us that you were going to be all right." Jaimer's pride showed in the softness of his voice.

"That's my baby," Vince said.

"Well, she loves you, man," Jaimer said, stating the obvious.

"Nah, she loves you. She just needs some time. If I've learned nothing else through all this, I've learned that patience is a virtue. Whoever said that was not lying. Jay, give her time, and be patient. But don't give up on her; she does love you."

"I love her, and she knows it. I'm not going anywhere. Check this out: I've been wanting Tonya Perkins for almost four years now. Does that sound like something that's just going to go away overnight? She's going to have a hell of a time getting rid of me. I'm right next door. If nothing else, I'll have to see her to give her the rent check."

"That's the spirit. She's not going to be able to ignore you or her feelings for you," Vince agreed.

"Well, man," Jaimer started, glancing at his watch, "I gotta head on out. You know how my sister can get."

"Hey, tell Eb to come visit me. Hopefully, I'll be out tomorrow."

"All right, brotha. Nairobi, nice to meet you, man." Jaimer shook both men's hands and left. After talking to Vince, he felt a little more confident about his future with Tonya.

~

"I'm coming," Tonya called, running down the stairs and to the front door. She could imagine Cindy standing on the other side with her hands on her hips, one foot impatiently tapping away.

"It's about damn time," Cindy said, rushing through the door and pushing her to the side. "I gotta pee." Dayton stood in the doorway with a solemn look on his face.

"Don't worry, Dayton, it won't be long now," Tonya said, putting a consoling hand on his shoulder.

"Who would have thought it would be this bad? I thought we were going to be the happiest people in the world."

"Women usually tend to get a little irritable towards the end of the pregnancy. Once she has the baby, she'll be back to normal—not that that was much better," she joked.

"I love her, Tonya, I swear I do, but sometimes, I just want to get in my car and go far, far away."

"Have faith, man, and buck up," Tonya urged, slapping him on the back. "You ain't seen nothing yet. You still got the labor to go through."

Dayton sighed in defeat. Just then, the source of his frustration returned.

"Come on, weeble-wooble," Tonya joked. "I'll follow you to the car."

"I ain't no damn weeble-wooble," Cindy snapped.

"Wow, you sure are in a good mood today. What gives?"

"This baby gives . . . gives a push on my bladder, a kick to my spine, a headache, and cramps."

"Are you sure you're not in labor?"

"Only if it were that simple. Jordan and Shawnique said they would meet us at the hospital."

"Did anybody call Rhashad?"

"Yeah, he was going to fly home, but Shawnique put Vince on the three-way this morning so they could talk. And since he knows Vince is all right, he's going to come down next week after his basketball camp is over. He'll have a week or two off then before starting practice."

CHAPTER 25

Jaimer kept the car quiet on the way to the airport, no CD and no radio as he thought about everything Vince had said. He still wasn't quite sure what he was doing. A little less confused than he had been, Jaimer still wished that he had never allowed himself to be so weak. Even though the morning's events were mind-blowing and more than he could have asked for, he wasn't sure if it was a good or bad for their already strained relationship. At this point, the way things were going, their little exchange wasn't going to have the positive effect he had hoped for.

"Finally," Ebony said, as soon as he pulled up to the curb, opened the car door and walked around to grab the heavy Louis Vuitton suitcase and carry-on out of her hands. "What took you so long? You know how I hate waiting at the airport."

"I'm not late, Ebony, you're early," he replied off-handedly, his voice tinged with annoyance. He was immediately sorry for his response. He had forgotten how good she was at picking up on things.

"What's going on?" she asked as soon as she slid into the passenger-side seat. "Why you in such a foul mood? It's got something to do with a girl, excuse me, woman, doesn't it?"

"No." He paused before continuing. Ebony tended to be a little dramatic. "Vince Perkins was shot yesterday."

"What? *My* Vince Perkins?" she asked, sounding shocked and horrified.

"Yeah. But he's alive and well. I just stopped by the hospital to see him. He wants you to stop in and see him before you leave."

"Of course, I will. You know I was in lust with him at one time, but he was too much of a dog."

"He wasn't a dog when you were seeing him. Did you know that?" Jaimer asked.

"Yeah, I know."

"He really cared about you."

"Yeah, but I was too young for that. I still had a little living to do."

"True."

"God does things for a reason. He puts you here or there because he has a greater plan for you in the future."

Jaimer remained silent. He knew that she was right, but he didn't want to start her on one of her sermons.

"You know you can talk to me about it," she stated simply, certain there was more to his story. Something was on his mind.

"I know I could—if I wanted to, but I don't."

"Oh, you don't? Well, if you got everything all under control, and you don't need any help, why you sitting here looking like a sore thumb?"

"Ebony, don't start—"

"Don't start? I'm just getting started. You never want to talk to me about your personal life. That's what I'm here for, right? If you can't talk to me, then who can you talk to?"

Jaimer sighed deeply and quietly weighed his options. His hands tightened and loosened on the steering wheel as he moved through traffic. "Okay, okay," he finally conceded, deciding to try. Besides, he and Ebony had always been close, always talked to each other about their problems. He just didn't want to hear her tell him how wrong he was to deceive Tonya the way he had. "But I don't want to hear anything from you until after I'm done. Not one single word, Ebony. I know how you like to cut in."

"Okay, I promise."

"Well, I met a young lady—"

"That's great. What's her—" Ebony became instantly quiet when Jaimer cut his eye at her.

"Her name is Tonya. She's Vince's younger sister."

"Did you know that Vince was my first?" She stopped again, this time of her own accord.

"I don't need to know that," he said. "Anyway, I've been kinda seeing Tonya since I moved next door to her a couple weeks ago. Things moved kinda fast, but everything was going nicely until something happened a few days ago that kinda messed everything up."

"What did you do?" she asked.

"I lied. Well, not exactly lied. There were some things that I should have told her and Vince about. Some things left over from the agency."

"This doesn't sound good, Jay." Ebony turned from looking out the window to stare at his face.

"It wasn't. I lied, betrayed her trust, and got the nerve to still want her in my life."

"Do you love her?" she asked.

Jaimer turned and looked at his sister, and told the truth. "I think I love her too much."

"Hah, there's no such thing as loving someone too much. Either you love her or you don't. God doesn't put a limit on love; people do. And if you love her, you got to give her time to get over the way you hurt her. See, what men don't understand about women is that the love of a strong woman isn't just a gift, it's a blessing. The problem is that most men don't realize when they've been blessed."

"Ebony—"

"No, for real. I don't know the ins and outs of your relationship or what you did exactly, but it all boils down to the same old, same old. You can't expect her to let you know today or tomorrow how she feels about things. You can't expect her to forgive and forget what you've done to her. At this point, the only thing you can do is be patient, and that's one of the hardest things in the world for a man to do. Be patient."

"Patient. It doesn't really seem as if I have a choice, does it?"

"If you love her, than no, I guess you don't. But should you have one? When you had the choice of telling her the truth, did you? No. Men don't do good with choices."

"Why you so hard on men? You almost sound like a male basher," he joked.

"Hey, I just call it like I see it."

He took her comments in, knowing she was right. About men and about him. Ebony's advice was always right—always given harshly—but always right.

The hospital door squeaked open slowly, bringing Vince out of his much-needed, well-deserved power nap. After using all of his strength to get out of bed and walk to the bathroom, he quickly took advantage of the silent room once Nairobi left. As he focused in on the small group of visitors coming into his hospital room, his expression changed from pleasure to excitement and pride.

Tonya walked into the room, her tearful eyes focusing in on her brother's medium frame nestled in the center of the hospital bed. It was funny how a hospital bed could make the strongest man look small and weak. But the joy she felt from seeing her brother alive and well with her own two eyes couldn't be suppressed. In a flash, she moved past Cindy and rushed to the side of his bed, bending down to kiss him on the cheek.

"Vince, don't you ever scare me like that again," she whispered close to his ear, holding him a little tighter than necessary.

Vince withstood the pain as she hugged him. "Tonya, look at you. They told me that you were here last night, but dang, girl, you're just outdoing yourself." He grabbed hold of her hand when she stood and moved his leg over so she could sit on the bed next to him. "I'm so proud of you, Tonya. I wish that I wasn't the cause of you pushing yourself to be here last night."

"That doesn't matter. Maybe I needed a jolt. Today wasn't so bad. There are a lot more people around, but I had to see you for myself."

"Cindy, how you feeling today?" Vince asked, finally turning his attention to the couple at the foot of his bed. "Here sit in the chair. Dayton just put those flowers anywhere."

"I don't want to sit down," Cindy grumbled. "It hurts too much. I swear I don't ever want to go through this shit again."

Dayton's expression darkened as he found a place for the flowers on the windowsill.

"Oh, you say that now, but after it's over, you'll forget all about the pain," Vince assured her. That's what he heard a lot of women say.

"How would you know?" she snapped. "You've never had a baby."

"Look, I'm going to go outside for a minute," Dayton said, his accent heavier than usual and disappointment and hurt visible on his face.

As soon as he left, both Tonya and Vince turned on Cindy so fast she didn't see it coming.

"What the hell is wrong with you, Cindy?" Tonya said first. "Why do you have to constantly make that man feel like he's done the worst thing he could have ever done to you?"

"What?" she asked innocently, flabbergasted by Tonya's sudden outburst.

"You got yourself a good man in Dayton. He caters to your every whim. You don't even have to work. He's busting his ass so that you don't have to. He loves your spoiled, bratty ass beyond belief, and you're treating him like dirt just because you're going through a little discomfort right now. That shit will be over soon enough. You only got another month to go. I personally don't see how he does it, puts up with your ass day after day, night after night, complaining about something out of your control. For all that man does for you, the least you could do is give him a healthy baby and be happy to do it."

Cindy stood there in shock for a minute, looking from Tonya to Vince. "What?"

"She's right, Cindy. The quickest way to lose a man is by hurting his pride. He's not going to take too much more of your shit. Then what you going to do? I know you're going through something right now, but so is he. He's trying to stand beside you, but you keep pushing him away. Pretty soon, he's not going to be there to push."

"I-I didn't realize I was doing that."

"No, of course not," Tonya said. "You're so used to it being all about you, Cindy. But it's not just about you anymore. It's about you all, now. You're about to be a threesome. You, Dayton, and the baby."

"All I'm saying," Vince interrupted, "is don't be a fool like me. Know what you got while you got it."

"You're right. Oh, God," she exhaled deeply, finally taking the seat that had been offered earlier. "I have been a bitch, haven't I?"

"Yeah," they both eagerly agreed.

Cindy looked at them both before turning to the door as it opened and Dayton walked back in carrying two Pepsis and bottled water for Cindy. When he handed it to her, she said, "Thank you, baby." Enough emphasis was placed on the last word to make Dayton do a double take before standing beside her against the wall.

"So what do you have planned for the rest of the day, Tonya?" Vince asked.

"Nothing. I'm going back home to finish some research for my book and then maybe sit on the porch for a while."

"Are you going to talk to Jaimer today?"

"I don't know. Why should I?" she asked, flashbacks of the morning's escapade dancing in her head. She wondered if Vince could tell just by looking in her face that she still loved him.

"I just think that maybe you two should go ahead and talk things over and get everything out in the air."

"Vince, don't start, okay? Now is not the time."

"I think now is the perfect time. If not now, when? You can't put this off forever. Believe me, I know. If last night taught me anything, it's that forever is not promised. You have to grab hold of your happiness when you can. Especially when love is involved."

"Let me take care of my own affairs, okay?"

"Of course, you're a grown woman. I'm just saying it's a fool who doesn't learn from the examples of others."

"Vince, let it go," Tonya insisted.

"It's gone. Just listen to me, okay? The same thing you just lectured Cindy on also pertains to your own situation."

~~~~~

The early-evening wind felt so good against the unusual calmness Tonya felt surrounding her. She allowed her mind to be at peace with the decisions she had made about her life. Decisions that were not easy to make, but were necessary for her to be happy. She smiled as she watched her neighbors taking their evening walk, many waving to her in a pleased but surprised manner. Her life had changed in so many ways over the last two weeks, and she owed a lot of it to Jaimer. For that she was going to be forever grateful to him.

We need to talk, she mused, thinking of their time together and feeling warm and comforted. *The sooner, the better.*

Grateful for her brother's recovery, she said a silent pray as she though over the advice he had given her at the hospital. Her mind was firmly made up. She sat outside for another fifteen minutes and then decided to go on inside.

Just as she was about to move off the porch swing, Jaimer's car pulled up. Now was as good a time as any, she figured, and stayed where she was. What she didn't expect to see was the tall woman he was helping out of the passenger side. Nor did she expect to see the several pieces of luggage he pulled out of the car's trunk. Tonya was surprised to feel a twinge of jealousy shoot through her. She ignored it as she scooted up further on the swing so that he could see her.

"Hey, Tonya," Jaimer said. "What are you doing out here so late?"

"It's only six-thirty, Jaimer. I wanted to take a break, and I felt like some air."

Both stood seemed to be wondering what to say next.

Ebony cleared her throat. They were so obviously enthralled with each other she presumed that this was the woman Jaimer had been talking about. "Excuse me, I'm Ebony, Jaimer's sister."

"I'm Tonya Perkins. It's nice to meet you."

"Tonya Perkins? I know you're Vince's sister, but that name sounds familiar for some reason."

"Tonya is a writer, too, sis. You've probably seen some of her stuff or something."

"Oh, you are? Well, I'm here for a few days. We need to talk. Right now, I gotta go to the little girls' room. Jaimer, just give me the key, I'll let myself in." She was trying to give them the privacy they didn't seem to know they wanted.

"Yeah, that's a great idea," Tonya called to her retreating form. "Tell her that I said anytime, Jaimer."

"I'm sure she heard you. She hears everything. She's just in town for some kind of book event. Maybe you should go with her."

"Oh, no," Tonya said, putting her hands in the air as if to ward off something dangerous. "I'm hardly ready for that yet. I remember how crowded those things are."

"So how are you doing today?" he asked, moving up the steps.

"I'm doing fine. I went to see my brother today. He looks good."

"I was thinking about you today," Jaimer started the conversation he knew they needed to have. "After this morning, I—"

"Wait, Jaimer, let me say something. This morning shouldn't have happened. I'm sorry for letting it go on, but—"

"You mean it shouldn't have happened or you didn't want it to happen?"

"Of course, I wanted it to happen. I want it to happen again and again. But right now, I know that's not the best thing for us. Me or you. This morning was a moment that neither of us was in control over, but it can't happen again. We can't let that be our relationship, one out-of-control moment after another."

"Tonya, I know what I did was wrong. How I let you find out was even worse, but I do love you."

"I know you do, Jaimer." She let out a long sigh, one that held a lot of hope and dreams. "I love you, too, but—"

"There's always a but, isn't there?" he laughed.

"But I need to work on myself before I can work on us. I still want to be friends, I still want to talk to you. I'll see you all the time. You're right next door. But I need time for me. I've just started getting back on the right track, and I don't want to have to worry about anything but staying on track for a while. I don't know. This might be a lot to ask, but I need you to be patient. I want to be friends. I can't start a relationship right now." Tonya didn't look at him for fear that she would change her mind. She kept her head lowered, wiping her eye to stop a tear from falling.

"Tonya, don't cry, please. You're right. I can't expect you to forgive and forget what I did overnight. And I don't expect you to trust me completely after the last few days. But what I do want you to believe is that I'm not going anywhere."

"I guess I'll be the second to know if you do," she joked.

"Hey, you mind if I sit out here with you for a little while?" he asked, putting his arm across the back of the swing.

"Not at all." Tonya leaned back into a more comfortable position, allowing the evening air to fan around her, around them and their new friendship.

ABOUT THE AUTHOR

Michele Sudler lives in the small East Coast town of Smyrna, Delaware. Busy raising three children—Gregory, Takira, and Kanika Lambert—she finds time for her second passion, which is writing, on evenings and weekends. After attending Delaware State College, where she majored in Business Administration, she began to work in the banking industry, where she is still employed. Recently she enrolled back in school and is currently working hard on her time management skills in order to balance family, work, and school.

Best Foot Forward is her fifth novel. Her other books are: *Intentional Mistakes,* and *One of These Days,* in which she introduced the Avery family, and *Stolen Memories,* which introduced the Philips family. *Three Doors Down* is her latest novel. It was released in September 2008. Her November 2009 release will be *Waiting in the Shadows,* another Avery family romance.

Besides spending time with her children and writing, Michele enjoys playing and watching basketball, traveling, and reading. She would also love to hear from you about her novels. Please send any comments to her email address: micheleasudler@yahoo.com

2009 Reprint Mass Market Titles

January

I'm Gonna Make You Love Me
Gwyneth Bolton
ISBN-13: 978-1-58571-294-6
$6.99

Shades of Desire
Monica White
ISBN-13: 978-1-58571-292-2
$6.99

February

A Love of Her Own
Cheris Hodges
ISBN-13: 978-1-58571-293-9
$6.99

Color of Trouble
Dyanne Davis
ISBN-13: 978-1-58571-294-6
$6.99

March

Twist of Fate
Beverly Clark
ISBN-13: 978-1-58571-295-3
$6.99

Chances
Pamela Leigh Starr
ISBN-13: 978-1-58571-296-0
$6.99

April

Sinful Intentions
Crystal Rhodes
ISBN-13: 978-1-585712-297-7
$6.99

Rock Star
Roslyn Hardy Holcomb
ISBN-13: 978-1-58571-298-4
$6.99

May

Paths of Fire
T.T. Henderson
ISBN-13: 978-1-58571-343-1
$6.99

Caught Up in the Rapture
Lisa Riley
ISBN-13: 978-1-58571-344-8
$6.99

June

Reckless Surrender
Rochelle Alers
ISBN-13: 978-1-58571-345-5
$6.99

No Ordinary Love
Angela Weaver
ISBN-13: 978-1-58571-346-2
$6.99

2009 Reprint Mass Market Titles (continued)
July

Intentional Mistakes
Michele Sudler
ISBN-13: 978-1-58571-347-9
$6.99

It's In His Kiss
Reon Carter
ISBN-13: 978-1-58571-348-6
$6.99

August

Unfinished Love Affair
Barbara Keaton
ISBN-13: 978-1-58571-349-3
$6.99

A Perfect Place to Pray
I.L Goodwin
ISBN-13: 978-1-58571-299-1
$6.99

September

Love in High Gear
Charlotte Roy
ISBN-13: 978-1-58571-355-4
$6.99

Ebony Eyes
Kei Swanson
ISBN-13: 978-1-58571-356-1
$6.99

October

Midnight Clear, Part I
Leslie Esdale/Carmen Green
ISBN-13: 978-1-58571-357-8
$6.99

Midnight Clear, Part II
Gwynne Forster/Monica
    Jackson
ISBN-13: 978-1-58571-358-5
$6.99

November

Midnight Peril
Vicki Andrews
ISBN-13: 978-1-58571-359-2
$6.99

One Day At A Time
Bella McFarland
ISBN-13: 978-1-58571-360-8
$6.99

December

Just An Affair
Eugenia O'Neal
ISBN-13: 978-1-58571-361-5
$6.99

Shades of Brown
Denise Becker
ISBN-13: 978-1-58571-362-2
$6.99

2009 New Mass Market Titles

January

Singing A Song…
Crystal Rhodes
ISBN-13: 978-1-58571-283-0
$6.99

Look Both Ways
Joan Early
ISBN-13: 978-1-58571-284-7
$6.99

February

Six O'Clock
Katrina Spencer
ISBN-13: 978-1-58571-285-4
$6.99

Red Sky
Renee Alexis
ISBN-13: 978-1-58571-286-1
$6.99

March

Anything But Love
Celya Bowers
ISBN-13: 978-1-58571-287-8
$6.99

Tempting Faith
Crystal Hubbard
ISBN-13: 978-1-58571-288-5
$6.99

April

If I Were Your Woman
La Connie Taylor-Jones
ISBN-13: 978-1-58571-289-2
$6.99

Best Of Luck Elsewhere
Trisha Haddad
ISBN-13: 978-1-58571-290-8
$6.99

May

All I'll Ever Need
Mildred Riley
ISBN-13: 978-1-58571-335-6
$6.99

A Place Like Home
Alicia Wiggins
ISBN-13: 978-1-58571-336-3
$6.99

June

Best Foot Forward
Michele Sudler
ISBN-13: 978-1-58571-337-0
$6.99

It's In the Rhythm
Sammie Ward
ISBN-13: 978-1-58571-338-7
$6.99

2009 New Mass Market Titles (continued)

July

Checks and Balances
Elaine Sims
ISBN-13: 978-1-58571-339-4
$6.99

Save Me
Africa Fine
ISBN-13: 978-1-58571-340-0
$6.99

August

When Lightening Strikes
Michele Cameron
ISBN-13: 978-1-58571-369-1
$6.99

Blindsided
Tammy Williams
ISBN-13: 978-1-58571-342-4
$6.99

September

2 Good
Celya Bowers
ISBN-13: 978-1-58571-350-9
$6.99

Waiting for Mr. Darcy
Chamein Canton
ISBN-13: 978-1-58571-351-6
$6.99

October

Fireflies
Joan Early
ISBN-13: 978-1-58571-352-3
$6.99

Frost On My Window
Angela Weaver
ISBN-13: 978-1-58571-353-0
$6.99

November

Waiting in the Shadows
Michele Sudler
ISBN-13: 978-1-58571-364-6
$6.99

Fixin' Tyrone
Keith Walker
ISBN-13: 978-1-58571-365-3
$6.99

December

Dream Keeper
Gail McFarland
ISBN-13: 978-1-58571-366-0
$6.99

Another Memory
Pamela Ridley
ISBN-13: 978-1-58571-367-7
$6.99

Other Genesis Press, Inc. Titles

A Dangerous Deception	J.M. Jeffries	$8.95
A Dangerous Love	J.M. Jeffries	$8.95
A Dangerous Obsession	J.M. Jeffries	$8.95
A Drummer's Beat to Mend	Kei Swanson	$9.95
A Happy Life	Charlotte Harris	$9.95
A Heart's Awakening	Veronica Parker	$9.95
A Lark on the Wing	Phyliss Hamilton	$9.95
A Love of Her Own	Cheris F. Hodges	$9.95
A Love to Cherish	Beverly Clark	$8.95
A Risk of Rain	Dar Tomlinson	$8.95
A Taste of Temptation	Reneé Alexis	$9.95
A Twist of Fate	Beverly Clark	$8.95
A Voice Behind Thunder	Carrie Elizabeth Greene	$6.99
A Will to Love	Angie Daniels	$9.95
Acquisitions	Kimberley White	$8.95
Across	Carol Payne	$12.95
After the Vows	Leslie Esdaile	$10.95
(Summer Anthology)	T.T. Henderson	
	Jacqueline Thomas	
Again My Love	Kayla Perrin	$10.95
Against the Wind	Gwynne Forster	$8.95
All I Ask	Barbara Keaton	$8.95
Always You	Crystal Hubbard	$6.99
Ambrosia	T.T. Henderson	$8.95
An Unfinished Love Affair	Barbara Keaton	$8.95
And Then Came You	Dorothy Elizabeth Love	$8.95
Angel's Paradise	Janice Angelique	$9.95
At Last	Lisa G. Riley	$8.95
Best of Friends	Natalie Dunbar	$8.95
Beyond the Rapture	Beverly Clark	$9.95
Blame It On Paradise	Crystal Hubbard	$6.99
Blaze	Barbara Keaton	$9.95
Bliss, Inc.	Chamein Canton	$6.99
Blood Lust	J. M. Jeffries	$9.95
Blood Seduction	J.M. Jeffries	$9.95

Other Genesis Press, Inc. Titles (continued)

Bodyguard	Andrea Jackson	$9.95
Boss of Me	Diana Nyad	$8.95
Bound by Love	Beverly Clark	$8.95
Breeze	Robin Hampton Allen	$10.95
Broken	Dar Tomlinson	$24.95
By Design	Barbara Keaton	$8.95
Cajun Heat	Charlene Berry	$8.95
Careless Whispers	Rochelle Alers	$8.95
Cats & Other Tales	Marilyn Wagner	$8.95
Caught in a Trap	Andre Michelle	$8.95
Caught Up In the Rapture	Lisa G. Riley	$9.95
Cautious Heart	Cheris F Hodges	$8.95
Chances	Pamela Leigh Starr	$8.95
Cherish the Flame	Beverly Clark	$8.95
Choices	Tammy Williams	$6.99
Class Reunion	Irma Jenkins/	$12.95
	John Brown	
Code Name: Diva	J.M. Jeffries	$9.95
Conquering Dr. Wexler's Heart	Kimberley White	$9.95
Corporate Seduction	A.C. Arthur	$9.95
Crossing Paths, Tempting Memories	Dorothy Elizabeth Love	$9.95
Crush	Crystal Hubbard	$9.95
Cypress Whisperings	Phyllis Hamilton	$8.95
Dark Embrace	Crystal Wilson Harris	$8.95
Dark Storm Rising	Chinelu Moore	$10.95
Daughter of the Wind	Joan Xian	$8.95
Dawn's Harbor	Kymberly Hunt	$6.99
Deadly Sacrifice	Jack Kean	$22.95
Designer Passion	Dar Tomlinson	$8.95
	Diana Richeaux	
Do Over	Celya Bowers	$9.95
Dream Runner	Gail McFarland	$6.99
Dreamtective	Liz Swados	$5.95

Other Genesis Press, Inc. Titles (continued)

Other Genesis Press, Inc. Titles (continued)

Other Genesis Press, Inc. Titles (continued)

Other Genesis Press, Inc. Titles (continued)

Peace Be Still	Colette Haywood	$12.95
Picture Perfect	Reon Carter	$8.95
Playing for Keeps	Stephanie Salinas	$8.95
Pride & Joi	Gay G. Gunn	$8.95
Promises Made	Bernice Layton	$6.99
Promises to Keep	Alicia Wiggins	$8.95
Quiet Storm	Donna Hill	$10.95
Reckless Surrender	Rochelle Alers	$6.95
Red Polka Dot in a World of Plaid	Varian Johnson	$12.95
Reluctant Captive	Joyce Jackson	$8.95
Rendezvous with Fate	Jeanne Sumerix	$8.95
Revelations	Cheris F. Hodges	$8.95
Rivers of the Soul	Leslie Esdaile	$8.95
Rocky Mountain Romance	Kathleen Suzanne	$8.95
Rooms of the Heart	Donna Hill	$8.95
Rough on Rats and Tough on Cats	Chris Parker	$12.95
Secret Library Vol. 1	Nina Sheridan	$18.95
Secret Library Vol. 2	Cassandra Colt	$8.95
Secret Thunder	Annetta P. Lee	$9.95
Shades of Brown	Denise Becker	$8.95
Shades of Desire	Monica White	$8.95
Shadows in the Moonlight	Jeanne Sumerix	$8.95
Sin	Crystal Rhodes	$8.95
Small Whispers	Annetta P. Lee	$6.99
So Amazing	Sinclair LeBeau	$8.95
Somebody's Someone	Sinclair LeBeau	$8.95
Someone to Love	Alicia Wiggins	$8.95
Song in the Park	Martin Brant	$15.95
Soul Eyes	Wayne L. Wilson	$12.95
Soul to Soul	Donna Hill	$8.95
Southern Comfort	J.M. Jeffries	$8.95
Southern Fried Standards	S.R. Maddox	$6.99
Still the Storm	Sharon Robinson	$8.95

Other Genesis Press, Inc. Titles (continued)

Still Waters Run Deep	Leslie Esdaile	$8.95
Stolen Kisses	Dominiqua Douglas	$9.95
Stolen Memories	Michele Sudler	$6.99
Stories to Excite You	Anna Forrest/Divine	$14.95
Storm	Pamela Leigh Starr	$6.99
Subtle Secrets	Wanda Y. Thomas	$8.95
Suddenly You	Crystal Hubbard	$9.95
Sweet Repercussions	Kimberley White	$9.95
Sweet Sensations	Gwyneth Bolton	$9.95
Sweet Tomorrows	Kimberly White	$8.95
Taken by You	Dorothy Elizabeth Love	$9.95
Tattooed Tears	T. T. Henderson	$8.95
The Color Line	Lizzette Grayson Carter	$9.95
The Color of Trouble	Dyanne Davis	$8.95
The Disappearance of Allison Jones	Kayla Perrin	$5.95
The Fires Within	Beverly Clark	$9.95
The Foursome	Celya Bowers	$6.99
The Honey Dipper's Legacy	Pannell-Allen	$14.95
The Joker's Love Tune	Sidney Rickman	$15.95
The Little Pretender	Barbara Cartland	$10.95
The Love We Had	Natalie Dunbar	$8.95
The Man Who Could Fly	Bob & Milana Beamon	$18.95
The Missing Link	Charlyne Dickerson	$8.95
The Mission	Pamela Leigh Starr	$6.99
The More Things Change	Chamein Canton	$6.99
The Perfect Frame	Beverly Clark	$9.95
The Price of Love	Sinclair LeBeau	$8.95
The Smoking Life	Ilene Barth	$29.95
The Words of the Pitcher	Kei Swanson	$8.95
Things Forbidden	Maryam Diaab	$6.99
This Life Isn't Perfect Holla	Sandra Foy	$6.99
Three Doors Down	Michele Sudler	$6.99
Three Wishes	Seressia Glass	$8.95
Ties That Bind	Kathleen Suzanne	$8.95

Other Genesis Press, Inc. Titles (continued)

Order Form

Mail to: Genesis Press, Inc.
P.O. Box 101
Columbus, MS 39703

Name _____

Address _____

City/State _____ Zip _____

Telephone _____

Ship to (if different from above)

Name _____

Address _____

City/State _____ Zip _____

Telephone _____

Credit Card Information

Credit Card # _____ ☐ Visa ☐ Mastercard

Expiration Date (mm/yy) _____ ☐ AmEx ☐ Discover

Qty.	Author	Title	Price	Total

Use this order form, or call 1-888-INDIGO-1	Total for books _____
	Shipping and handling:
	$5 first two books,
	$1 each additional book _____
	Total S & H _____
	Total amount enclosed _____
	Mississippi residents add 7% sales tax